80AD
The Yu Dragon

(Book 5)

Aiki Flinthart

ISBN-13: 978-0-9945660-7-2
Computing Advantages & Training P/L

Discover other titles by Aiki Flinthart at: http://aikiflinthart.weebly.com/

Cover Art by : Jason Seabaugh

Review:
"This story is very unique. The premise is immensely entertaining. It's a great story!".......Chilli Tween Reads October 31st 2011

NOTE: this series is written with the young adult agegroup in mind. Having said that, thousands of adults have read and enjoyed them as well. Please bear this in mind when reading and leaving feedback.

80AD

Level Five

The Yu Dragon.

FENG ZHUDAI

Feng Zhudai dipped the tip of his brush into a small pot of ink. His lips twitched into a faint, satisfied smile. With his left hand, he caught up the silken sleeve of his robe so it wouldn't smudge the calligraphy. The brush hovered for an instant over a narrow strip of bamboo. Then, with graceful strokes, the Emperor's advisor penned an order to execute his prisoner.

Carefully replacing the brush, he allowed the ink to dry before summoning his servant. The man entered timidly, his nose almost touching the floor. Irritated, Zhudai threw the order onto the polished wood.

"Ensure that is carried out before the end of the day." He paused, dark eyes narrowed in thought as the eunuch scrabbled to pick up the bamboo slip. "And if General Ban Chao or Emperor Han Zhangdi find out, I will know who to blame. This must be done in secrecy. Do you understand?"

The top of the servant's head bobbed as he bowed and nodded his nervous understanding. Satisfied, Zhudai waved him out and turned back to his desk. He smiled again but anyone watching would not have felt comforted by his expression.

Zhudai moved his long fingers in a curious, twisting

motion and a small, dark, red-purple flame danced for a moment on the palm of his hand. As he watched, it curled into the shape of a slender woman who sat with her arms wrapped around her knees and her head buried in them. A miniature chain encircled her ankles and wrists.

The flame twisted and reformed into the image of a man; sprawled on an invisible floor and also chained. Zhudai's unpleasant smile broadened. He moved his hand as though to dismiss the dancing light but, before he could, it shifted again into another shape. This time, a broad-shouldered warrior stalked purposefully across the sorcerer's narrow palm. He looked...brooding, angry. A sword glinted in his hand.

With a snap of Zhudai's fingers, the dusky-red flame vanished. His fine, black brows drew together in a frown. He stared blankly at his own hand for a moment then turned to look at the floor as though seeing through it to the levels below. He rose to his feet in a sudden, decisive movement. Sweeping long, black robes around himself, Zhudai strode toward the door on silent, soft-shod feet.

Outside, his secretary eyed the execution order with misgivings. It was the third one this week. At this rate, the Emperor had to hear of Zhudai's doings. Anyone with any brains could sense a confrontation coming between the Emperor and his pet warlock. General Ban Chao, the only possible stumbling block to Zhudai's ambition, had been sent on a sudden posting to India. It dawned on the hapless servant that he wanted to be well out of Xijing before Zhudai's plans came to fruition.

As he pondered how he could arrange to have himself sent to Luoyang before the *ri shi,* his master appeared suddenly at his side. He jumped and almost made the fatal mistake of looking Zhudai in the eye. He knew it to be fatal, because the name of his masters' previous secretary had been on an execution list three weeks before.

"Bring me the prisoner," Zhudai demanded.

His servant glanced in confusion at the death sentence lying on his desk.

"Not that one, you imbecile. The girl. Yajat's captive. Bring her to me. I think I have a use for her alive, after all." Without waiting, the warlock vanished back into his rooms, leaving the secretary to stare after him in fearful bewilderment.

CHAPTER ONE

Phoenix gritted his teeth, wishing his horse came with shock absorbers. Every jarring hoof-beat lanced pain through his arm. Marcus had set the bone well enough but he really needed Jade's healing powers. How was he supposed to swing a sword now?

Pushing the thought aside, he stretched out one leg, easing a bruised butt cheek off the saddle. It didn't help much. They had ridden non-stop since before dawn in an effort to reach Karla Caves. It was taking longer than he'd expected to make their way west. The road toward the coast seethed with refugees from the recently-ended war between the Kshatrapa Bhumaka and the true king, Guatamiputra Sakatarni. Their pathetic footslogging pace made for slow going on the narrow path through the mountains.

Several times, Phoenix had to physically bite his lip to stop himself from shouting at the peasant-soldiers trudging homeward. He just didn't have the patience to deal with this right now. They had to get to Karla Caves and the portal gate to China quickly, or any hope of rescuing Jade would be gone.

For all he knew, she could have already lost her three remaining lives and be dead. A spasm of fear twisted his guts. His mind shied away from the thought but Phoenix forced himself to consider the possibility. If Jade had lost all her lives and was really dead then he was stuck here.

Forever.

He glanced around at the dramatic, tropical, humid landscape. A rugged mountain range rose before him, signalling an abrupt end to the enormous Deccan Plateau at his back. So different from the soft, cool greens of England. The heat of the sun; the dark greens of the forest; the heavy, cloying scents of the jungle; even the food wasn't like Indian food at home in the twenty-first century.

It seemed a long time since he'd seen his mother, his home, his own time. Memories of his old life were fading: being a thirteen year old at school, aikido training, playing computer games and even the harsh reality of his fathers' death and his stepfather's stupidity were all more like a dream. Reality was here in 80AD, India: wars, gods, magic, friends and foes. It wasn't even that great a reality any more. What had been a brilliant adventure to start with now, frankly, sucked.

He'd just about had enough.

A wave of despair swept through him and he had to swallow hard to keep down a groan. He had come to rely on Jade in the last few weeks. She'd been gone just one day and he felt her absence keenly. Everything seemed harder without her quick wits, magical abilities and commonsense. He even missed her pointless worrying. They'd been unwillingly and unwittingly thrown together in this surreal game-world over three weeks ago. During their first few days here Phoenix had, in his carefree impatience to be adventuring, wished her away a dozen times or more. In the past day, since her kidnapping, he'd begged every god he knew, and he'd met several now, to bring her back.

It hadn't worked.

After a full-scale war the day before and hardly any sleep since her abduction, Phoenix now ran on faint hope and sheer determination. He looked across at his grim-faced companions and realised they must be just as weary;

just as worried.

Marcus, the battle-hardened son of a Roman Governor, looked older than his sixteen years. His dark, curling hair stuck to his forehead as the sun baked them all in its tropical heat. With soldier's train alertness, his dark eyes swept the surrounds constantly, seeking danger.

Glancing to his left, Phoenix saw Vasi, son of Guatamiputra, riding easily beside Brynn, the youngest of their group. Vasi was clearly tired but Brynn looked worse. The ten year old boy-thief from ancient Britain winced with every hoofbeat. His usually-cheerful, thin was face screwed into a bizarre cross between determination and pain. The pony tossed its head and Brynn's eyes widened in alarm. He wasn't a very good rider.

Prince Vasi, a native of the area, looked the most comfortable in the afternoon heat. His brown skin barely glowed with sweat and he still moved effortlessly in the saddle.

It was due to his father's generosity and gratitude that they were on the road so quickly this morning. Vasi knew the way to Karla Caves and his father provided fresh horses and supplies. Even if they kept going at this slow pace, they should be at the caves before dark.

That hope was dashed the very next moment. Vasi threw up a hand and pulled his mount to a halt. Behind, a servant, leading six spare horses, followed suit. Phoenix frowned and dragged back on the reins. Vasi swung down from his horse, leading it off the track, into the shade of an enormous fig tree. His servant followed.

"What are you doing?" Phoenix demanded. "We don't have time for this. We're already a night and most of a day behind Jade. If we don't reach the Caves soon, we may as well have climbed over the Himalayas into China to get to her." He flung his good hand at the distant, purple mountains to the northeast.

Vasi calmly sank into a cross-legged position on the

ground and nodded to his man.

"We need to eat and the horses need to rest. There's a stream over there. We'll water them and move on when we are all recovered."

Phoenix slipped awkwardly off his horse, holding his broken right arm out so it wouldn't be knocked. His foot caught in the stirrup and he had to hop a few times before it came loose. Brynn snickered, hiding his mouth with his hand. Phoenix glared at him.

"You think this is funny?" He heard the angry edge to his own voice and snapped his jaw shut.

Brynn sobered, staring back at him with solemn, dark eyes.

"Sorry," Phoenix muttered, turning away.

Out of habit, his left hand rested on the hilt of his sword, Blódbál. Its berserker song of glory and death swelled in his head, trying to take over his thoughts and emotions; trying to turn him into the ultimate, amoral warrior. He snatched his hand away, shaken by the power of the song. His emotions were all over the place and the enchanted sword was trying to seize the opportunity to use him as a weapon against his enemies. He had to be careful. If he let it take over he would turn berserker – no longer able to tell enemies from friends.

Right at the moment, though, he would welcome a few enemies to go berserk on. Inaction was driving him nuts.

Sitting down with a thump, Phoenix dropped his head into his good hand and scrubbed fingers through sweaty hair. His right arm throbbed, the fingers fat and stiff. Sharp shafts of pain shot up into his shoulder, dragging at his resolve and strength. Sighing, he closed his eyes. Despair tightened like a band around his chest again. He pressed his lips together.

This couldn't be happening. It just couldn't. Jade couldn't have lost all her lives and have left him here alone. Surely, when he opened his eyes, she would be sitting right across from him, looking anxious, ready to fix his arm and tell him exactly what he'd done wrong so he could argue with her.

Half-hopeful, Phoenix opened his eyes. There, sitting across from him looking faintly concerned, was not her fair, green-eyed, Elven face but Marcus' handsome, square-jawed one.

"Gaaah!" Anger burst free and flooded his belly with fire.

Phoenix sprang up. Marcus stood as well, laying a hand on his own sword, his expression watchful. His friend's caution inflamed Phoenix's mood further. He glared at the Roman, grabbed awkwardly at Blódbál and wrestled the magic sword from its sheath with his left hand.

"Get out of my way, Marcus," he warned.

Sitting around was pointless. If Jade was stupid enough to get herself captured and Vasi wasn't going to help then he would have to go find her, himself.

Marcus eyed him, circling to stay between him and the horses. "What are you going to do?"

"Go get that stupid girl on my own, since you lot are too pathetic to do it with me," Phoenix growled.

Blódbál's music rose and fell in his head; a symphony eagerly urging him on, feeding his anger at Jade and turning it toward Marcus as the nearer target.

"You can't save her on your own," Marcus reasoned. "You're injured and exhausted. You wouldn't be able to fight anyone at the moment and you know it."

His logic annoyed Phoenix further. Marcus was *always* calm. Faced with death and danger, he barely even blinked an eye. It was irritating. In fact, he decided, it was about time someone taught the arrogant Roman a thing or two.

"Y'think, do you?" he sneered. "I can beat you any day."

Marcus slid his sword free, his eyes following

Phoenix's slightest movement. "Maybe, right-handed but left-handed? I doubt it." His derisive chuckle inflamed Phoenix's rage until it consumed his thoughts.

"Marcus?" Brynn's question was loaded with doubt.

"Shut up," the Roman gestured the boy back, "I know what I'm doing."

"Somehow, I doubt that," Phoenix mocked. "You're always letting Jade do the thinking for you. What are you going to do now she's not here? No-one to worship and slobber over now. She's *gone*. She's left us to fend for ourselves. She's probably dead by now and I'm *stuck* here with you. That's what people do. They leave when you need them. So why don't you go, too, Marcus? I know you only came with us because of *her,*" Phoenix taunted, his mind filled with fury - anger at Jade for being stupid; anger at Marcus for turning against him. He would leave too, so what was the point in prolonging it? He wasn't needed anyway. Phoenix didn't need anyone.

He lunged, stabbing with the tip of his sword. Marcus twisted aside but Phoenix had seen the flash of real fear in the Roman's eyes and he exulted at it. Blódbál urged him on, flooding his mind with the desire to give in to the blood-rage. If he did, Blódbál promised, he would never be unhappy again; never be frightened; never be alone.

Finally, tired of fighting it; tired of being scared and alone, Phoenix did what he had sworn to Thor and his friends he would not. He let go. Letting down his mental barriers against the sword, he felt its full power pour into his soul and rejoiced in the molten, mad energy it gave him.

Now, his enemies would see his *real* power. The time had come to kill them all. Starting with this cocky little Roman in front of him. Phoenix bared his teeth in an animal growl and advanced on his friend, the red light of battle glowing in his eyes.

The two antagonists prowled around each other. Phoenix was only vaguely aware that Vasi grabbed at

Brynn as the boy took a half-step forward.

He heard the prince mutter: "Not now," as he backed away and dragged Brynn with him.

"But they'll kill each other," Brynn's protest sounded distant and muffled.

"I don't think so," Vasi shook his head. "Phoenix is grieving for his lost friend. Anger is just one of the stages of grief. Beneath it, he knows Marcus is his friend."

Brynn shook himself free. "You don't understand. Phoenix's sword is magic. It feeds his anger. I've never seen him quite this bad before. I don't think he's in control anymore. I think the sword is."

Vasi frowned. "Then we must watch closely. If Phoenix looks like he is going to hurt Marcus, we will intervene. In the mean time, let him get it out of his system if he can."

Brynn crossed his arms mutinously but stayed put.

For some reason, Brynn's lack of faith in his ability to control Blódbál stoked the flame of fury in Phoenix even higher. The red mist of wrath narrowed his vision until all he saw was Marcus' glittering sword dancing in front of him. What right did Brynn, Marcus or anyone else have to question him; to curtail him; to try and stop him? None. They had none. He was their leader.

With Blódbál in his hand, he was invincible.

Phoenix lunged again, his lips curling into a sneer of disdain. Marcus deftly turned the blade aside and danced out of reach. Phoenix went after him, slicing with a flurry of overhead blows from every angle. Marcus blocked them time and time again, metal clanging against metal in the dusty afternoon heat.

Phoenix spun, dropping low and slicing at Marcus' legs. The Roman leapt back, barely avoiding Blódbál's razor edge. By the time his feet were on the ground again, Phoenix closed the gap between them, fury consuming all reason and thought of friendship. He flicked limp, dark hair out of his eyes, snarling.

Brynn shivered and glance fearfully at Marcus.

The Roman boy was sweating, a frown furrowing his brow as he concentrated. He barely kept Phoenix's furious sword-strokes from connecting. With the power of Blódbál fully unleashed, Phoenix's disadvantage in fighting left-handed was all that kept Marcus alive. Phoenix's exultation grew as Marcus' breath became fast and ragged. His parries slowed and twice Blódbál's tip skimmed close to his chest as he sidestepped to avoid a strike.

Phoenix drew more energy from the sword and redoubled his efforts. His arm seemed to move of its own accord. The song of death blotted out the world. It was only a matter of time. Marcus only just managed to get his sword up in time to block the next vicious overhead blow. He couldn't last much longer.

Marcus lost his footing. He stumbled and fell onto one knee. A triumphant laugh escaped Phoenix's stretched-thin lips. It didn't sound like his voice but he didn't care. He stepped closer and raised the bloodthirsty sword over his head to deliver the final blow.

Blódbál descended from on high, straight toward Marcus' unprotected head.

Brynn shrieked a warning.

Marcus leaned to one side, surged to his feet and brought his shoulder and left arm into Phoenix's chest as they collided. For a few seconds, Phoenix stood frozen, leaning into the Roman; Blódbál still raised to strike.

His mind shrank back into his skull. Pain blossomed. He dropped his arm to his side and staggered back two steps. The berserker rage drained from his limbs, swept aside by astonishment and blinding agony. He stared in disbelief at Marcus and looked down at himself. A knife handle protruded from his chest.

Blódbál fell from nerveless fingers as Phoenix sank to his knees. Brynn gasped. Beside him, Vasi said Marcus' name in soft incredulity. Marcus dropped his own sword and came to Phoenix's side as he sagged. He eased Phoenix to the ground.

Phoenix looked up at Marcus in numb shock. His friend's dark eyes were filled with pain.

"I'm sorry, Phoenix," Marcus said quietly, "but I had to do it. Do you understand?"

Phoenix opened his mouth but nothing came out. A blessed feeling of utter relaxation spread throughout his body. For the first time in days, he felt like he could actually get a good night's sleep. He was a bit cold, though. Maybe if he just closed his eyes…

CHAPTER TWO

Jade awoke feeling distinctly unwell and extremely uncomfortable. Wisely, she kept her eyes closed for a few moments to get her bearings. She had no patience with people in movies who, on getting kidnapped, immediately gave away their wakeful state and started to ask stupid questions like "where am I?" and "who are you?". No self-respecting kidnapper would tell their victim that sort of information. Plus, if you're going to escape, letting the badguys know you're awake is just plain dumb.

So she lay still for awhile, listening, feeling, trying to work out where Yajat had brought her and whether he was still nearby.

She lay on her side, with her wrists and ankles bound. Her head rested on cold, unforgiving, hard stone. No light penetrated her eyelids, so it was either night time, or the room was dark. With each breath, she smelled dampness, death and decay. A faint trickle of water somewhere nearby made her both incredibly thirsty and desperate to go to the bathroom. There were no other sounds at all. Her ears rang with the silence.

Emboldened, she opened her eyes. It made little difference. A dim square of light in one section of her vision revealed at least one window but it was too dark to see outside. With a suppressed groan, she wriggled and squirmed until she could sit up. Shuffling backward, she eventually hit a stone wall and stopped.

A dungeon then, she realised. Hard on that thought followed a flicker of black humour: that brought her one imprisonment closer to Brynn and Phoenix's totals of what, six or seven now? Amusement fled as the reality of her situation sank in. Alone, captured, bound by iron chains that burnt her skin like fire; she felt weak, tired, hungry and scared. She'd lost count of how many lives she had left but it couldn't be more than two or three at the most. Now, worst of all, she was separated from her friends.

Leaning her back against the damp wall, Jade finally allowed herself to succumb to the emotion that swelled in her throat. With a quiet sob, she dropped her head onto her knees and cried.

It felt good.

She'd had never been the type to cry for long – it didn't solve anything and got little sympathy in a big family – so she soon gave up and wiped her face on her sleeve. The chains around her wrists clanked. She pulled at them experimentally but only succeeded in burning the palms of her hands on the hot-cold iron. At least someone had wrapped her wrists in cloth first, so her skin wasn't blistering. With a deep, determined breath, she got control of her emotions, leaned her head against the wall and tried to work out how she'd got into this stupid situation. Maybe that would give her an idea for getting out.

The last thing she remembered was Yajat materialising out of the darkness in the temple grounds in Pune in India. Phoenix had been about to activate the portal that would take them all to China for Level Five of this damnable game. Instead, Yajat had appeared, thrown a thin iron chain around her neck and arms and dragged her through the portal with him.

She had a vague impression of some sort of explosion then nothing. This was 80AD. How could there be explosives? Had her friends been hurt? Was she hurt? Jade sniffed again and focussed on the last two questions.

A quick assessment of her body showed no injuries, just a few bruises and general weakness that nothing but time, food, sleep and her herbs would fix.

Next she concentrated on the Binding Spell she'd put into place in Albion. The iron chains around her wrists and ankles muffled her Elven abilities but, through the fog of weakness and iron, Jade faintly sensed the unbroken Binding. With a sigh of utter relief, she slumped back against the wall. If the Binding remained whole then the others were still alive. She didn't have the power to find them yet but at least they were alive and would come for her – eventually.

In the mean time, she should take stock of whatever tools she still had and try to escape this dungeon. She slid one manacled hand across her chest, patting at her clothes, wincing as the chain scorched exposed skin with each movement. Knife: obviously gone. Staff: gone. Amulet: still around her neck.

Relief flashed through her. Her link to the real world was there. The jade and pearl yin-yang ring Cadoc had given her was still on her right hand, too, but that was of little importance. Just one more thing… Her fingers darted in and out of her shirt as a horrible, sinking feeling took over.

Gone. The Hyllion Bagia. The bottomless black hole bag that held anything and everything without getting bigger or heavier; gone. It held not only weapons, money and spare clothing but also the Horn of Aurfanon. As long as she had the Bag and the Horn, Jade had had hope.

Without the Horn, there was no way of summoning help; there were no hidden weapons; no money to bribe her way free. Nothing. Even worse, Zhudai now held a valuable magical object in his possession; one that could give him enormous power if he worked out how to use it.

Misery descended and tears once more welled in her eyes. What was she supposed to do now? No weapons, no bag, no friends. She missed Marcus' solid reliability, Phoenix's impetuous strength, Brynn's sly comments and cheeky grin.

Brynn! Jade sat up abruptly, eyes wide in the darkness. Frowning, she replayed the last day or so in her head. Yes… yes! The Bag wasn't lost at all. She'd given it to Brynn during the height of the war in India. He had kept it with him after he'd blown the Horn to summon Garuda to their rescue. She sagged against the wall. OK. So *she* didn't have the Bag but at least their arch enemy didn't have it, either. That was something, anyway.

With her heart lightened a little, Jade took more of an interest in her prison. Using the wall, she managed to shove herself upright, though every muscle protested. The thin iron chains dragged strength from her very core. She clenched her teeth against pain and weakness with every step. Hands outstretched in the darkness, she moved cautiously toward the small, dim square of light in the distance.

Before she reached it, a flickering, orange glow told her someone approached. Quickly, she backed away until she was once more up against the cold, damp stone wall. Ignoring the pain, she twisted the iron chain between her hands like a garrotte, although she had little hope of being able to use it effectively in her weakened state.

The door creaked cautiously open and golden shadows flickered into the dark cell. A small, elderly Chinese man smiled at her and bobbed his head in a series of small bows. Behind him stood a taller, younger man with the muscles and deadpan expression of a soldier or bodyguard.

"Come, come." The old man gestured at Jade. "The master wishes to see you but first you must bathe and rest. He sends his apologies for the poor accommodation you have been put into. His servant misunderstood his instructions. You are our *guest,* not our prisoner." The wrinkled face screwed up in distaste as he eyed her cell.

He smiled.

Jade glared at him in extreme mistrust. It could be a trick but what need was there for tricks when Zhudai already held her prisoner? Was it possible that there had been a mistake? That she wasn't meant to be imprisoned? It made no sense.

The man nodded eagerly. "Come. You will not be harmed. Come. There is food and drink waiting for you in your proper quarters and those chains will be removed." He held out a hand toward Jade, dark eyes crinkled at the edges as his smile broadened.

She weighed up the pros and cons rapidly. Chains gone, food, drink, bath, rest against deprivation, damp, cold, iron chains and stone walls. No contest. Even if it was some sort of trick, at least if the chains came off there was *some* chance she could escape.

Nibbling at her bottom lip, Jade followed the old man out of her cell toward the hope of freedom.

*****

Phoenix swam up from the blood-red depths of hell, back to the hellish world of consciousness. For a bizarre fraction of a second, he thought he heard his mother's voice, thought he smelled a strange, harsh, chemical scent. Then it faded. He opened his eyes and blinked blearily.

Marcus knelt over him, looking faintly worried. Behind him stood Brynn, apparently about to be stabbed by Vasi. Or maybe Brynn was holding Vasi back from stabbing Marcus. Yes, that made more sense. After all, Phoenix had wanted to stab the Roman, so why wouldn't Vasi? Part of him realised that was very fuzzy logic indeed and he wasn't yet thinking clearly, so he concentrated on waking up.

The Indian Prince caught sight of Phoenix's face and his jaw dropped, followed by his arm.

"What?" Vasi stumbled back, his expression horrified.

Brynn followed, murmuring some explanation of

Phoenix's miraculous return to life that must have soothed their friends' fears somehow. Vasi sat down on a log and gaped at Phoenix.

Phoenix switched back to Marcus and found the Roman watching him.

"Are you well?" Marcus asked in a low, tense voice.

Memory of the fight, his hatred, his determination to kill Marcus, flowed back into Phoenix's now-clear mind. He groaned. With an oath, he sat up, grabbed at his knife and checked the life-rubies on the hilt. Sure enough, one more of the seven he'd started this game with glinted dull and broken. He had just three red stones left intact.

"You…you killed me, Marcus." He fingered the ragged, bloody tear in his shirt. "You deliberately goaded me on and…and you killed me." Confused and hurt, he looked at the palm of his left hand. It was blank. "But…I don't understand."

Marcus gripped the hand with his own and squeezed. "There was no betrayal intended, my friend, so Jade's Binding Spell remains unbroken. We are still bound, the four of us, on this quest to kill Feng Zhudai. Yes, *four* of us." He nodded as Phoenix stared at him dazedly. "If you'd stopped to think, you'd know that Jade can't be dead if the Binding is whole."

Phoenix groaned and closed his eyes. "I'm an idiot."

"Only sometimes - when you let your anger and grief control you." Marcus smiled, standing up. "Now if you're finished being one, we can get on with our rescue mission."

Unthinking, Phoenix put his right hand down to push himself off the ground. Only as he brushed dust off his pants did he realise his broken arm no longer hurt. He looked at it in surprise, unwinding the rough cloth that held the splint in place. Flexing his fingers, he prodded the bone.

"It's healed!" He blinked at Marcus.

The Roman nodded. "I thought so."

"Bit of a drastic way of fixing a broken arm, isn't it?"

Marcus shrugged, handing him a water skin. "We need your sword arm and clear head if we're going to find Jade and defeat Zhudai. It seemed like a good idea at the time."

Phoenix choked on the swallow of water he'd just tipped into his mouth. "A *good idea*? I could have killed *you*, and then where would we have been?"

Marcus raised an eyebrow at him. "I was never in danger."

Phoenix opened his mouth, and shut it again. Even through the hazy, blood-red memories of the fight, he realised Marcus was right. The Roman had been cool and controlled throughout the fight, acting fearful for Phoenix's maddened benefit only. Phoenix, on the other hand, actually fought worse under the arcane influence of the sword, than when he thought straight. Twice now, Marcus mastered him when he'd given in to Blódbál's insidious song.

Frowning, Phoenix picked up the sword and turned it over in his hands. It hummed a smug, satisfied little tune in his head. He eyed Marcus. The Roman returned his look without expression. Phoenix sighed and slid the blade back into its sheath.

"I'm not sure whether I should thank you, hit you or apologise." He clapped Marcus on the shoulder.

"We should water the horses and keep moving," his friend replied, unfazed.

A short while later, as the mountain-shadows began to stretch far out across the plains behind, Vasi turned the group north, off the main path, onto a narrower one. With the refugees left behind, the travellers moved faster. The track wound precariously along ridge-crests, deeper into the mountains.

Just as jagged teeth of the mountain peaks ahead began to nibble at the edges of the sun, the path levelled out and they saw a deep-set curve in the vegetated hillside. Amongst the lush trees and vines, a cliff of bare, exposed volcanic rock came into view. Sheer and vertical it was punctured by regular, and obviously man-made, holes in the dark face. The sounds of hammer and chisel echoed down into the valley below.

Vasi drew rein. "The Caves of Karla." He waved a hand. "Inside you will find only a few Buddhist monks and craftsmen who work on construction of the many temples. If this 'portal' you speak of is in there, I do not know where it is. I've been here only once, as a boy."

"Aren't you coming in with us?" Phoenix peered at the blank, black cave-mouths. Memories of the Naga shivered down his spine.

"I must return to my father." Vasi shook his head. "This war has left our kingdom in chaos and, with the death of my brother, I am now heir. I cannot be away long or my father will be uneasy. These are a peaceful people. You will be safe."

Marcus pushed forward and reached out to grip the Prince's arm. "We are deeply grateful for your help in getting us here. May the gods protect you."

Vasi bowed his head regally. "And all of you, my friends." He released Marcus and took Phoenix's proffered hand. "If...*when* you find Jade, please tell her I...wish... I...would like..." The young prince flushed in the dwindling light.

Phoenix grinned at his discomfort. "I get it. I'll tell her. She has that affect on men, I've noticed. But you do know we aren't coming back this way? If our final Quest is successful then we'll be going home to our own land and we'll never see you again."

Behind, Phoenix heard Brynn's soft, sharp intake of breath and cursed his own stupidity. He'd forgotten that they'd never actually discussed the end of this game-play with Brynn. Oh, they'd mentioned 'going home' offhandedly but never really bluntly stated that they'd never be seeing friends again. Now he'd let the cat out of the bag and there was no Jade to smooth over his thoughtlessness.

Unaware of the blunder, Vasi grimaced. "I feared as much but who knows – stranger things have happened than old friends reuniting."

"In this world, you have no idea how much stranger," Phoenix murmured as he released his hand, waved and kicked his horse into a weary walk.

Vasi and his servant turned and began their long trek home, leaving the three companions to forge ahead alone.

An awkward silence fell between the friends as they approached the entrance to the Karla Caves.

"Are you really going away if we kill Zhudai?" Brynn sounded young and unsure.

Phoenix sighed and nudged his horse over to walk beside the boy's. "I'm sorry, Brynn. We should have made it clear to you earlier. You know we came to this world by accident. Our goal is to get home to our own lives and families in our own world by completing all the Quests we've been set. I'm sorry." He glanced at Marcus but the Roman boy's face remained blank, his gaze stoically ahead.

Brynn turned his face away and scrubbed at his cheeks. Phoenix laid a hand on his thin shoulder and squeezed it, not knowing what to say. The boy shrugged it off.

"You ok?" Phoenix asked hesitantly.

"I'm fine." Brynn hunched a shoulder. "I was fine before you two arrived. I'll be fine when you're gone. I can look after myself. Have done for awhile now, in case you'd forgotten." He sent Phoenix a scathing look and kicked his pony so it trotted ahead a little.

Marcus came alongside. "I'll look after him." His eyes were on Brynn's stiff back.

"Thanks." Phoenix's throat was tight. There was so

much more to be said but he couldn't say any of it. Where was Jade when he needed someone good with words and people?

The thought of her pulled his mind back to where it should be. As much as he liked Marcus and Brynn, he had to remember that he and Jade didn't belong in their world. The problem was, if he couldn't find and rescue Jade quickly, they may end up belonging here whether they wanted it or not. A sense of urgency in his gut told him time was running out - and quickly.

A minute later, all thoughts of his home vanished as Phoenix and his friends rounded the last corner and saw Karla Caves in all its glory. Half-lit by the last shafts of sunset, the caves cut into the volcanic cliffs took his breath away with their magnificence and sheer scope.

All around lay the evidence of hard work over many years. High in the curving black wall, narrow steps lead to long, low cave entrances, split by carved pillars left to hold the roof up. Down these stairs hurried dozens of monks, clad in flowing orange robes. In the centre of the cliff, at ground level, gaped an enormous, rectangular cave entrance, flanked by two huge pillars. Atop each, lions stood proud and behind them arched a massive window surrounded by intricate carvings of people, animals and geometric designs.

As the travellers dismounted wearily from their horses, a small group of orange-clad monks emerged from this structure and shuffled toward them. As they approached, they moved apart to reveal a bent and frail old man at the centre. Also wearing faded orange robes and with his head clean-shaven, the wizened monk put his hands together and bowed deeply.

"Namaste. Welcome to our home, Phoenix Carter of Cambridge," he intoned. "The portal is waiting within. You must hurry. There are only three days until the *ri shi* and Long Baiyu is weak. Even worse, without your strength, Jade Lockyer is in danger of losing the path."

CHAPTER THREE

Jade followed the old servant up several flights of stairs. Her surroundings became progressively more pleasant along the way. The steps went from slippery, dark stone, to polished marble then to polished red wood. Smells changed from damp decay to the enticing aromas of exotic food. From somewhere nearby floated the melancholy sounds of a stringed musical instrument; the unseen musician plucking a strange but pleasant tune. The walls on either side of the stairs began as rough black rock, altered to gleaming wood and then to something translucently white that she suspected was nothing more than thin cloth framed in black wood.

This last change reassured her. They couldn't possibly hold her prisoner in walls that she could put her finger through. Maybe it had been all a big mistake, like the old man said.

At last, the servant and soldier ushered her through a sliding door, into a huge room. Jade stopped, staring in surprise. The door slid shut behind as the soldier took up a post outside. This was far from the misery of her cell. Smiling, the old man bowed and gestured for her to inspect the place. After a moment's hesitation, she did so.

A raised bed was half-hidden behind an exquisitely decorated screen in one corner of the room. She ran a hand over the intricate silk coverings and drapes that decorated it. They were in every imaginable colour and embroidered with brilliant designs of birds, clouds and lotus flowers. It was beautiful.

In another area, a low table, surrounded by silken cushions, invited her to relax. Placed perfectly on it was a tea set of the palest porcelain, delicately painted with blue birds. They were paired with a small bowl and set of chopsticks. Her nose caught the enticing scent of fish and vegetables in two gently steaming, covered bowls. Her mouth began to water. Unconsciously, she moved toward the table.

The servant stepped in front of her and she shied back. He smiled reassuringly and held out a key.

"Let me take those off of you," he tut-tutted at the iron bands around her wrists and ankles. He unlocked the chains and hurried to hand them out the door to a waiting servant.

Jade glanced longingly at the food.

"Soon, soon," the old man said. "First you must bathe. Through here." He waved her toward another sliding door. "There are towels, fresh clothing and creams for those burns. Take as long as you need. The food will still be hot when you are ready. Eat, sleep. The Master will see you in the morning. I will send a maid to help you finish dressing." Bowing again, he slid the door closed behind her and she heard his soft footfalls patter into silence.

Listening hard, Jade slid the door open and tiptoed out. Glancing around, she saw the silhouettes of two soldiers standing outside the main door. Assessing her inner strength, she realised she didn't have enough magical ability at the moment to put a narcoleptic cat to sleep, let alone two guards.

Biting her lip, she turned to look for other exits. There were none. All of the other walls were solid wood. There was one, wide window but a quick look outside revealed she was high above an enclosed, ornate courtyard garden with no easy way down and no obvious exit. Golden afternoon sunlight shafted through the room from a pierced wooden screen high up in one wall. If another way out existed, it wasn't an easy one. In the mean time… she cast another longing look at the food and the bathroom. She might as well regain her strength and get *clean*.

Within a few minutes – after first working out how to use the hole-in-the-floor toilet facilities - she shed her filthy trousers and tunic and slid blissfully into a standing tub of warm water. Now *this* was more like it.

*****

Far away to the west, Phoenix, Marcus and Brynn followed their escorts into the grand Chaitya of the Karla Caves temple complex. They passed between the lion-topped columns, beneath the arched window, into a vaulted, colonnaded room that made even Marcus blink in astonishment. Sixteen metres overhead, curved wooden beams supported a stone ceiling, mimicking an upside down boat hull. Marching down both sides of the wide hall were rows of hand-carved stone pillars topped by intricately carved figurines. Just this hall alone represented thousands of hours of labour with the basic hand tools Phoenix had seen so far. If their guides were to be believed, there were dozens of other halls carved out of the very guts of the mountain; hewn with love by the monks who followed the peaceful path of the Buddha and all he taught.

The sound of their horses' hooves echoed like gunshots in the enormous room, making Phoenix uneasy. There had been some contention amongst the monks about allowing the animals inside the hall but their objections were overruled by the elderly Lama. He listened to every argument with a benign smile then bowed to his advisors and calmly told them his decision: the travellers and their animals were to pass through the great prayer hall. It was necessary. Silenced, the monks followed their aged leader.

Ignoring them, he shuffled ahead to catch up with

Marcus; murmuring into the Roman's ear. Phoenix eyed them suspiciously, wondering what was being said but unable to overhear without being obvious.

Finally, deep inside the hall, the monk stopped. They had reached the farthest corner, behind a large, domed stone structure that shadowed the end wall in darkness.

"There." He pointed with a bent finger. "The Portal is in the far wall. You know how to use it and where to go. Good luck, young ones."

"Don't we even have time to stop and eat?" Brynn whispered at Phoenix's elbow.

His young face was pinched with exhaustion and hunger. None of them had slept much the last few days and their meals had been sketchy at best.

Phoenix cast an inquiring look at the Lama, who shook his head regretfully, bowed and said: "The diamond can only be polished by friction; the man perfected by trials."

After mulling that over for a few moments, Phoenix turned to Brynn. "I'd have to say that meant 'no'."

The Lama sighed. "I am sorry, young man but your friend is in danger and it is up to you three to save her. The *ri shi* coincides with the Qingming Festival and Zhudai will be greatly strengthened at this time. If you wait, it may be too late and the balance of the world will be upset forever."

Brynn groaned. "So we have to go save the world again, huh? Seems to be a regular thing in my life since I started travelling with you. It'll be nice to get back home where the only thing I have to worry about is how to pick the purse of the nearest Roman without getting caught."

Phoenix caught the faintest flash of fear and hurt beneath the boy's bravado.

Marcus and Brynn moved over to the doorway and Marcus stretched out his hand to touch the stones. Phoenix hesitated, looking back at the old monk.

"Hang on." He folded his arms across his chest. "We *do* know where to go and how to use it but how do *you* know so much about us and about Jade? Are you some sort of magician? Do you have special powers that told you we were coming?"

The old face crinkled in childish delight. "Dear boy, I am nothing special, but you and your friends are. I have known you were coming for many years. When your friend, Cadoc, arrived through the portal a few days ago and asked for you, I knew your arrival was imminent. I do hope you met with him?"

"Oh yes," Phoenix growled.

He still had mixed feelings about the Player Prince who had befriended them, betrayed them then redeemed himself by helping them against Yajat.

"Oh good." The monk rubbed his hands together with glee. "Please tell Long Baiyu when you see him, that I am so glad I was able to fulfil my foreordained task correctly. Now you must hurry." He ushered him toward the three-stone portal that could be seen dimly in the corner of the hall. "If you do not, both your friend and mine will be lost forever and you will be trapped in this realm."

"Hang on," Phoenix repeated. "That's twice you've mentioned this Baiyu guy. Who is he and what does he have to do with Jade? I thought Zhudai had her."

"Yes, of course he does," the lama blinked in surprise, "but he also holds Baiyu prisoner and it is your task to free my friend as well as your own."

"Oh no." Phoenix backed away, shaking his head. "Freeing Jade is fine but our job after that is to master the Yu Dragon and defeat Zhudai. I'm not getting involved in anyone else's little problems again, not after the war we've just been through."

The old man smiled enigmatically and bowed. "Of course. You must do what is right and only you can decide that."

"Oh man!" Phoenix threw up his hands in defeat. "You sound like my father."

The monk's grin broadened. "Where do you think Alex Carter got his ideas from, son? And while you're thinking about that, consider one more thing: *the beginning of wisdom is to call things by their true names.*"

There was a bright flash of light as Marcus activated the portal to China. Distracted, Phoenix looked over. When he turned back, the old man was gone, the great hall echoed emptily and he was left with nothing but mysteries and enigmas.

"Dammit," he muttered, irritated and unnerved, "I really hate it when they do that. 'Their true names'? Whose names? What names? 'Fred'? 'Mary?' They're names. How did he know my dad's name? How could he possibly know my dad at all? Great. More riddles." With a growl of frustration, he dragged his reluctant horse into the shimmering portal.

*****

Jade emerged from the bathing room almost an hour after she'd entered. Her fingers were prunes but she felt really clean for the first time since they'd left Heron's bathhouse in Alexandria. It took a few tries to get dressed in the exotic, silken wrap gown left out for her, but it suited her well enough. A pale blue under-robe showed at the hem and throat, beneath an over-robe of delicately embroidered silver and blue silk. Flowing sleeves fell almost to the ground. She wondered if she'd be able to eat without getting them dirty.

There were a number of combs and jewels that seemed to be for her hair but she had no idea how to use them, so she left it loose. One of the longer, jewelled pins, however, now nestled in the front of her robe – just in case she needed a weapon in a hurry. The bath had been nice but Jade wasn't about to forget that Yajat had kidnapped her, chained her in iron and pushed her into a dungeon.

As promised, the food on the table still steamed. After a moment's thought about the possibility of poison and drugs, Jade shrugged and fell to. She couldn't remember the last time she'd eaten – or even felt like eating. If Zhudai wanted her dead, he could have killed her already.

After she'd eaten her fill, she wandered toward the inviting bed and thought hard about taking a nap. Darkness had crept in sometime during her bath and someone had lit lamps around the room. It was later than she realised. She sat down on the edge of the bed, running her hand absently over the smooth silk bedspread. The servant had said something about seeing his Master in the morning. She could only assume he meant Yajat's master, Zhudai. But he was the arch-nemesis of this game, so what did he want to see her for? Why was he treating her so nicely?

Kicking off her slippers, Jade slid backward until her spine pushed up against a pile of cushions at the head of the bed. She frowned, nibbling on a fingertip as she tried to work out exactly what Zhudai and Yajat were playing at. Why try to kill her then kidnap her instead? Why throw her in a dungeon then treat her like an honoured guest? Was this some sort of bizarre mind game? What did they want from her?

What had Cadoc said? Something about rumours in Xijing; rumours that Zhudai wanted to make himself immortal; that the Han Emperor himself was coming from his capital in Luoyang to speak with Zhudai. What on earth did that have to do with *her?*

Jade stretched her stiff neck and wriggled a bit lower so the cushions supported her head. The hairpin prodded her stomach, so she took it out of her robe and laid it on a side table. Maybe Zhudai thought her Elvish blood could somehow transfer Elven longevity to himself? She shook her head, dismissing that idea. Cadoc said immortal, not long-lived. Even Elves died eventually, so the blood of a mere half-elf wouldn't be of any use in helping Zhudai become immortal.

So what would? Jade let her mind drift, trying to

access all the lore her avatar knew regarding magical ways to become immortal. Somewhere in between contemplating drinking the Water of Life, the blood of the White Wyrm, or the Elixir of the Gods, exhaustion fogged her mind and muffled it with sleep.

She dreamed, briefly, that Phoenix, Marcus and Brynn were somewhere close by and in trouble: outnumbered by faceless warriors. Calling their names, she ran through darkness to reach them but a barred door slammed shut in front of her face. She was trapped in a cage made of gold. It burnt her skin like iron. Then her mother and sisters appeared, pointing at her through the bars and laughing, mocking her. Even the beauty and skill of her avatar was not enough to impress them. Behind them, Phoenix, Marcus and Brynn just stood watching. Behind *them* stood a shadowed figure gesturing urgently to her as though he or she wanted help of some sort. Frustration made her grip the bars unthinkingly. Pain pierced her sleep.

With a cry, she awoke to a dark room, convinced her hands were burnt; that her friends were really there after all, ready to rescue her. When the room remained silent and empty, her hands unmarked, she clutched at a silken pillow and hid her face in it until she slept again.

*****

Far below, in a cell not unlike the one from which she had been released, Long Baiyu struggled upright, his eyes wide in the darkness. When Jade was close, he had hoped to speak with her. By removing her, Zhudai had also removed that idea. Baiyu was once again alone. He tried reaching her in her sleep, as she had been reached once before when she was between-lives, but she was too caught up in her own fears to hear his thoughts.

Now, he sensed her weakening; and sensed also that Phoenix was in trouble. Jade now walked a path only she could choose. Baiyu could not help in the decision she had to make. He could only hope she chose wisely, for all of their sakes.

Phoenix, however…

Baiyu closed his eyes and reached out mentally to contact someone close by who might be able to help the young warrior.

CHAPTER FOUR

Phoenix, Marcus and Brynn all stepped through the shimmering surface of the portal at the same time, blades drawn. Once through, Phoenix caught only a fleeting glimpse of close walls and a low ceiling before the horses crowded through and the portal schlorped out of existence. Shadows closed in immediately, as though they had been waiting to pounce. Darkness blanketed everything so absolutely that he reached up and touch his own eyelashes to make sure his eyes were open.

For several seconds the three companions stood in front of the portal in silence, ears and eyes straining to hear anything beyond restless animal sounds made by the horses. Nothing. Phoenix decided he was glad the horses weren't silent. Their stompings and huffing breaths were the only feeling of normality about this oppressive place. In an effort to dispel his own sense of unease, he cleared his throat.

"So," he tried for light and cheery but didn't quite manage to suppress the uneasiness in his voice, "we've come through into a small, dark, enclosed space...what an astonishing surprise."

Brynn snickered but there was an edge of nervousness to his tone as well.

"Yep. You'd think they'd come up with something original."

" 'They' who?" Phoenix reached out to lay a hand on

the boy's shoulder, fumbling in the dark.

"These 'programmers' of yours." The boy sounded offhand, as though he didn't really care much. "The magicians who sent you two here and who keep throwing all these obstacles in our way. I have to admit, whatever you did to offend them, it must have been bad. Do me a favour and apologise to them, would you?"

Phoenix shut his mouth with a snap, realising Brynn couldn't see his astonished look anyway. Obviously the boy had sharp ears and had put together snatches of his and Jade's conversations in an interpretation that made some sort of sense to him. There was no point in trying to explain that Phoenix had never met the game programmers and had no way of contacting them, so he just nodded then added aloud,

"I'll do what I can. In the mean time, let's get some torches lit and find a way out of here."

"Does this count as number seven?" Brynn's question was slightly muffled as he dug into his backpack.

Disconcerted, Phoenix had to think before he realised what the boy was talking about: being trapped or imprisoned. He and Brynn had a sort of competition going; counting how many times it had happened now. He grinned and shook his head.

"Nah – we have to be accidentally trapped or deliberately imprisoned. That's the rules."

Brynn's incredulous reply echoed dully, as though the sound was being sucked up by the walls. "There are rules now?"

Phoenix shrugged. "We can't claim every dark place we end up is on the list or we'd be up to about ten by now. Besides," he peered into the darkness, "we don't even know where we are. It might be easy to get out."

"Just spare me the rock falls this time, huh?"

Phoenix chuckled. "No guarantees."

Brynn made a triumphant sound, which was shortly

followed by the click of flints being knocked together. Very quickly, he had a small flame going and then a torch lit. Handing it to Marcus, the boy lit a second and kept hold of it himself. Phoenix eyed him askance. Brynn cocked his head.

"I figured you'd need your hands free to chop things up when they leap out at us."

"Oh, way to be positive," Phoenix groaned.

Brynn sent him a quirky grin. "Oh, you know me. I'm positive – positive something big and nasty will jump out at us any time now. Just wait."

As one, all three turned outward, holding torches and weapons high and peering into the darkness beyond the pool of light. Nothing leapt. Phoenix and Marcus glanced at each other then down at Brynn. The boy raised one shoulder.

"Give it a minute."

"I'd rather not." Marcus glanced up. With an oath, he snatched his arm down, lowering the torch to head height.

Phoenix looked up to see what had caused the reaction. Little smouldering sparks glowed on the ceiling. The sparks struggled then died. Marcus let out a soft sigh of relief. The ceiling was wood, though not timber bearers and joists like a house. It was just raw timber. Whatever this building was, it was very basic - just packed earth walls and dozens of enormous logs laid side-by-side overhead. They were obviously covered by something, since no light filtered through, but any gaps were too small and packed with dirt to tell what the roof covering might be.

He took in the space around them. The room measured roughly five metres wide and only just over head height. Ahead, its earthen walls turned abruptly to form a solid wall only a few steps away. All in all, a very small, bleak and exit-less place to emerge.

OK. Not time to panic. What would Jade do in this situation? How would she find a way out? The Portal?

The last few times, the Portal had been firmly set into a wall, so it wasn't with any great hopes of escape that Phoenix and the others pushed the horses to one side and turned around to look at the gate.

"Aaaah!" Brynn's strangled shriek died almost as it was born, absorbed by the earth walls.

A dozen or more soldiers faced them from beyond the empty stone gate. Fully armoured and armed with long, wicked, levelled spears, the men stood in perfect formation and utter silence, eyeing the newcomers without expression. Behind them, in close configuration, stood another rank and another and another.

Instinctively, Phoenix drew Blódbál into the guard position. Marcus' sword glinted in the torchlight as well. Together, they faced their enemy with one thought: there were just too many.

If Jade were here, or if there were another exit, they may have a chance but two warriors and a boy-thief against dozens or even hundreds of trained soldiers? Impossible. They would meet their deaths here in this airless little room, without even getting a chance to save their friend.

For a long moment, Phoenix stood, semi-crouched, awaiting the soldiers' charge. Nothing happened. The men continued to stand motionless and stare. Perplexed, he straightened up and exchanged puzzled looks with the others. Still the soldiers didn't move.

"Is it my imagination," Brynn whispered, "or are these guys really, really good at being very, very still."

"A little too good, perhaps," Marcus agreed.

Brynn edged forward, his torch outthrust. The soldiers remained where they were. Boldly, he waved the torch beneath the outstretched hand of one man. The soldier didn't even blink. Phoenix frowned. None of them blinked, actually. A dim memory scratched at his mind, asking for attention.

"Hey," he lowered Blódbál and took a few steps closer,

edging past a lethal-looking speartip, "I know what these are."

Brynn was already there, tentatively touching a dusty arm. "They're made of clay!" he said wonderingly. With a knuckle, he rapped on the body. The chamber rang with the clear, bell-like sound of fired clay.

"They mean we're underground, not in a building. They're the Terracotta Warriors," Phoenix finished, awed. The other two looked at him in bewilderment. "The first big ruler of China...Emperor Chin...Chin-something... when he died, he had thousands of life-sized warriors made out of clay to be buried with him. This must be them. Jade's going to be majorly annoyed she missed these guys." He opened his mouth to add that he hadn't recognised them because, in his time, all the beautifully-painted details had worn off, leaving plain, red clay. He shut it again, deciding it was too hard to explain he'd seen them that way on television.

Luckily, Brynn turned away, exclaiming in amazement over the detailed form and paintwork.

"They look so *real*. Their armour looks like leather and," he moved his head from side to side, staring at an impassive face intently, "I'm *sure* his eyes are following me." It didn't take him long, either, to discover the uniqueness of every face and the sharpness of every bronze weapon.

Sucking on a punctured thumb, the boy frowned. "But what are they supposed to do? What are they for?"

Phoenix shrugged, once again pondering the more important issue of getting out.

"They're meant to guard the Emperor's treasure and serve him in the afterlife, I suppose."

"Treasure?" Brynn's eyes lit up and he peered into the gloom beyond the soldiers with interest.

"No time, remember?" He laid a heavy hand on the boy's thin shoulder. "Besides, in this world, they're probably spelled to come to life if you try and raid the Emperor's tomb."

Brynn rolled his eyes and nodded. "That sounds like something that would happen to us. You owe me." He wagged a finger at Phoenix, who grabbed it and twisted it upside-down until the boy yelped.

"Just remember what happened last time we raided the chamber of a dead king?"

"Yeah," Brynn said cynically, "I picked up some seriously cool treasure – which Jade then gave away again while trying to save your life, as I recall."

"That would be the life *you* then took away?" Phoenix snapped, getting irritated.

"Enough." Marcus admonished, laying a hand on each of them. "We need to work on getting out of here, not rehash past mistakes. Ideas?"

"We could put the horses into the Hyllion Bagia again and dig our way out," Brynn suggested.

"Jade had the bag, remember?" Phoenix sighed. "Which means Yajat and Zhudai have it."

"No she didn't, I do." Brynn pulled out the shiny, black cloth and waved it like a flag. "She gave it to me to get the Horn of Aurfanon out back in India when we were losing the war. I never got a chance to give it back."

"The Horn!" The idea of instant salvation bolstered Phoenix's spirits immediately.

"No." Marcus shook his head. "We have to be in dire peril for the horn to work and we can only use it one more time, anyway."

"You're right. This doesn't qualify as dire – yet." Phoenix scrubbed a hand through his hair. "So what else was in there?"

Brynn cocked his head and squinted at the bag. "Umm…Roman spears and money, Egyptian treasure, clothes, the Horn. Nothing else I know that would help."

"OK. So that brings us back to the original question."

Phoenix glanced at the others. "How do we get out of here?"

Marcus raised his torch again, staring at the ceiling. "Could we move the logs and dig out?"

Phoenix shook his head. "If I remember rightly, the logs are laid across these pits and buried under about ten feet of dirt. There's not enough space to move one and not even Blódbál could chop through one of those suckers. Pity we don't have Thor's hammer any more."

Marcus shrugged and pointed toward the terracotta warriors with his torch. "In that case, we have to hope there's a way out behind them."

Brynn tilted his head, examining the ranks of soldiers. "We'll never get the horses through without knocking them all over. Although," he shrugged, "we've never let the destruction of a few ancient monuments stop us before."

"There is a gap down the side." Marcus indicated it. "If we can get past the spears, we should be able to squeeze through."

"Sounds good," Brynn agreed. "Let's turn them around." He ducked in between two soldiers, and grabbed one by the waist and heaved. It teetered slightly then rocked slowly back to its original position.

"Err," Phoenix began.

Brynn glared at him. "They're heavy! I thought it would be hollow – light, y'know?" He grunted, trying again. This time, when the figure rocked to one side, Brynn pulled to turn it as well. The man-sized clay soldier tilted and twisted to one side; its spear now pointing almost toward its neighbour. Brynn gave it one more push, just to turn it completely. The spear now posed no danger to them or the horses. He grinned back at Marcus, who smiled faintly and shook his head.

"What?" Brynn asked in an aggrieved tone. "This isn't easy. You guys could help, you know."

The Roman stepped forward and grasped the long

wooden handle of the nearest spear. With a quick jerk, he pulled it free of the earthenware hand that held it and dropped it to the ground at his feet. Phoenix laughed aloud at Brynn's expression, smothering the sound with a hand. It felt good to laugh.

Brynn grimaced and rubbed his forehead with a grubby fist. "Well, I suppose you *could* do it that way, too. Would you please stop laughing at me?" He glared half-heartedly at Phoenix, who grinned back.

Marcus pulled another spear free. Phoenix followed suit, still expecting the lifelike pottery man to object.

"Man, we could use one of Jade's bright ideas about now," he muttered, sobering as he eyed the long rank of soldiers. "What if we get to the other end and find it doesn't lead us out, either?"

"Then we come up with another plan," Marcus said equably. "You're starting to sound like Jade, anyway."

"There's sure to be a way out through the tomb of that Emperor," Brynn added with a grin.

"You're just saying that because you want to find the treasure," Phoenix rolled a scornful look at the boy as they lead the horses past the first line of figures. It was a tight squeeze but they could just scrape by without knocking any of them over.

"Who, me?" Brynn tried to look innocent and failed.

They walked on for awhile in watchful silence.

Marcus held up a hand. "I feel a breeze."

Sure enough, the faint scent of open air brushed Phoenix's cheek as he turned his face. The torch Marcus held guttered and jumped, its light casting weird shadows of distorted warriors on the walls and low ceiling.

"Smells like rain." Brynn sighed with relief.

"Did you hear something?" Marcus' sharp question was lost in Phoenix's next eager words.

"I think I see something – a ramp, maybe." He tugged his horse onward.

"Phoenix," Marcus glanced back over his shoulder, "I'm sure I heard…"

"It was nothing. C'mon, we're almost there. I can see the stars." Phoenix hurried ahead.

It was a ramp of sorts. Several logs had slipped off their moorings and dropped one end into a large, open space in the entombed warriors' pit. Dirt had tumbled down, making a steep, slippery exit from the darkness, into the overcast, moonless night above.

Phoenix frowned at the exit, trying to work out the best way to get five reluctant horses up it. Brynn made an excited sound and vanished into the darkness beneath the logs. Marcus stared back the way they'd come. He drew his sword.

"Right," Phoenix decided. "I'm pretty sure it's stable enough but I'm going to climb up myself, just to test it. If it won't hold the horses, we can always do the Bag thing again. You guys wait here." He looked around. "Where's Brynn gone?"

"I don't know," Marcus' reply was tight with strain, "but I'm *sure* I heard something back there."

"You're imagining things," Phoenix assured him. "There's no-one there but a bunch of fake clay soldiers. Now where's Brynn?"

"Hey!" Brynn's voice sounded faintly from beneath the earthen ramp. "I've found a door here. I bet it leads to the Emperor's tomb. It's all covered in gold and there's writing on it. I've picked the lock, easy. I'm just going to-"

"Don't open it!" Phoenix and Marcus yelled at the same time.

There was a faint squeak, followed by several ominous twangs and thumps; then silence.

"Brynn?" Phoenix called out. "Are you ok?

"Um," the boy's voice was faint and sheepish, "help?"

"I'd better go get him," he said in aside to Marcus.

"Sounds like he's got himself in trouble again."

Marcus' hand gripped his arm and Phoenix almost yelped in shock. He looked at the Roman boy's face, white in the torchlight.

"What?"

"I don't think he's the only one. Look."

Phoenix looked into the darkness where the clay soldiers stood. There was nothing but rank upon rank of blank Chinese faces staring at them, spears levelled, bronze tips and painted eyes glinting in the torchlight.

"What? I don't see anything."

Marcus' fingers tightened. "We can see their *faces.*"

"So?" Phoenix shrugged. "We could always see their faces. So what?"

"We're behind them now. We should only see their backs," Marcus whispered. "They've *turned around.*"

His words were followed by the creaking, musical, thunderous sound of a thousand clay hands tightening on a thousand spears; and a thousand clay feet taking a step forward, toward the intruders.

CHAPTER FIVE

"Oh man!" Phoenix groaned. He raised a fist and shook it toward the ceiling. "C'mon! An army of clay soldiers coming to life? Even *I* know that one. A little originality here, please?"

"Who are you talking to?" Marcus dropped into a fighters crouch, his eyes never leaving the slow-moving wall of automatons.

"Nevermind," Phoenix muttered.

"You were the one who said they were spelled to come to life if the tomb was raided," Marcus reminded him.

"It was a *joke*, ok? I didn't expect them to be *this* predictable. Brynn! Get out here!" he yelled, backing up against his horse. The animal snorted at him and pushed back.

Marcus cast a quick look at the steep, mud-covered ramp. It glistened with rain.

"We'll never get the horses up that, or into the Bag in time."

The terracotta men took another ponderous step forward.

"Do we fight or run, then?" Phoenix looked at Blódbál dubiously. It was a magic sword but he wasn't sure even it could stand up against a thousand ceramic enemies who didn't feel pain and probably couldn't be killed.

"Without Jade's skills, I don't think we have what it will take to stop these magical things," Marcus replied evenly.

"Brynn's door then?" he suggested. "Through the undoubtedly-cursed and probably booby-trapped tomb of a dead Emperor?"

"So it seems," the Roman agreed grimly.

"Of course," Phoenix sighed.

Together, they snatched at the horses' reins and hauled them beneath the broken timber roof, into the unknown. The sound of heavy, synchronised footfalls echoed loudly behind.

Brynn's torch lay on the floor, sputtering in the dirt. By its smoky orange light, Phoenix saw the boy's predicament. In spite of the danger that dogged their footsteps, he had to laugh.

The tomb entrance had been boobytrapped with loaded crossbows. Ten bolts had been flung at the intruder who dared to open the tomb. Luckily, Brynn was a little smaller than the trap-builders expected and the crossbows were old, so he was uninjured – except for his pride. Three of the bolts speared through his loose clothing and he stood pinned to the wooden door. He'd managed to tear himself free of two of them but the third stuck through the thickest part of his pants-hem and the material wouldn't rip.

The clatter and clink of clay soldiers resounded in the small space.

"Quit playing around, Brynn." Phoenix yanked the bolt free and handed it to the glowering boy. "And find a way out of this mess you got us into."

Brynn opened his mouth but movement over Marcus' shoulder caught his eyes – which widened into horror at the sight of the first clay soldiers stepping out of the darkness.

"I thought you were joking!" he yelped, backing into the tomb opening.

"So did I." Phoenix snatched up the torch and thrust it at him. "Let's go."

They barely managed to get the horses inside and the

door closed before the first speartip thrust through gaps in the wood of the door. It emerged inches from Marcus' nose. The Roman flinched backward.

"There's no lock on this side," Brynn wailed, scrabbling around for something to jam into the door.

"There's got to be some way of blocking the door. Go further in if you have to but find it," Phoenix ordered, leaning all his considerable strength against the wood. Something heavy and hard slammed into it, jarring him to the teeth as he braced himself. His feet slid a couple of inches on the dirt. He shifted to get better purchase on the dusty floor.

A few seconds later, Brynn called out to Marcus. After a quick glance at Phoenix, the Roman ran toward the sound, towing the frightened horses behind him. The door jolted beneath Phoenix's shoulder again and again. Wood began to splinter.

"Phoenix!" Marcus' deep voice echoed down the tunnel. "Run. We can block this entrance."

With one uneasy look at the door, Phoenix jumped back and ran. Behind him, the door flew open, wood shattering and metal clashing on stone. A bronze-tipped spear flew past his head. Gulping, he sped up. An arrow zipped by, scraping his arm. The deafening thump of pottery feet grew louder again. When was this tunnel going to end?

There, ahead! The orange blaze of a torch lit the regular outline of a doorway. Brynn's head was silhouetted against it.

"C'mon! Hurry!" the boy shouted. "They're right behind you."

Phoenix grimaced. His lungs burned. So close now. Four more paces.

Pain ripped through his ribs and left shoulder.

He stumbled, falling through the exit to land on his knees on a hard, cold surface. Dragging a shallow, painful breath, he coughed.

Behind, a stupendous, grinding crash was followed quickly by three more, equally as loud, then deafening silence.

Marcus and Brynn appeared at his side.

"We released a drop-stone designed to block the entrance. It was probably meant to trap us in the tunnel but the mechanism had corroded. They won't get through. Now don't move," Marcus ordered, his brow furrowed with concern.

"That bad, huh?" Phoenix coughed again. Something dark sprayed from his mouth.

Gently, Marcus and Brynn lay him down on his stomach. There was a jostling, painless tug and a spear clattered to the floor beside his head. He eyed it resignedly. The tip glistened with blood in the torchlight. A loud ringing in his ears blotted out the words he saw Marcus speaking. His toes and feet were cold. This was getting to be way too familiar a feeling. Dammit.

The world went dark. Again.

An unknowable time later, Phoenix awoke. Marcus crouched beside him but Brynn had disappeared. Phoenix eased himself up and sighed.

"One more down. Two to go," he joked, trying to ignore the sickening sinking feeling in the pit of his stomach. There were now only two life-rubies left in the hilt of his dagger.

"You must guard them more carefully," Marcus said, holding out a leather water bag for him to drink from. "We have yet to rescue Jade, master the Yu dragon and defeat Zhudai."

"I know, I *know*," Phoenix returned irritably, raking back his long hair. "This stuff is a *lot* harder to do without Jade around to help with the magical stuff, you know."

Marcus sat down, re-capping the water and stowing it away.

"I know," he echoed.

There was an odd note to his quiet reply that made Phoenix look sharply over at his friend. Realisation dawned. How had he missed it?

"You… you *like* her, don't you?" he murmured, glancing about for Brynn.

The boy wandered a little further away, torch raised high, inspecting what looked like regular piles of stone on the floor of the room they occupied.

Marcus turned bleak, dark eyes on his friend then looked away, his lips pressed hard together.

"But…" Phoenix faltered, not knowing what to say. He wasn't exactly big on experience in these matters. "You know we have to leave at the end of all this, don't you?"

"Yes."

For once, Marcus' minimal conversational style annoyed him. "So what are you going to do?"

The Roman raised his brows and stood up, brushing his pants off. "I'm going to keep you alive so we can rescue her, finish your last Quest and send you both home."

"But…but what about you?" Phoenix blurted. "If we don't finish then she can stay here with you. Isn't that what you want?"

Marcus shrugged. "It's not about what I want." He shook his head. "It's about doing what's right. There's more to your Quests than simple treasure hunts and revenge against Zhudai. I know that much by now. The lives and happiness of many, many people are at stake. Surely my own happiness is a small matter compared to restoring Balance to the whole world, possibly two. I will do what's right, and so will you."

He turned to stare off into the darkness, as if seeing into the future. "Jade, however…"

"What about her?" Phoenix was confused. This emotional, talkative Marcus was unsettling.

The Roman's eyes were hard now. "There may come

a time when Jade has to choose the right thing over what she wants and she will find it difficult. We must be there to help her."

"What are you talking about?" Phoenix demanded, rattled. "She's the one who's always going on about helping people. She already had to choose when Arawn offered to let her stay with the Elves. If anyone knows the right choice, it's Jade, not me."

When Marcus didn't answer, Phoenix spoke again, more urgently. "Do you know what she's going to do? How? What is it?"

Marcus picked up his horses' reins and those of the pack horse. "The old monk told me..."

"What did he tell you – exactly?" Phoenix grabbed his friends' arm.

Those dark eyes lifted again. "He told me… just what I said: that Jade will need help to make the right choice sometime soon." He shook off Phoenix's grip. "Now let's find a way out of here before Brynn finds something to steal and awakens *that.*" Pointing into the gloom, he marched away, leaving Phoenix to stare after him uneasily.

He glanced at where the Roman had pointed and swore. By the flickering glow of a torch, Phoenix made out the enormous shape of a stone dragon statue. Its ruby eyes glittered strangely in the half-light and shifting shadows gave it the illusion of movement. With half-furled wings, it's long, snaky body coiled and wound about a sarcophagus of pure jade in the centre of the room.

Startled, Phoenix took in his surroundings for the first time. They must be inside the Emperor Chin…no, Qinshihuan, that was it…'s tomb.

The domed ceiling darkened into gloom overhead but where it could be seen, star patterns of pearls and diamonds glittered in the torchlight. All around the base of the jade sarcophagus lay what looked like a vast map. It wasn't flat but three dimensional – like a miniature world. Knee high mountain ranges were painted green to simulate forest. At their foothills, silvery rivers shone smooth in the torchlight, winding toward a beautifully-laid out, walled city.

Brynn, looking exactly like some sort of giant in a bad monster movie from the fifties, stepped gingerly between the buildings. He crouched down and dipped a finger into a river, examining the shining silver digit curiously. Poking out his tongue, he was about to taste the liquid when Marcus knocked his hand away.

"Quicksilver. It's poison."

Unabashed, Brynn shook his finger and dried it on his shirt. Tiny droplets of mercury flew through the air like silver rain and ran down the walls of perfect little dolls' houses.

"It's incredible," Phoenix said, awed. Every building was exact: every tile in place; every door hinged; every interior perfectly furnished; every wall decorated with minute murals and paintings. Apart from a thick layer of dust, it could have been made yesterday. He half expected tiny people to come out and run screaming from the invading monsters who towered over them.

"Hey," Brynn called out excitedly, beckoning them over toward the jade sarcophagus. "There's sure to be treasure in here, don't you think?"

Phoenix reached out and swatted the boy lightly on the head. He pointed up at the dragon. Its white teeth and red eyes gleamed down at them.

"What's the bet that great big lizard would wake up the minute you touch the coffin?"

Brynn, whose hand had already been outstretched, turned his gaze upward. Slowly, his hand fell back to his side.

"Maybe you're right." He swallowed and stepped away. "Maybe we should find a way out, instead. I don't really need any more treasure."

Phoenix and Marcus exchanged amused looks.

The three investigated the tomb with sinking hearts. There seemed to be four exits – one in each wall. Or at least, there used to be four. Marcus' trick with the drop-stone must have triggered the other three to close the same way. All four exits were now blocked by enormous chunks of stone.

"Uh…ok then." Phoenix spun around, looking for other ways out. "*Now* you can say we're up to number seven, Brynn. Only Five for you, though Marcus," he added mock-patronisingly. The Roman raised an eyebrow at him but disdained to answer.

Phoenix sighed. "So where's one of Jade's secret exits when you need one?"

"Hello? Hello there? The secret exit is this way, please. You come now. Yes?"

The three companions stared at each other in confusion.

"Who said that?" Phoenix peered into the darkness beyond the torchlight.

Out from behind the dragon, tottered a wizened, bent old woman. Narrow, dark eyes sparkled up at them from a face like scrunched up brown paper. She wore a plain, dark, long sleeved shirt with a high collar and matching loose pants. In one hand she held a knobbly wooden cane, on which she leaned every once in awhile to aid a particularly tricky step through the miniature city. She didn't look dangerous.

"Long Zhi Hui," the old woman said, smiling so hard that her eyes were just black slits.

"Pardon?" Phoenix asked, feeling stupid.

Whatever those words were, they sounded like incomprehensible gibberish. He slapped himself lightly on the side of the head, wondering what had happened to the translation spell that had been cast on them all back in Svealand. Had it stopped working?

The elder hobbled forward and bowed. "My name.

Long Zhi Hui. You may call me Zhi Hui."

"*Oh*, now I get it. Phoenix," he pointed to himself, "and my friends Marcus and Brynn. Umm… how did you get in here?" For some reason, he had a nagging feeling he'd met this old woman before somewhere but couldn't for the life of him think where or when.

Zhi Hui smiled and bobbed her head. "I told you: the secret entrance. I am the Tomb-sweeper. It is the first day of the Qingming festival."

When they looked blank, Zhi Hui shook her head. "You are from far away. Maybe you don't have this day in your year. It's a celebration of Spring and also a time to tend the graves of the departed. It's my job to clean the tomb of the Emperor Qinshihuan. This tomb."

"Ah ha." Phoenix hoped he sounded like he understood. "Well, I'm sorry we messed it up a bit. We came here by accident and the terracotta warriors kind of…er… came to life and started chasing us. We weren't going to steal anything, if that's what you're worried about."

Zhi Hui grinned, showing worn, yellowing teeth. "I was not worried. If you had stolen anything, you would have awakened the Dragon god and we would not be having this conversation."

Phoenix looked sideways at Brynn who managed to look both sheepish and a picture of outraged innocence.

"Come," Zhi Hui waved a gnarled hand, "you must come to my house and rest. You are tired and have a difficult task still ahead of you."

The companions had nodded and gathered up their gear before the full import of the old woman's words broke on Phoenix.

"Hang on." He stopped in his tracks, glaring at the bent figure. "What difficult task do we have ahead of us? Who sent you here?"

"Why, Long Baiyu, of course." Zhi Hui spread her

free hand. "He was worried you would be eaten by the Dragon if young Brynn succumbed to temptation." Chuckling, she turned away again, her cane tapping on the stone floor.

Stunned and lacking any other options, the three travellers followed. Behind the dragon, Zhi Hui tapped on a certain carved stone with the tip of her cane. A dark, low door opened in the stone plinth, under the dragon's tail.

Brynn looked up and stifled a giggle. "If the dragon was intending to eat us then we're going in the wrong end."

CHAPTER SIX

Jade awoke slowly. She kept her eyes closed and stretched languorously against the smooth, silk sheets. A slight smile of contentment curved her lips as she smelled the delicious aroma of breakfast drifting through the air. If it weren't for the fact that her bladder was bursting, she might have been tempted to stay in bed all day. It seemed like forever since she'd had a good sleep in.

That thought banished the last fog of lazy sleep and she sat bolt upright in bed, eyes wide. What was she thinking? She wasn't home! Somewhere out there, her friends were searching for her, battling who knew what dangers to try and rescue her from Zhudai's clutches and here she was, revelling in the comforts of her jail.

Disgusted with herself, Jade slid off the bed and padded toward the bathroom. Once she'd relieved the most pressing of her needs, she'd find her old clothes and find some way to get out of here. She felt strong again. The effects of Cadoc's poison must have finally worn off. There had to be a way.

There was someone else in the main room: a woman with her back to Jade, hands busy laying dishes on the low table. Jade stopped, hoping the stranger hadn't heard her.

"Your breakfast is ready, miss." A shy voice disabused that hope.

The girl turned around and bowed deeply. She wore a plain, dark-blue silk robe and flat slippers. Her skin glowed porcelain pale, her dark, glossy hair was swept up and pinned on top of her head in an ornate style that looked as uncomfortable as it was beautiful. Two long hairpins stuck out from one side, their jewelled tips dangling and sparkling in the morning light.

"Ummm…" Jade faltered, her determination derailed by this unexpected politeness. "Thanks. I'll just…" She edged past, toward the bathroom.

The girl bowed deeper. "Yes miss. I'll help you dress and do your hair when you finish."

Jade fled to the privacy of the bath-room. She glanced down at the blue robe she'd put on last night. Sleeping in it had crinkled it beyond wearability. After using the facilities, she washed her hands and face then glanced around. A clean robe had been laid out for her. Her own clothes were nowhere to be seen.

This one was even prettier than the blue one. All in silver-grey silk with a long-feathered bird embroidered in pale green across the back and wrapping around onto the front panels. The material floated, soft and thin, around her body. A matching pair of loose silk trousers went with it. Jade slid everything on and tied the ties and sashes as best she could.

When she emerged, the girl looked at her and giggled a little before casting her almond-shaped dark eyes down.

"I am Li Lei, miss, your maid." She gestured for Jade to sit at the table.

"Thanks. I'm Jade," Jade said politely, sinking down crosslegged onto a cushion.

"In our language, your name would be Lin," Li Lei said meeting Jade's eyes shyly. "It means 'beautiful Jade'."

Jade blinked, taken aback. "Lin." She rolled the name around on her tongue and smiled. "I like that. Thankyou."

"I'm glad, miss. Now you eat while I do your hair properly," Li Lei ordered.

Jade relaxed a little and picked at the various exotic foods laid out on the table. There was little she recognised, except the rice, so she ate cautiously, not knowing what would taste good and what wouldn't. There was nothing like cereal or toast to be seen. Two types of soup, dumplings, small cubes of what she thought might be tofu, plus various steamed vegetables. Wonderful for restoring her Spellweaver strength but a very strange fare for breakfast – to Western eyes, at least.

Li Lei brushed, tugged, twisted and pinned Jade's hair until Jade felt like her head weighed twice as much as it had before. When she was done, Li Lei held up a large, round mirror of polished bronze.

"Do you like it, miss?"

Jade stared at a stranger in the mirror. She'd been dressed up several times now: as a concubine, as an Elven princess, as an Indian Lady; but this was different again. Her pale hair swept smoothly up into an ornate knot on her crown. Three silver, jewelled pins sparkled in it. She looked, somehow, older; serene; elegant; more beautiful.

"It's…it's very nice." She wasn't exactly certain. This was getting harder and harder to understand. She stood up, shaking her head - carefully. "But I have friends waiting for me. I'd like my clothes and gear back so I can join them as soon as possible."

Li Lei gazed at her for a long time, her black eyes wide. Then she bowed.

"I'm so sorry miss but the Master has asked for you to visit with him now. Maybe you can speak with him about your friends. Please," she moved toward the door, "this way."

Jade hesitated. What did she do now? If Zhudai wanted her dead, he could have ordered Yajat to do it or just left her in that miserable cell, chained with iron. He was the ultimate badguy; the endgame of this digital scenario. Why was he treating her like an honoured guest when all he had to do was kill her to put paid to any opposition to his plans? None of this made any sense.

She bit her lip, wishing she could talk to Marcus and Phoenix. She needed to bounce ideas off them. They often thought in terms of strength, strategies and tactics that would never occur to her. Brynn's devious thinking would be handy too. Maybe they would understand Zhudai better than she. Maybe all this would make sense to them.

For the first time, Jade truly felt the gap left by her friends' absence. Without knowing it, the four of them had become a team – each one shoring up the weaknesses of the others; supporting; pushing; helping. Without them, she felt all her old sense of inadequacy rushing back. Self-doubt took her in its grip and fractured her thin veneer of confidence.

Reluctant but unable to think of an alternative, Jade followed Li Lei out of the room. Two heavily armed guards fell into step with them as they emerged into a long, white-cloth-walled corridor. She walked in numb silence awhile, eyes downcast, mind skittering in all directions, chased by worry and fear.

She looked up as they passed through an awe-inspiring hall. Huge pillars, painted red and ornamented with golden dragons, supported a high ceiling decorated in red, green and gold geometric patterns. The floor was an intricate pattern of parquetry, festooned with more golden dragons. From the ceiling hung immensely long banners of white silk marked with hundreds of black, Chinese characters proclaiming the Emperor's achievements and brilliance. They drifted and fluttered in each wayward breeze; hiding and revealing the darker areas beyond the giant pillars. At one end, on a raised dais, was a gilded, much-carved throne covered in gold cushions.

It was empty.

Jade breathed a silent sigh of relief. Perhaps Zhudai was out and Li Lei would take her back to her rooms now.

Li Lei did not pause in the throne-room. Instead, she continued, exiting through a narrow door behind the throne, into another long corridor. Helplessly, Jade followed. She briefly considered putting both guards and the maid to sleep with a *Command* spell. A glimpse of a parade ground outside ruled that idea out. It swarmed with black-armoured guards. Hundreds of them. The sheer size and complexity of the buildings surrounding the courtyard was also daunting. If the small section she had already traversed was any indication, this palace was an enormous maze of rooms, courtyards, and corridors – all alike. Finding her way out without being caught seemed impossible. She could hardly leave a trail of sleeping people behind her without being noticed.

Then there remained the small matter of Zhudai being in possession of her ruby-studded Life-dagger. She wasn't entirely sure what the implications of being separated from the dagger were but she had a feeling they wouldn't be good.

As if reflecting her thoughts, the first thing she saw on entering Zhudai's apartments, was her dagger. It lay, in plain view, on a desk in one corner of the room. Otherwise, the room was empty. Unlike her own ornate rooms, Zhudai's were plain to the point of being austere. It came as a shock after the over-lush silk-and-gold style of the rest of the palace. Jade decided he probably did it on purpose to make people uncomfortable. He'd succeeded. She felt decidedly ill-at-ease.

Without another word, Li Lei and the guards bowed and left her alone in the den of her worst enemy in this world.

Keeping an eye on the door, Jade edged toward the desk. As she drew nearer, her heart raced, thumping against her chest. Gingerly, she picked up the dagger, examining the handle with a sinking feeling in the pit of her stomach. There were only two whole rubies left.

Somehow, probably during her capture or captivity, one more of her lives had been taken. She now had only one spare 'death' left.

There was a slight noise behind her. She whirled, hiding the dagger behind her back.

Zhudai entered the room.

On silent feet, Jade backed up until her shoulders hit a wall and she had nowhere to go. She held her breath, waiting for him to challenge her; to demand her dagger back. Instead, he turned away, seeming not to even see her in this darkened corner. Bemused, Jade stared at the arch-nemesis of her game. Something was wrong.

It was Zhudai, and yet, somehow, different from last time she'd seen him, in Egypt. Here, he looked…younger, almost…handsome. Gone were the long, black fingernails; gone the severe, black silk robe; gone the sneering look of arrogance. Now, he wore a loose-fitting robe of dark blue, embroidered with a red, long-feathered bird similar to that on her own robe. His dark hair was tied back at the nape of his neck. On his head sat a red and black hat – round and with bits sticking out over his ears. Three rows of rubies dangled from each side. He looked…pensive, worried – but not angry or evil. She had to look closely to be sure it really was him.

Apparently still oblivious to her presence, he took off the odd hat and smoothed his hair with long, strong fingers. Laying the hat on a narrow table, he clasped both hands behind his back and paced away to stare out the window.

Jade withdrew the dagger from behind her back and looked at it in the palm of her hand. What if he just hadn't seen her? Could it be this easy? Could she possibly end this whole game here and now? She had, many weeks ago, made a pact with Phoenix that if either of them got an unmissable chance to kill Zhudai, they would do so. This seemed to qualify as an unmissable chance. If only she'd learned from Cadoc how to throw knives.

Folding her fingers tightly around the hilt of her knife, Jade decided she had to try.

She slipped around the desk, circling until she stood directly behind the warlock and he could not possibly see her. Her heart pounded so loudly she feared he would hear it. Drawing a long, slow breath, she stalked nearer, trying to steady her hand and heart. Palms slick with sweat, Jade held the dagger horizontal, aiming to slide it neatly between the second and third ribs on the left side. It would take just one sure stroke to kill this man; to end this Quest once and for all; to send herself and Phoenix home to England.

Just one, well-placed strike to the heart.

She swallowed. She'd never killed anyone like this: one on one. Phoenix and Marcus had killed many in battle and in self-defence; even Brynn had; but Jade had only ever struck to incapacitate.

Certainly people had died in this game as result of her actions – an exploding cauldron, an overheated furnace. They had been more by accident than intent. Something in her avatar's Spellweaver upbringing stayed her hand from a killing stroke, whenever possible, each time she actually did battle with an enemy.

That same hand trembled, now, when faced with the prospect of cold-blooded murder.

"Why do you hesitate?" Zhudai swung to face her, his expression curious and calm.

Jade gasped. The knife fell from nerveless fingers, clattering on the polished wood floor. Zhudai retrieved and examined it. He caught her wary gaze with his fathomless black one.

"You had an opportunity to kill me and end your Quest." He raised arched brows at her and tilted his head to one side. "Why didn't you?"

When she didn't answer, he smiled faintly. "I don't think you lack the courage – I've seen what you are capable of, many times. Perhaps you just lack experience. Would you like to try again?" Flipping the knife over, he held it by the blade and offered it back.

CHAPTER SEVEN

Jade stared at the knife as though it would bite and slowly shook her head.

Zhudai grimaced, glancing down at the bronze blade. "Perhaps you are right not to gain this particular experience. It gets much easier after the first one, though – as your friend, Phoenix, has found."

She rediscovered her voice, harsh though it sounded. "You don't know anything about Phoenix."

The sorcerer's mouth twisted. He gestured toward a pair of low-backed divan seats nearby. "You'd be surprised how much I do know about all of you. Remember that I watched you through much of your travels in Albion and again in Egypt. Please, sit."

Not knowing what else to do, Jade sat on the very edge, poised to flee. He placed the dagger between them on a low, glossy-black table. Several plates of fingerfoods were spread out there but her stomach rejected the thought of eating. She sent the sorcerer a quick look from beneath her lashes, wondering what to do; what *he* was going to do.

Zhudai tilted his head again, eyeing her with undisguised curiosity. He leaned back, folding his hands over his stomach in the most casual manner imaginable.

"Brynn is the youngest; a thief and mischief-maker; not terribly constrained by the morals that seem to prevent you from taking action. He admires you and Phoenix immensely but sometimes resents your mothering and enjoys provoking Phoenix. He has secretly stolen many more things than you realise."

Jade blinked at him in astonishment. He had hit Brynn's character exactly and only confirmed other things that she'd already suspected anyway. It was unnerving.

He continued, seemingly oblivious to her reactions. "Marcus," he raised a finger, "now Marcus is a different beast altogether. Strong, quick to think but slow to speak. Impressive swordsman and archer, brilliant tactician. He admires you too," the sorcerer threw Jade a swift, amused glance, "but in a completely different way."

She flushed and looked away, raising her chin and shutting her mouth firmly.

"Marcus has, however, one flaw," Zhudai continued.

Almost against her will, Jade's curiosity stirred. She stilled, awaiting the rest.

"He is a Roman, raised by a Roman general to think as a Roman soldier does. In his heart, he believes the rest of the world to be barbaric and inferior." Zhudai shrugged. "Marcus is more like his father than he realises. He enjoyed leading the vast armies of India into battle; and one day will do the same for Rome. He finds it difficult to follow Phoenix, whom he considers inexperienced and sometimes rash."

Jade fought to prevent herself from returning a hot denial. Her fingernails bit into the palms of her hands and she allowed the flare of pain to distract her until she could control her anger.

"Very good," Zhudai admired. "You have much better self-control than Phoenix. Poor boy." He sighed and shook his head. "He really was not well prepared for the realities of this realm, was he?"

This time, Jade had to bite back the urge to agree with him. It was true. By treating it as a great, fun game, Phoenix had coped well with the world of 80AD to begin with but he struggled as it got harder. He had improved, though – they both had. She pressed her lips together.

"So *angry*," Zhudai murmured, seemingly to himself. "Phoenix, I mean," he clarified. "He carries such deep anger and it spills out so often.   Did you know that he almost killed Marcus again, in India, after you came here? He let his anger at your capture overcome him and Blódbál took control."

Startled, Jade glanced up.   Zhudai's gaze was sympathetic, almost kind. He nodded gently. Picking up a slice of fruit, he examined it before nibbling on the end.

"Luckily, Marcus was the better swordsman, it seems. He killed him."

"Marcus killed Phoenix?"   Sheer, disbelieving astonishment forced the words from her lips. She ran a thumb across the palm of her left hand.

"Oh," he assured her, "it was all in a good cause, apparently. Phoenix had broken his arm and without you there to heal him, Marcus felt it was the simplest way. At least, that's what my spies tell me."

Jade looked at him for a long time, trying to read whether he told the truth. His face gave nothing away. It did sound horribly plausible. That explosion when Yajat captured her. Phoenix could well have been injured and he definitely would have been angry at her for being dumb enough to get kidnapped.

A rush of guilt made her bite her lip. If she had been more careful; if she had fought off Yajat; if she hadn't trusted Cadoc, who had betrayed them...

"Tell me," Zhudai interrupted her tumultuous thoughts, "would you like to go home?"

"What?"   The change of subject left her confused. "You mean back to my room?"

"No, home. To your world. Your time. Your family. Home."

His words triggered an overwhelming longing. Jade's mind filled with images: her real father; her plants and books; even her sisters and mother. To be free and home again; back in her thirteen year old body; back in her house; back with her father; back with no overwhelming worries and responsibilities. It was what she'd been working toward for the last four weeks. She was tired of the hardship and bloodletting; tired of the fear and worry; tired of being a kid in an adult world and adult body; tired of being tired.

Slowly, she nodded. "Yes."

He leaned further back on the divan, holding his head up with one hand and curling his legs beneath him, casual and relaxed. Not at all the evil, villainous warlock she expected.

"Then we have that in common, for I would like you to leave this realm. I can do it, you know." He inspected the back of one hand. "I can send you home."

Jade sprang to her feet, hope, anger, resentment and hurt all warring in her chest until she was surprised she could speak at all. Fists clenched at her sides, she forced the words out through gritted teeth.

"You're lying. You can't. We have to win to get home. It's the only way. And anyway, what about Phoenix and the others?"

Sitting up again, Zhudai leaned forward, a slight smile on his lips. "I can send all of them home. Think about it. You don't *know* that defeating me is the only way to get home. You're only guessing, aren't you?"

"No!" she shot back.

Somewhere, however, a tiny seed of doubt sprouted. What if he was right? Only the mystery woman in the gray limbo world had ever actually *told* them the only way to go home was to win the game. What if she had lied? They didn't even know who she was. What if it weren't true at all? What if all this fighting and dying had been for nothing?

"No," she repeated, appalled at the possibility.

What if the person they thought was the badguy, was actually the source of their escape from this realm? What if they had guessed wrong?

Zhudai remained silent, watching her with eyes full of sympathy.

Jade shook her head, trying to rediscover the determination; the wary anger at her supposed enemy.

"No. You can't be telling the truth. Otherwise, why would you have tried so hard to stop us? Why did you have me killed and kidnapped? No. Our task is to defeat you. If we do that, we'll go home. It's that simple."

He shrugged. "If you say so. But, just so you know, I was only trying to stop you because I thought you wanted to kill me. Once I found out you just wanted to go home, I kidnapped you instead. You're a bright girl. I thought you, more than Phoenix, might be open to reason." He stood and bowed. "I can see I made a mistake but I'll give you time to think about it anyway. Li Lei will escort you back to your room now."

Turning on his heel, he strode from the room, his blue robes fluttering. Jade stared after him, more confused than ever.

She glanced down. Her knife still lay on the table.
*****

"Good morning. Feeling better now?"

Phoenix pried his sleep clogged eyes open.

"Gaark!" He flung up a hand, startled by the wrinkled apparition just inches from his face.

Zhi Hui chuckled and stood up, nodding her greying head amicably. Her sparkling eyes vanished in a mass of wrinkles. Still chortling, the old woman hobbled out of the room and disappeared into another.

He sat up, scraping his long hair back and rubbing gritty eyes. It was morning but only just. He glanced around the dwelling. After a long trek through muddy farmland, they'd arrived late and in the dark, so they hadn't had much of a look at where Zhi Hui lived. He remembered tripping over a ridiculously high doorstep and sprawling ignominiously into a paved courtyard. After that, it had just been a blur of sliding doors, rooms and a bed on the floor. He hadn't cared much past the bed.

By dawn-daylight, he saw the house wasn't grand but it wasn't a mud hut, either. Zhi Hui had left the door open and the courtyard was visible. There were three wings to the house, all facing into it. What would have been the open, fourth side, was not. Instead, it was a high wall, pierced only by a large, round wooden double-door set in a round, brick frame. Across the red doors danced an ornately carved dragon, painted white with gold eyes and talons. More dragons, ceramic this time, perched on top of the sweeping, sharply peaked, tiled roofs of the house.

Phoenix smiled to himself. It was exactly the sort of building he'd expected to see in China. Very cool.

Somewhere, close by, a gong sounded. Breakfast? Phoenix's stomach rumbled at the thought. He struggled off the floor-mat, shivering. It was cooler here than in India. He grabbed his cloak and threw it over his shoulders, pausing only long enough to strap Blódbál to his hip. A quick glance around showed two more sleeping mats – empty. Presumably Brynn and Marcus were already up.

Following his nose, Phoenix found his way to the kitchen area. Marcus and Brynn were there, seated crosslegged around a low, black table. They glanced up and nodded in greeting without stopping their steady inhalation of food. Zhi Hui smiled again and waved him toward a seat. Phoenix sat cautiously, kneeling in seiza, still not sure whether or not to trust this strange old woman. She placed a steaming bowl of something in front of him.

"Eat. Eat. You are safe here for awhile." She bowed and turned back to her cooking.

"S'good," Brynn said thickly, wiping his mouth with a

sleeve. "No idea what it is but it tastes good." He'd given up trying to use chopsticks and used his fingers instead.

Phoenix looked at Marcus, who nodded and shrugged as if to say he didn't think it was dangerous, anyway. Phoenix ate. It was good and he was hungry.

After they were finished, Zhi Hui lead them into a spartan lounge area where they sat in conference around another low table. The old woman's face was now serious.

"There is much for you to know and do before your quest will be complete," she said, "and little time for it. The *ri shi* is now just three days away."

"What?" Phoenix demanded. "What do we need to know? Who are you, anyway? Why do I feel like I know you?"

"Of course you know me. I came to you when you first arrived in Albion and told you of your task." Zhi Hui matter-of-factly poured herself a cup of tea.

"That was you in the gray limbo place!" Phoenix pointed an accusing finger at her. "You're the one who told us we had to complete these quests to be able to get home."

The old woman nodded serenely, offering him tea.

"But why? What does Zhudai have to do with you? Why do you care if we defeat him?" Phoenix couldn't see the connection and it irritated him to think he'd been manipulated by this meddling old lady.

"I am Long Baiyu's mother," she said simply. "And it is your task to free my son from his imprisonment. Doing so will also free my granddaughter and dozens of others of the Light, who go in fear, hiding from Zhudai's notice for fear of their lives. She must be protected from him at all costs."

"Oh no. No way." He shook his head emphatically. "You've already had your go at telling us what to do and I'm doing that and nothing more. Our job is to free Jade so we can master the Yu Dragon, defeat Zhudai and end this insanity once and for all. There was no mention of breaking anyone else out of jail."

Zhi Hui's solemn gaze didn't change. "There are many paths to the top of the mountain but the view is the same in the end."

Phoenix met her look with a cynical one of his own. "I'm happy to listen to you when you start making sense again."

She looked mildly affronted but only folded her hands in her lap. "Only by freeing my son will you have a chance to prevent Zhudai from succeeding. Without Baiyu's help, your quest will fail," she stated.

"Oh come *on*." He groaned. "It was going to be hard enough without this as well." He sighed, scrubbing his hand over his face. "Alright, alright. Why do we need him? We've done pretty well up to now."

"Baiyu and Zhudai were once friends." Zhi Hui's face sagged with remembered sadness. "Almost brothers. They grew up together, trained together, learned together from the greatest of our wizards and wise men. Then, seven years ago, something broke between them. An argument over a woman they both loved divided the harmony of their friendship and they went their separate ways. Zhudai vanished. Baiyu remained here as tutor to the young Prince Zhang."

Phoenix jumped at her use of the word 'harmony'. It cropped up too many times during this adventure to be just a coincidence. In every level, their task involved restoring balance and harmony, somehow. He decided the old lady was worth listening to.

"Five years ago, young Zhang became the Emperor Han Zhangdi. At that time, Baiyu refused the role of Grand Vizier and, instead, went into the western mountains for a time, studying and meditating with the Buddhist monks there."

She sighed, picked up the kettle and continued.

"Zhudai, we now know, went south seven years ago and studied with a great warlock. He returned last year and the young Emperor immediately appointed *him* Grand Vizier in his court in Luoyang." Zhi Hui paused, pouring them each a cup of green tea."

Phoenix turned his cup, staring into its clear depths. "I knew it," he muttered. "It's *always* a Grand Vizier who's the badguy."

Zhi Hui cast him a faintly puzzled look before going on as though he hadn't spoken. "Baiyu returned only a few months ago. That was when he first heard the rumours of Zhudai's plans."

"What plans?" Marcus prompted.

Brynn sipped his tea and made a face at its hot bitterness.

"On the day of the *ri shi*, Zhudai will carry out his scheme. To complete it, he must kill my son at the precise moment of the full *ri shi*. If he succeeds, nothing will stop him from doing whatever he wishes - in both your world and this one," Zhi Hui said bluntly.

Phoenix thought hard, wondering if *everyone* in this benighted world knew about his world and wishing for a less fuzzy brain.

"*Ri shi*, that means…um…solar eclipse, doesn't it?"

Zhi Hui bowed her head. "The eclipse co-incides with the last day of the Qingming festival of death and rebirth. Only on such a day: a day of death and life; a day where darkness overcomes light, will Zhudai be strong enough."

"Strong enough to do what?" Brynn asked.

"Make himself immortal," the old woman replied.

There was long, weary silence as the three travellers considered this revelation. Brynn sipped noisily at his tea again, apparently unfazed.

Finally, Phoenix spoke. "Um…are we talking 'immortal' as in 'unable to be killed' or 'immortal' as in just 'lives a really long time as long as nothing bad happens to him'?"

"Unable to be killed," Zhi Hui nodded. "Invincible. Immortal. Evil. A sorcerer of unimaginable power. He will control vast armies of men. They will sweep across the world like a plague. He will be unstoppable."

"Uh huh. Figures." Phoenix shook his head. "So explain to me why nobody's stopped him already. Y'know. One good shot with a bow and arrow would do it."

"His powers protect him from ordinary weapons. The only man who could have stopped him now lies in the prison beneath the Emperor's palace here in Xijing."

"Wait," Phoenix held up his hand, "let me guess. That would be Long Baiyu."

She bowed. "He is of the Light, as Zhudai is of the Darkness. Killing the Light at the moment when Darkness is strongest will upset the Balance and imbue incredible powers upon Zhudai. Held in the dark for so long, Baiyu is too weak to challenge his blood-brother."

"So what does that have to do with us?"

Zhi Hui pursed her wrinkled mouth and shot him a shrewd look. "Only when all contribute their firewood can a strong fire be built."

He threw up his hands in disgust. "In Engli…unenlightened-people speak, please,"

With a shake of her grey head, the old woman tucked her hands into her wide sleeves. "Baiyu cannot defeat Zhudai alone any more. He will need your help, just as you will need his. You must release him. It is the only way you can save our land, your world – and yourselves."

"And where does Jade fit into this?" Marcus' low voice intruded.

"She is in the Palace as well." Zhi Hui nodded. "She has been moved from the cells and is in a guest room on the second floor. She is in grave danger."

The friends exchanged glances.

"Er...doesn't sound like she's in danger if she's in a guest room," Brynn put in hesitantly.

She shook her head again. "She was safer in the dungeon. Now, she is too close to Zhudai. She falters. If you do not reach her soon, she will give in and all may be lost. When faced with an open treasure chest, even the virtuous man will be tempted."

"Tempted? Give in?" Marcus sat up straighter, gripping his sword hilt. "To what?"

"Hope," Zhi Hui said quietly. "She will give in to hope and all will be lost."

CHAPTER EIGHT

Back in her room, Jade sat on a low couch overlooking the garden far below and nibbled on her thumbnail. In one hand, she held her dagger, its two remaining gems gleaming like drops of blood. No-one had tried to prevent her from reclaiming it. Li Lei had even returned the small sheath Jade usually kept it in when it hung from her belt. Jade turned the blade over in her fingers, staring but not seeing it at all. She'd been told she couldn't let Zhudai get his hands on her dagger or amulet, yet he'd had access to both and hadn't taken them.

What should she do now? Zhudai's proposition was ridiculous. He couldn't possibly be able to send her and Phoenix back home. He was the villain. He wasn't trying to help her. He couldn't get them out.

Could he?

Doubt crept further into her mind, overshadowing everything she'd felt certain of before. Nothing about this world was real and yet here she was. She'd accepted that they were here…somehow. Why did she find it so hard to accept that there might be an easy way out? Just because all the fantasy books she'd read said there had to be a big finish to a Quest, didn't mean there *really* had to be one. Who made up that rule? What if Zhudai wasn't the badguy he'd been made out to be? What if he was actually capable of what he said? Why shouldn't she just say 'yes, send us home'? What would happen if she and Phoenix left now?

Jade grimaced, shaking her head. This was just a dumb computer game, not a real world. Nothing would happen. The game would just be over and she'd be home. She'd been here so long she was forgetting that essential fact. She was over-analysing things again, just as her father always told her.

At the thought of her father Jade's shoulders slumped. Her father must be absolutely frantic. She could almost see his anxious face, hair greying at the temples, worry lines creasing his forehead; almost hear his voice calling her name. A tear slid down her face. She wiped it away and licked it off her finger, tasting the salt.

If only there was some way she could consult with Phoenix, ask him what he thought of Zhudai's proposal.

She sat up straight again, staring blindly at an ornate painting on the wall. What an idiot she was. Of course she could contact Phoenix. The *mind-talk* spell from the Svear spellbook. She'd used it over and over in India. She'd regained enough strength now. It should be a simple matter to contact Phoenix, tell him where she was and what Zhudai wanted. Then they could get this over and done with one way or the other.

Excitement brought hope back again. Beneath her breath, Jade whispered '*heili tala*' and closed her eyes. Feeling the Binding Spell that attached her to her friends, Jade sent her mind drifting out along its tenuous, green connection, seeking them. In her mind's eye, she floated through palace walls, over gardens and courtyards, heading west toward the great stone wall that enclosed the entire Royal Palace.

Reaching the wall, she pushed through it as she had the internal walls – only to be brought up short by an invisible barrier of some sort. The Binding Spell went straight through. She could feel it; sense Phoenix, Marcus and Brynn's lives still connected to it. She pushed again and was, again, repelled. Once more, harder this time, she focussed on breaking through. Again she was denied; repulsed by a backlash of magic - this time all the way back to her own room and mind.

Half-stunned, Jade opened her eyes. It was no use. She knew the 'feel' of that spell. Zhudai had some sort of protective shield up around the Palace that prevented her from reaching out to mind-talk with her friends. She remained alone.

A soft knock fell on the door and the panel slid open to admit Li Lei. The girl bowed deeply.

"I'm sorry to interrupt miss but the master has asked you to attend him again, if you are not busy."

Jade hesitated. She really needed time to think; time to plan an escape; time to work out a way to get past Zhudai's shield.

Li Lei saw her indecision and bowed again. "The master asked me to tell you that he apologises for the inconvenience. He is aware that you tried to contact your friends. He forgot to warn you of his defensive walls. If you would like to reach them, he asked me to tell you he is happy to help you do so now. He will take down the barrier for you."

Gaping in astonishment, Jade rose to her feet. "Are you saying he'll let me talk with Phoenix?"

The girl bobbed her head, smiling. "He is waiting for you in his study. The defensive spells around the Palace are complex and can only be dropped partially or we will be vulnerable to attack. If you would like to speak with your friends, the master requests you come quickly."

Jade shut her mouth with a snap and gathered the skirts of her robe in her hands. "Well…alright, I guess. Take me to him."

The girl bowed and Jade followed her.

This time, Li Lei lead her on a much shorter path to a different room, just a few halls down from her own. When she opened the door, Jade walked straight in without hesitation; fear gone in her eagerness to contact the others. She barely noticed the sparse furnishings or the workbench covered in odd instruments and sealed jars.

The room was dark and window-less; lit only by a dozen lanterns hung from the walls and low ceiling. Zhudai sat at a desk, writing something with a small brush in elegant calligraphy on crackling, yellow paper.

As Jade approached, he looked up with a faint smile. Nodding at a seat opposite, he took the paper between two fingers and blew gently on the ink. Looking at it critically, he nodded again and handed it to a small, deeply-bowing man who shuffled in and out of the room without a word.

"So much easier to use than bamboo and so much cheaper than silk." Zhudai studied a blank sheet of paper curiously.

"What, paper?" Jade asked, confused.

"Yes." Zhudai ran his fingers gently over the surface of the thick sheet under his hand. "One of our most brilliant scholars, Cai Lun, a eunuch at the Emperor's court, invented it a few months ago. I just had some delivered. The ingenuity of the human race never ceases to amaze me. Speaking of which," he smiled again at her, "I believe you have a rather ingenious Binding Spell you use to connect to your friends."

She eyed him, wondering where he was going with this. "Yes," she admitted. "So what?"

He shook his head and shrugged. "Nothing, really. I'm just impressed that it seems to work even through my defensive shields. I felt it but I couldn't tell what it was until you tried to use it a short while ago."

"I couldn't get through your barriers, though," Jade pointed out.

Zhudai waved a long, languid hand. "Nevermind. Your Binding is quite remarkable, especially for a young, inexperienced Spellweaver. I really am most impressed. It would, however, take something much stronger to penetrate my defences, so I will help you."

Jade flushed, trying to ignore the unexpected rush of pride that accompanied his words. "But why? Why should you want to help me contact Phoenix?"

"I told you," the sorcerer raised his brows in mild surprise, "I'd like to help you go home. You can hardly make a decision like that on your own, can you? Of course you want to discuss the idea with your friends. The sooner the better. Shall we begin?"

She bit her lip uncertainly. She wanted to reach Phoenix but Zhudai must have a hidden agenda; he must mean to harm her or the others in some way. Surely though, if he'd wanted to kill her he could have done it easily by now. She had only two lives left. Nothing could prevent him. Perhaps he really was trying to help them get home. He certainly didn't *seem* like an 'ultimate badguy'. There was no manic laughter or plans of world domination, anyway. The more she saw of him, the more she wondered if there had been some big mix-up in all this. Besides, he couldn't hear her telepathy with Phoenix. Could he?

She would have to take the risk. This was too important for her to decide on her own. Phoenix had to be given the choice, too.

"Alright," she agreed. "I'll contact him." Nervously, she scratched at the palm of her left hand.

*****

"So explain to me how you know where Jade is, in the Palace?" Phoenix demanded of Zhi Hui, suddenly suspicious of the old woman as she hurried them back to their room to gather their gear.

She seemed very anxious for them to rush to her son's rescue. Phoenix buckled on the last of his leather armour and faced her. He'd been burned once by a supposed ally. This time he needed a really good reason to trust.

"And maybe you could also explain how Baiyu contacted you, from inside the dungeon but Jade hasn't reached us. How did he tell you to come and get us in the tomb yesterday? How do we know we can trust you? How do we know you're not a spy from Zhudai, sent to trick us?"

The old lady grinned, busily rolling up their sleeping mats and stowing them in an ornately carved cupboard. "You cannot know, of course, and you are wise to ask such questions."

"Maybe you'd be wise to answer them," he growled, losing patience with this verbal cat-and-mouse game. He laid a hand on Blódbál, feeling its eagerness for battle course through his fingertips.

Zhi Hui sighed. "Still so much anger, young Phoenix. Great anger is more destructive than the sword. You must master that if you are to be free."

"What?" He blinked at her, sidetracked by the change of subject.

"Nothing. You will understand, later." She chuckled at his bewildered expression. "I'm a cleaning lady. That's how I know where Jade is and how I can communicate with my son. Nobody pays attention to a harmless old cleaning lady. I come and go to the Palace as I like but I do not have access to the upper floors, where Jade is held. When I'm inside Zhudai's defensive magic shields I can speak with Baiyu anytime." She tapped the side of her head meaningfully.

"You mean he uses a mind-talk spell like Jade?" Brynn stretched out on a pile of cushions, hands linked behind his head, at home as usual.

"And are Zhudai's shields the reason Jade hasn't been able to reach us the same way?" Marcus paused in his packing to ask.

"Yes and yes." The old lady nodded, solemn once more. "The only way your Jade could bespeak you is if Zhudai dropped his defences, which he will never do, for it would make him far too vulnerable."

Phoenix?

Phoenix spun, drawing Blódbál as he stared into the darker corners of the room, searching for the source of the voice.

Can you hear me, Phoenix?

Eyes widening in surprise, he nodded. He spoke aloud for the benefit of the others, finally realising that the words were inside his head, not outside.

"Jade? Is that you? Are you ok?"

Of course it is. Who else? I'm fine. I can only talk for a moment, so don't interrupt.

Marcus, Brynn and Zhi Hui were all gazing at him in astonishment. Phoenix shrugged and tapped his head.

Zhudai has offered to help us get home. He's partly dropped his shields so I can talk with you. He says he doesn't want to kill us – he was just trying to stop us killing him. I... I think he means it. I think he really might be able to send us home without any more bloodshed.

"Are you insane?" Phoenix blurted, forgetting that he wasn't supposed to interrupt. "Zhudai is the *badguy*; ultimate villain; corrupter of Roman governors; manipulator of gods and all that. Remember? Our Quest is to defeat him, not shake hands and say 'we're off now, thanks so much'."

There was a sense of impatience, doubt and hope all intertwined. *I know but what if we were wrong about that? What if we don't have to have some big battle to get out of here? What if he **can** send us home? We were just following someone else's orders to finish the game to get out. What if we were wrong? Isn't it worth a try?*

"Jade, you can't be serious." He struggled to keep calm. What the hell was going on in that mind of hers?

I'm tired of the fighting and killing, Phoenix. Surely if there's a peaceful way to just get home, we should take it. Her mind-voice sounded desperate.

"But how can we trust him?" Clenching his fists, he

sought for patience. "Why should we believe him?"

I...I just do. He's had every chance to kill me and he hasn't. I've been treated like a VIP guest. I think he's telling the truth.

"Based on what?" The words came out more sarcastically than he meant and Phoenix could feel her hurt reaction.

Don't you trust me?

"You, yes. Zhudai, no," he stated flatly.

Will you at least meet with him...us? In the square in front of the Palace in two hours. Just you. Leave Marcus and Brynn behind. They're too emotionally tied up in trying to kill Zhudai. I have to go now. Please be there. For me?

Suddenly his head felt emptier. Phoenix screwed up his face. Feeling extremely uneasy, he faced his friends. "Somehow, I don't think you're going to like what she had to say."

CHAPTER NINE

"It has to be a trap." Marcus was calmly logical, as usual. "Don't go."

Phoenix scratched his scalp. "I know but what else can I do?"

He paced the small room restlessly. Zhi Hui perched on a small stool in one corner, watching. Marcus leaned against the doorframe, fingering the pointed tip of one of his arrows. Brynn busily hauled things out of the Hyllion Bagia and worked out what might be useful in rescuing Jade. There were two piles of trinkets, clothing, coins and weapons growing in front of him. He looked critically at a small Egyptian glass phial of blue liquid for a moment then placed it on one of the piles. A crystal prism went on the other pile. Finally, he began tucking things into his copious pockets. The rest he stowed in the cupboard with his sleeping roll.

Phoenix paused in his pacing, looking at the boy without really seeing him. "It's probably our best chance of rescuing her, anyway. Even if we could disguise ourselves as workers and get in through the servants' entrance with Zhi Hui, we don't have any way of getting Jade *and* Baiyu out of a palace held by hundreds of guards and eunuchs. Worst of all, she may not even want to come with us. Getting her outside, in the open, is probably our *only* chance."

"She can't be so thoroughly bewitched by Zhudai as

that, can she?" Marcus murmured. "Doesn't she remember what he has done?" His expression hardened.

Phoenix sighed. "She does but she says she's tired of fighting. She just wants to go home and Zhudai has offered an easy way to do it. I can't entirely blame her."

Marcus hitched himself off the wall, frowning. "You don't believe him, do you?"

"N…no." Phoenix grimaced. "At least, I'd like to but I just can't see it being that easy. Not after all we've been through to get this far. It wouldn't make sense. Jade's just blinded by…"

"Hope," Zhi Hui interpolated. "As I said. She has given in to hope. Zhudai cannot fulfil his promise. Now you must decide what the right thing to do is."

"We have to get her back," Marcus stated.

"Well," Phoenix shrugged, "we'd better come up with a damned good plan, fast. There's only an hour and a half left until we're supposed to meet her and Zhudai. Can you give us any advice Zhi Hui?" He turned to the old lady.

She shook her head. "Only he that has travelled the road knows where the holes are deep."

"Helpful." He sighed, turning away.
*****

Jade opened her eyes. A wave of weariness swept through her. She wasn't as fully recovered as she thought. Zhudai's study shimmered before her. She reached out a hand to steady herself. Zhudai caught it, holding her firmly upright, a look of concern on his angular face. Then he smiled, his expression softening as he looked at her.

"Here. Sit before you fall." He guided her to a silk-covered divan.

She sat, grateful for his support. "I can't believe I'm still so tired."

He bowed apologetically. "That is my fault, I believe. I gave the poison to Cadoc and I instructed Yajat to take your life. I am deeply sorry."

She said nothing, staring at her own hands in her lap. What could she say?

Covering the awkward silence, Zhudai took her right hand in his own, examining the yin-yang ring there. "I see Cadoc gave you his ring."

"How did you...?" She looked at the ring apprehensively, wondering if it were somehow a thing of evil.

Laughing softly, the sorcerer shook his head. "No, it's nothing uncanny. It is simply that I saw Cadoc in the markets when he purchased it. I'm glad to see it being worn by someone as beautiful as it deserved."

Blushing, Jade withdrew her hand and leaned away.

"Come, child," Zhudai tilted her chin up, examining her face in surprise, "why do you blush? Surely you know you are exquisitely beautiful. I shall have to make sure our young Emperor does not lay eyes on you or he shall demand you as his concubine."

She looked at him in horror, only to see a gleam of humour in those black eyes. She smiled uncomfortably back.

"I know I'm pretty here," she admitted, "and I've always wanted to be but it doesn't seem to really do much good."

He laughed and stood up, pacing around behind his desk. "Then you are not yet using your beauty to its full extent."

"What?" Jade raised her eyebrows at him, taken aback.

Picking up a single sheet of paper, Zhudai held it lightly in the palm of his hand. "In any extreme, there is potential power. Extreme strength," he crushed the sheet into a ball, "intelligence, skill, magical talent." Now the paper burst into silent, purple-blue flame and vanished. "And extreme beauty."

Zhudai sent her a quick look. "You have the ability, with just a look, to change men's minds; to manipulate their desires; to control their decisions. Isn't that what you really wanted when you chose this body to inhabit? To have people like you; treat you as something special; be swayed by your opinions?"

Dumbfounded, horrified and yet strangely drawn to the idea, Jade held his gaze for a moment then looked away uneasily. He was too close to the truth for comfort. It made her motivations sound selfish and small. She wasn't really like that, was she?

"Come." The sorcerer waved a hand at a low table. Food had appeared from somewhere and Jade discovered she was ravenous. "Eat and tell me what your friend, Phoenix will do."

She shifted closer and picked up a small, doughy steamed bun. Biting into it, she frowned. "I'm not sure. I think he'll probably come to meet us but I don't know if he'll come alone. I doubt it. Marcus and Brynn will be around somewhere."

Zhudai grinned wryly. "I would be astonished if they were not."

"He'll probably try some stupid rescue attempt," she warned, trying not to feel guilty. Phoenix had to at least *talk* with Zhudai. He could ruin everything if he came rushing in at his normal level of bullheaded anger.

"Again," he bowed, "I would be amazed if he did otherwise."

"You won't hurt him?" Jade was suddenly unsure; worried that she might be making the wrong decision.

"I do not intend to hurt him, my dear," Zhudai assured her. He sat down and began to eat as well.

Jade watched him narrowly but if he lied, she couldn't sense it. Absently, she rubbed the palm of her left hand on her knee. It itched.

*****

"Right," Phoenix said, "do we have everything now?"

He stood at the front gate, waiting impatiently for

Brynn to complete his preparations. Nearby, Marcus calmly picked at his fingernails with the point of his knife. Zhi Hui vanished into the house, leaving them with nothing more than a resigned shake of the head and a hope that she would see them again.

Nodding in wide-eyed innocence, Brynn spread his hands. "Sling, lots of rocks, dagger, lockpicks. What else do I need?"

"That's what I'd like to know," Phoenix growled. "Did you bring the Hyllion Bagia and the Horn of Aurfanon, just in case?"

"Of course I did," the boy returned indignantly, "and a bunch of other useful stuff." He patted his bulging pockets and grinned.

"Well," Phoenix shrugged, "let's go, before you decide you have to bring the whole house."

Together, the three flipped up the hoods on their cloaks and eased through the dragon-painted doors. Cautiously, they looked east then west along the cobbled, narrow street toward the Palace. There were very few people abroad. Most, it seemed, were attending various events for the Qingming festival. The streets would be relatively safe for three foreigners.

Zhi Hui gave them clear directions and even drew a sketch of the open, tree-lined courtyard before the Palace gates. The best vantage point for Marcus and Brynn to hide, and still be within bowshot and slingshot range, was the roof of a nearby house. The old woman had given them a slip of bamboo, covered in cryptic marks, which supposedly asked a friend to lend them roof-space. Phoenix was a bit nervous about that. It just looked like a bunch of squiggly black lines. Jade was the only one who could read other languages, as well as speak them. There was no way of knowing if their elderly helper had written what she said she had.

Phoenix shrugged off his misgivings. He had to trust

someone, sometime, didn't he? Zhi Hui could have turned them in last night if she'd wanted to. Besides, she needed them to save her son.

First, though, they had to save Jade.

As they neared the Palace, they slowed and began watching for guards. A beggar scurried out of their way. A small child watched them with wide, dark eyes. A skinny dog slunk by. Otherwise, they were alone.

Reaching the house to which Zhi Hui had directed them, they sheltered in the doorway a moment. It was a much larger, more grand residence than Zhi Hui's. The tiled roof angled steeply to a peak covered in ornate, ceramic animals. Brynn eyed it with misgivings.

"Those tiles will be pretty slippery after the rain. Do you think you're up for a bit of roof-walking, Marcus? Not really a soldier's forte." He elbowed the Roman sharply in the ribs.

"I'm sure you've had more experience sneaking about on roofs in the dead of night," Marcus returned, "but I think I can manage."

He laid a hand on Phoenix's shoulder. "Are you sure you want to go alone?"

Phoenix nodded. "I'll be fine. You two watch my back from here. Whatever happens, I'm sure Jade won't let them kill me. At least, if we're taken, you can get us out of prison – which you can't if we're *all* locked up. I know this is dumb but it seems extra-dumb to deliberately put all four of us in the firing line."

Marcus grimaced. "I still think you're underestimating Zhudai."

"Maybe he's underestimating me, too." Phoenix grinned then shrugged. "Believe me, if I could think of another way to get her out of there, I would. From what Zhi Hui says, the palace is just too well guarded by men and magic to try a rescue without Jade's help."

Brynn knocked on the door and handed over Zhi Hui's

message to a servant. He and Marcus were ushered inside. They went, Marcus looking back over his shoulder dubiously.

Phoenix took a deep breath and squared his shoulders. With one hand lightly on Blódbál's hilt, its war-song loud in his mind, he marched into the open Palace square. His feet kicked up the pink and white petals of cherry and magnolia tree blossoms that floated gently to earth all around.

*****

Jade walked out of the enormous Palace gate and into the open square outside with Zhudai on one side and Li Lei on the other. The entire square was surrounded by pink-wreathed trees, their branches laden with flowers and the tiny green buds of new leaves. Its grey-paved expanse was littered with petals but empty of people. She breathed a faint sigh of relief. If Zhudai had soldiers here, they were not in sight. It seemed he was going to keep his word after all. Now, if only Phoenix showed the same faith and came alone.

She looked up. There he was, striding toward them from the eastern side of the square. He held himself confidently, the hood of his cloak pushed back, one hand resting almost arrogantly on the hilt of his sword. With his long, dark hair unkempt and leather armour scuffed from recent battles, Phoenix looked barbaric compared to the sleek elegance of Zhudai's dark robes and Li Lei's delicate beauty.

As Phoenix neared, Jade ran ahead. She hugged him hard, searching his face for clues as to what he intended to do. He stared back at her blandly then inclined his head in the merest hint of a bow, toward Zhudai. It was deliberately insolent and Jade wondered how the sorcerer would react. Zhudai's eyes narrowed fractionally but he kept a serene smile in place and bowed in return – deeper than Phoenix had.

"So," Phoenix ploughed straight in, "I'm here. Talk."

Zhudai straightened slowly, his hands sliding into his wide sleeves. He shrugged. "You know my proposal. I will send you home."

'How?" Phoenix's retort was brusque to the point of being rude.

"The same way you got here," the sorcerer returned without heat. "Magic."

"Why?"

Zhudai smiled faintly. "Because I don't want you here any more than you want to be here."

"What about our friends?" Phoenix jerked his head back the way he'd come.

Jade peeked over his shoulder, wondering where Marcus and Brynn were hiding; hoping that they didn't have any stupid plan to interfere.

The sorcerer shrugged. "They can travel home by the portals as easily as they got here, if they wish. I will not prevent it."

Phoenix glanced at Jade. She tried hard to look cool but knew she must look like a small child, pleading for a treat. It was such an easy decision. They could go *home*. Surely he would say 'ok'.

A gust of wind swirled pink and white petals around them and plastered the thin silk of her clothing against her legs. Jade shivered, gripped by a sudden sense of unease. Something was wrong. She looked uncertainly at Zhudai but his expression was unchanged.

Phoenix turned slowly back toward the emperors' advisor with a poor impression of innocence. "And what about Long Baiyu?"

Jade glanced quickly between him and Zhudai in bewilderment. Who was Long Baiyu? Zhudai stiffened, his angular face hardening into an arrogant, sneering expression reminiscent of when they had first met him in the halls of the Norse Gods. Appalled, Jade shrank back toward Phoenix, who reached out and dragged her to his side, glaring at the sorcerer.

"When were you going to tell Jade about your plan to kill Long Baiyu on the day of the *ri shi*, in order to attain immortality?" Phoenix demanded. "Or were you just hoping you could get rid of us now so we wouldn't interfere with your little quest for two-world domination?"

His overly dramatic words tickled Jade's funnybone. She laughed nervously.

"You have to be kidding, Phoenix. World domination? That's so clichéd." She turned to the sorcerer, a hand outstretched. "Zhudai, tell him: you were just trying to protect yourself against us when you thought we were going to kill you. Right?"

Zhudai smiled again but this time, his smile made Jade shiver more than the chill wind had. His eyes darkened to black pits. He slid a look across to Li Lei, who nodded imperceptibly. The sorcerer withdrew his hands from his sleeves. His fingertips crackled with reddish, purple-blue light. He stepped toward them. Phoenix drew Blódbál and shoved Jade to one side.

Finally, their arch-enemy replied. "No, my dear. He is right. You are wrong."

"No!" she whispered, backing away. "You promised. You said you wouldn't hurt my friends. You said you would send us home. That's why you brought me here: to convince Phoenix."

Zhudai's expression of amused disdain became more pronounced. "Yajat did say you were extremely gullible. I didn't quite believe it but it is true. You were so desperate to believe; so keen to impress me. Well, your need to be liked has blinded you, you foolish girl. I used you to draw Phoenix out. I knew that if I just killed you, he would seek revenge and I don't have time for that."

"No." Jade shook her head, not wanting to hear it.

"Yes." He nodded, raising his hands. "I cannot send

you home. Only the one who brought you here can do that.
I didn't lie, however, when I said I didn't intend to hurt
your friends. I don't. I intend to kill them, and you.
Quickly. Right now. Then, with your amulets and knives,
I will have the power to control both worlds."

CHAPTER TEN

When it happened, the attack came from an unexpected direction: not from Zhudai but from Li Lei. The girl's hands blurred as she threw a long, silver hair ornament straight at them. Instinctively, Jade threw up a shield spell around herself and Phoenix but her timing was fractionally slow. The lethal point arced past her and plunged its full length into Phoenix's chest.

Jade choked his name and caught him as he sagged sideways. Angrily, he yanked the thin metal blade from his body and flung it aside. It bounced off the inside of the shield spell and clattered to the paving stones. He took half a step toward Zhudai then sank to his knees with a look of annoyed surprise on his face.

"Dammit. Not again." He coughed and grabbed Jade's arm for support. "I was too busy watching the monologuing badguy. That'll teach me to ignore the sidekick." Collapsing, he fell to the ground with Jade kneeling beside him. Angry tears burned her eyes.

"I'm so sorry, Phoenix," she murmured. "This is my fault. I'm so, so sorry. He used me as bait to get you here and now..."

He managed a weak grin. Blood trickled from the side of his mouth. "I'd say I'm getting used to it but I'm not. This is my last spare one, too." He coughed again. "Sorry Jade. You're on your own until Marcus and Brynn get here or I wake up. Some rescue, huh?" His eyes closed and he sighed as his last spare life slipped away.

Jade leapt to her feet. Rage pulsed life through her veins: anger at herself for being so completely stupid and self-absorbed; anger at Zhudai for manipulating her feelings so easily; anger even at Li Lei for pretending to be a friend. Mostly, though, it was a kind of black, despairing pain that she had allowed her old desire for approval to blind her to what was happening. She felt sick to the stomach at how easily Zhudai had twisted the situation to suit himself.

Well, not any more. He was not going to kill them without the fight of his life. Whatever happened, she could not let him have their amulets. Maintaining the shield, she moved between Phoenix and Zhudai and lifted a hand.

The sorcerer raised his thin brows at her contemptuously. "Do you really think you can beat me with magic?"

"I can try," she grated. "*Sky-hiti!*"

The bolt of lightning she drew from a cloudless sky surprised all of them. It snaked and crackled to the ground, detonating on the pavingstones with a deafening *crack* that sent a shower of debris in all directions. When it cleared, blue smoke curled out of a blackened hole in the ground a mere foot from Zhudai.

He remained where he was, disdainfully motionless. "You'll have to do better than that. Try this one."

His long fingers crackled with energy. Jade strengthened her shield and drew it closer to conserve strength. Zhudai whispered a word and made a throwing motion. Something hard and invisible hit her shield, sending tremors through both it and her body. Jade gasped, clutching at her stomach. It felt like someone punching her. She could hardly breathe.

Before she could recover, he struck again with the same spell. She dropped to her knees, struggling for breath; angry and scared. On the merest whisper, she cast another spell, *lauss hond,* hoping to distract Zhudai long enough to gather her wits and breath.

Instantly, the feeling of being breathless vanished. Jade straightened, glancing down at Phoenix.

Still dead.

Zhudai glared at her. With his left hand, he held his right wrist in a death grip, trying to keep it still. Jade's 'unsteady hand' spell worked but for how long?

Dismay clutched her as the great, gold-coated palace gates swung outward. With a thunder of matched steps at least a hundred palace guards marched forth, all wearing Zhudai's personal crest of a red bird on a black background.

Jade pointed a finger at the front row and Commanded: *"Sleep"*. Ten men dropped like stones, unconscious. The rest simply stepped over them. Seconds later, the sleeping men staggered upright, her magic countered by Zhudai's.

She tried again, this time with a different word: *vomit.* A dozen men spontaneously threw up on their companions. It caused confusion and disgusted outcry for almost a minute before Zhudai again broke the spell and the soldiers recovered.

Desperate, Jade cast a mind-talk spell and broadcast a cry for help in the direction she hoped Marcus and Brynn were hiding. Even as she thought, a stone whistled through the air, taking Li Lei in the head. The girl collapsed in a pathetic heap of fluttering silk. An arrow followed, aimed at Zhudai. For one heady second, Jade thought it might hit but it stopped dead in mid air and combusted in a flash of red-purple flame. Another stone soared past, this time heading for the contingent of guards but they were too far away for it to be effective. It rebounded uselessly off their armour. They marched on.

At her feet, Phoenix groaned and sat up, holding his head. The guards came closer. Zhudai released his hand with a smile of satisfaction. The tips of his fingers glowed again as he regained full control.

Hurriedly, Jade cast the first spell that came into her head: *laufsblad hrid.* Leaf-storm. Wind whistled into the open courtyard. Picking up magnolia and cherry petals, debris and small rocks, it howled toward Zhudai and the guards. Increasing in speed, the winds formed into a miniature tornado, spinning a blinding spray of pink and white into their faces.

Phoenix scrambled to his feet, staring in amazement at the chaos beyond Jade's shield.

"Sweet," he admired. "Can we use it to hide our retreat?"

Jade shook her head, frowning with effort. "Zhudai is too strong. See, he's already stopping it. The guards are almost here and they have iron weapons. My shield won't hold against them and Zhudai's magic for long. Where's Marcus? Where's Brynn? Why hasn't he blown the Horn?"

Phoenix rubbed his forehead. "I don't know. Can you reach them with telepathy?"

Jade whispered the mind-talk spell again and reached out to her friends.

Marcus?

Coming.

Faintly, she heard running footsteps coming from across the courtyard behind them. Her heart sank. He was running right toward the guards and there was no way she could drop the shield to encompass him. Even a moment's vulnerability would give Zhudai time to destroy them. Brynn and the Horn of Aurfanon were their only hope now.

Brynn? Where are you? Blow the Horn.

There was a pause; a sense of hurry and breathlessness then Brynn's hollow voice sounded in her head.

Busy running. Guards everywhere. Right on my tail. They took us by surprise. Hold on. I'll blow it as soon as I can find a spot to hide.

Realising Brynn was in no position to hold a conversation, Jade frowned at Phoenix. "Brynn's dodging guards. They must have been watching for him and Marcus. I don't know if he'll be able to blow the horn without getting caught."

"Damn," Phoenix swore. "Tell him he can't let it fall into Zhudai's hands no matter what happens to us."

Jade grabbed at Phoenix's arm. "I think we may have run out of time, anyway. Look."

The leaf-storm had settled. Above the palace, dark clouds gathered. Purple-blue lightning zipped ominously between them. Even through the shield, the air felt thick with power and intent. Zhudai's exultant, arrogant expression was triumphant. His whole body glowed and crackled with magical energy. His contingent of guards spread out to surround them. Jade and Phoenix stood back to back, facing overwhelming odds.

With a battlecry that rang across the courtyard, Marcus fell on the nearest guards, taking them by surprise. Steel struck steel and sent a shower of sparks into the air as Marcus attacked without mercy or fear. Phoenix started forward, gripping Blódbál – only to be brought up short by Jade's shield.

"Drop it so I can help him," he ordered, watching their friend's swordplay.

"I can't," she cried. "The second I drop the shield, Zhudai will attack us. Can't you see he's just waiting for the chance?" She glared at the vizier, who returned a gloating smile then went back to watching both her and Marcus. There was no doubt - he waited only for her to break.

"Dammit, Jade," Phoenix growled, "I can't just stand here and watch him get slaughtered. Think of something."

She casted around for something, anything that would give Marcus and advantage over his opponents; something that Zhudai couldn't immediately counter. Ah! That would work.

"Bresta vapn" she muttered, pointing at the man Marcus fought. Marcus struck again and the guard blocked. This time, his sword didn't ring true. The Roman's sword hit it and, with a muted *crack*, the Chinese blade shattered into five shards that tinkled dully to the paving below. The guard stared at his broken blade in astonishment. He backed away before Marcus could follow through with a killing blow. Another took his place.

Again Jade pointed and repeated the spell. Again a weapon shattered. And again; and again. Five times she cast the *break weapon* spell before it suddenly stopped working. A quick look over her shoulder showed Zhudai smiling smugly at her. He had offset her magic. His soldiers once again closed on Marcus – this time on all sides.

"Jade!" Phoenix warned. "Come on. Marcus is good but if you don't let me out of here, he's going to be overwhelmed any second. We haven't got time to wait for Brynn. Drop the shield now!"

"Hang on!" She held out an arm to stop him, thinking hard. Time! That was it. There had been something in the old Svear magician's spellbook. Two spells about manipulating time. What were they? Jade wracked her tired brain, trying to recall the spells she'd thought too powerful and dangerous to try out before. Yes! That one.

Drawing a deep breath, she carefully formulated the words. If she got this one wrong, the results could backfire in a disastrous way.

"Skjotr oevi," she murmured, twisting her fingers and drawing a circle that encompassed herself and Phoenix.

For a moment, nothing happened and Phoenix growled as Marcus traded blow after blow. Jade watched anxiously. The Roman flinched and a spreading stain of bright red blood appeared on his side.

Then, the world outside the shield seemed to thicken

and slow. The air grew murky. Overhead, clouds boiled sluggishly; swords swung in freakish slow motion; battle yells sounded like a too-slow soundtrack – deep and incomprehensible. Each blink of a soldier's eye and turn of a head took longer and longer.

"What the...?" Phoenix sent her a puzzled glare.

She closed her eyes, trying to maintain the thread of concentration needed for this difficult spell. Sweat broke out all over her body, such was the effort.

"I…can't… hold this for long," she grated. "I'm…not strong enough to slow time for a large area.…like the druids did, so I've sped us up a little. Just enough to get over to Marcus and let him into the shield without giving Zhudai enough…time to cast a spell. Help me."

She held out a hand and Phoenix grabbed it. Together, they stumbled over the hard ground toward their friend. A sword descended, ever so slowly, toward his head from behind. Marcus' own was raised to block a blow from the front. He couldn't possibly defend against both. Inch by inch, the blades came closer.

"Hurry up, Jade," Phoenix urged.

"Ha…ha," she replied, breathless. "Get ready. I can't hold both spells any longer. I'm going to have to drop both at once and then raise the shield spell fast. There's a chance I…won't be able to do it quick enough. Be ready to stop…that sword."

"Right," he raised Blódbál. "Shut up!" he muttered.

Jade blinked at him, startled.

"Not you," he pointed at the sword, "this stupid thing. It keeps singing at me."

She grimaced. "OK. Be ready...Now!"

There followed a brief, bizarre sensation of inertia; like being in a car when the driver hits the brakes quickly. All around them, the rest of the world sped up to normal. Jade saw Phoenix brace himself to not run into Marcus. He only just managed to get Blódbál up in time to catch the stroke aimed at the Roman's back.

With an almost-visible flash of purple-blue, Jade's domed shield sizzled into life around them again. Unfortunately, it included the guard, whom Phoenix now fought.

To Marcus, it must have been as though his friends had simply vanished then miraculously reappeared right beside him. The sword he had been about to block rebounded off Jade's new shield. He staggered back, colliding with Jade.

She slipped his arm around her shoulders as he fell against her. "I've got you," she smiled up at him.

He nodded at the shield. "So I see. Thanks." Straightening, he grimaced. With a quick smile down at her, he disengaged himself.

"Shall I heal this?" Jade tore a strip from the bottom of her silk shirt and knotted it around the deep slash on Marcus' side.

"Save your strength," he advised, pointing with his sword. "I don't think Zhudai's done with us yet."

She glanced up. Sure enough, the Chinese sorcerer glowered at them. He paced back and forth, hands clasped behind his back, yelling directions at his soldiers, who scurried to do his bidding. Dark clouds above built into the mother of all thunderheads. An ominous green tinge suggested hail and all sorts of other nasties were in store, should he unleash his full fury. At his direction, Zhudai's guards assaulted Jade's shield; striking repeatedly with their iron swords and spears.

Behind, Phoenix dispatched his opponent in three short strokes then joined them. Jade pulled the shield in closer.

"OK?" he asked Marcus.

The Roman nodded. "Thanks for the rescue."

Phoenix jerked his head toward Jade. "All Jade's doing, that one."

Jade didn't reply. She couldn't. Every fibre of her being was focussed on her shield as Zhudai and his men struck it over and over. Her clothes clung to her, her elaborate hairstyle had tumbled free and sweat stuck tendrils to her face and neck. She trembled at each painful blow.

Glancing at Zhudai's soldiers, fruitlessly striking at the invisible dome, Phoenix ran a hand through his sweaty hair. "Think you can hold Zhudai off much longer, Jade?"

She shook her head jerkily. "I'm…only just keeping this shield…intact. You can't see it but, as well as the iron outside and your swords inside, he's…throwing something magical at it every couple of seconds."

"Can you do the time-thingie again so we can get away?" Phoenix looked back over his shoulder. "At least that might give Brynn time to blow that damned Horn."

"No." She drew a short, gasping breath. "And I've been…trying to reach Brynn…but…I can't get him. I think…we're on our own…this time."

From the corner of her eye, Jade saw him catch Marcus' solemn look and nod in return.

"So this is it then," he said.

"So it would seem." The Roman shrugged. He gripped Phoenix by the forearm. "If we die here, today, my only regret will be that it is by Zhudai's hand and not a more honourable enemy."

"*My* only regret will be the dying part," Phoenix muttered. "I'm out of lives."

"It's been fun." Marcus sent him an ironic smile.

Phoenix grinned back and turned to face their enemy. "You have a truly warped sense of fun but I agree."

Jade whispered. "Give me your Life-blade, Phoenix – and your amulet."

"Why?" He drew the knife from its sheath. A single ruby glittered in its hilt. He pulled his necklace off over his head, yelping as it caught in his hair.

"No time to explain. We can't let Zhudai get his hands on them." She gritted her teeth and drew her lips back in a snarl, feeling her energy slip away.

Phoenix handed her both. She now held hers and his all in one hand. Swiftly, she turned away from Zhudai's penetrating gaze and knelt on the ground. Feeling Phoenix's puzzled gaze on her, she looked at the sun, high overhead, muttered a spell and mimed putting the blades and amulets into something. They vanished. She felt a strange moment of disorientation, as though her mind was somehow linked to the objects and was now split in two.

"What the…?" Phoenix stuck at foot out, kicking at the place the knives had been. His foot met empty air.

Jade struggled to her feet, her legs like rubber. "If there's a later, Phoenix, I promise to explain. I just know we'd be stupid to let them fall into Zhudai's hands. At least I can do this much right." She swayed and Marcus steadied her, thrusting a long, staff weapon into her hand; a trophy from the fallen Chinese guard. She leaned on it, gasping for breath. "But now…get ready. I can't hold the shield any longer."

With a fizzling soundless, purple-blue almost-flash, her shield collapsed. They now stood alone, surrounded by dozens of enemy warriors and vulnerable to the magical onslaught of the most powerful sorcerer in the realm.

CHAPTER ELEVEN

Zhudai's triumphant laughter rang out across the courtyard. Phoenix saw Jade shiver at the sound. She gripped her new staff as though to keep from collapsing. She looked drained: her lips almost blue; magical reserves probably exhausted. Zhudai could do whatever he liked now, and she was as helpless as Phoenix felt. Where was Brynn? Where was the Horn? Where was their eleventh-hour rescue from dire peril?

The first guards approached cautiously, waving their weapons in the air; testing for Jade's now-vanished shield. Emboldened by its absence, they advanced more quickly, slipping into fighting stances with swords, spears and knives at the ready. Behind, a rank of ten crossbow-wielding men stood, awaiting Zhudai's command to fire.

"You *sure* there's no more spells you can cast to save us, Jade?" Phoenix tried to keep as many of the enemy in sight as possible. "Can't you even reach Brynn?"

"I'm sure," she replied. "I'll be doing well to even lift this staff, let alone cast a spell. I'm sorry I got you both into this. I'm sorry I've been such an idiot."

"You are not to blame," Marcus' deep voice behind them assured her. "We all would have made the same choices, I'm sure. Let's just take as many of them with us as we can."

"Deal," Phoenix said grimly. "Bring it on."

That was the last chance they had to speak. The attack began and Phoenix was too busy defending himself to wonder how they would escape – or even *if* they would escape.

He caught a downstroke on Blódbál's edge and redirected the blade just enough to avoid it. Turning, he slipped out from beneath the descending sword and swung high overhead. Blódbál sliced easily through the iron-and-leather armour, killing instantly. Phoenix grimaced as his opponent collapsed and another took his place. Crouching and blocking at once, Phoenix rose up with a new dagger in his left hand, taken from his fallen enemy. He used it and the second guard went down.

From the corner of his eye, he saw Marcus' sword swinging, falling, cutting and killing with rhythmic efficiency. On his left, Jade held her own with the staff. The sound of hollow skulls being cracked echoed across the courtyard. Man after man fell, unconscious, at her feet.

Two guards came at him together. Phoenix ignored any rules of nicety and kicked one of them in the nuts. The man went down with a groan, clutching at himself. The other overreached his strike just a fraction – enough for Phoenix to pull him offbalance forward. He cracked him over the back of the head with Blódbál's hilt, shoved him aside and turned to the next in line.

This time, not two but four swords jabbed at him. He managed to deflect two and catch the third on his dagger but the fourth slid under his guard and into his body. It glanced off his ribs, leaving a long, shallow cut across his chest. With a gasp of pain, Phoenix jumped backward, out of reach. His new mortality suddenly hit home. He had absolutely no spare lives left. He could not afford to be reckless any longer. A fatal blow was, this time, going to be truly fatal. If he died here, he had no idea if his body would die in his own world, or if he would just wake up. It was a risk he wasn't prepared to take.

Frowning in concentration, he took a deep breath and tried to put pain and Blódbál's insidious song out of his thoughts. Various bits of his sensei's advice came to mind. He relaxed his shoulders and extended his senses, feeling the ground beneath his toes; hearing the movement of enemy and friend alike. Unfocussing his gaze, he allowed peripheral vision to catch any sudden movements. Then Blódbál sang in his head and jerked at his hand, distracting him with its dreams of bloody glory. His moment of awareness shattered. Growling, he swung the sword again. It rejoiced in the blood spilled.

Jade laid about her with the staff like a wild thing. She had to be running now on sheer adrenalin. One, *crack*, two, *crack*, three, *crack*; the guards fell like wheat beneath her weapon. She jabbed the staff into the stomach of one man, twirled it above her head and brought it down like a hammer on the sword-arm of another guard then spun to sweep the legs of a third so he crashed into his neighbour. Phoenix knew that desperation lent temporary strength but it wouldn't last for either of them.

How long until Brynn blew the Horn? How long until Marcus fell beneath so many swords? How long until either he or Jade was killed for the last time and the game was, truly, over? How long could they last beneath such an onslaught?

There was a brief hiatus around them as Zhudai's men paused, surprised by the ferocity of their defence. They fell away, leaving the three friends temporarily alone, in ringing, ominous silence. The smell of blood, vomit and death rose sickeningly from the warm ground. Zhudai waved a languid hand. The footsoldiers moved back. Twenty bowmen stepped forward and knelt, raising their weapons. Twenty bowstrings creaked in unison. Twenty bolts pointed in their direction.

Unexpectedly, Jade turned her back, grabbed Phoenix and Marcus by their shirts and hauled them close. She closed her eyes. Phoenix saw the faintest shimmer of purple-blue as she drew on the last of her strength to cast a feeble Shield spell. Could it work? Could she save them?

"No!" Marcus tried to push her aside.

She opened her eyes and glared at him, holding her place with Elven strength. "Don't be so stupidly noble, Marcus. Shut up and stay still!"

Then Phoenix heard the sound he had been expecting; dreading: Zhudai's voice. The sorcerer spoke just one word but it was the word that meant doom and the end of everything they had fought for; a word that spelled utter disaster and death.

With an expression of supreme boredom and irritation, Zhudai called out to the crossbowmen, "Fire."

The sky rained oblivion as twenty bows released their bolts.

The shafts struck and pain lanced through his body. Jade gasped, her back arching as she dragged all three to earth in a helpless, bloodsoaked tangle of arms and legs. The world vanished in sparkling darkness.

*****

In a distant part of town, Brynn dodged into a noisome alley and crouched behind a pile of garbage, shivering. His body jerked in response to blows he couldn't feel as bolt after bolt struck his friends down. Biting his lip to prevent a cry of pain, he fought to hold still; to ignore the awful, overwhelming knowledge that he had failed.

When Zhudai's guards zeroed in on the rooftop where he and Marcus lay hidden, Brynn knew their only chance was the Horn. He'd reached into the bag for it, only to be diverted by Jade's call for help. By the time his flung stone felled the Chinese girl beside Zhudai, guards swarmed into the house and chased him over the roof. He ran, trying to give Marcus time to get into the courtyard to help the others.

Every time he stopped; every time he reached into the Bag; every time he *tried* to help his friends, more guards appeared, hounding him. There'd been no chance to get the

Horn out, let alone blow it. Past experience told him that help wouldn't arrive immediately anyway. He *had* to find somewhere safe and fast. Even now he could hear the guards getting closer. He'd have to move again.

How could it have come to this? How could Jade have believed Zhudai's lies? How could Phoenix have lost another life without even a fight? They were his heroes and yet they were going to fail at the last Quest through stupidity and fear. Didn't they realise what was at stake?

Hearing marching footsteps approaching, Brynn slunk further into the alley. Guards patrolled every street. There was no way he could get back to Zhi Hui's house during daytime. He would have to wait until night and hope Phoenix, Jade and Marcus could hold out until then.

Anxiously, he rubbed at the palm of his left hand. The Binding Spell had not yet broken. Surely that meant they weren't dead…yet.

He peered cautiously around the corner.

A sword tip pricked at his throat. A deep chuckle sounded from behind. He raised his hands slowly, heart sinking. The Hyllion Bagia dangled enticingly in plain view.

*****

Jade awoke, slowly and painfully, to a dark, cold, smelly and unpleasantly familiar place: the dungeon. Easing her eyes open, she saw nothing but darkness – again. Hard rock cushioned her aching head. Water trickled somewhere nearby. At least her hands were not chained this time. That was something, anyway. That, and the fact that she seemed to actually be alive.

It took a lot of effort to push off from the floor. The world momentarily danced with pretty, sparkly lights as she sat up. Blood rushed away from her head, leaving it throbbing. Jade patted at herself, feeling shredded silk, clinging and unpleasantly tacky with blood. Her injuries seemed to be healed but she felt like she'd been hit by a truck. Well, there went her last spare life. Now, what about the others? Had she managed to save them?

"Marcus?"

She stretched out into the blackness, inching to the right. Nothing. It could take forever to find them at this rate. Annoyed with herself for sheer stupidity, she cast a light-spell. A single, feeble little greenish ball of light danced on her palm. She sent it floating away, searching for the others.

After a few moments, it hovered above a still form.

Jade crawled over, peering at the face in the gloom. Marcus. She felt his neck. There. A faint, thready pulse beat beneath her fingertips. He lived but only just. The light-spell now danced above another figure close by. A quick touch told her Phoenix, too, survived. She laid a hand on each and hung her head, sucking in and letting go a deep breath of relief. They were alive. All of them.

Beneath her palm, she felt Marcus stir and moan. His eyes fluttered open and he stared vaguely up at the green light-ball then at her face. He smiled, faintly.

"You're ok." His words were the merest whisper.

"Yes." She smoothed back a lock of wayward hair from his forehead. "We're all ok. You're going to be fine. I'll look after you. We'll be out of here soon, you'll see. This makes six times in a prison for me, you know. I'm catching up to Phoenix and Brynn."

He chuckled, ending on a painful cough. "We're even then." There was a long pause. She wondered if he'd fallen asleep again.

"How's Phoenix? Can you heal him?" He drew a shallow, shaky breath, coughed and winced.

Jade glanced over at their friend. "I can't tell yet but he's alive. I'll regain some strength and heal you both in a little while, you'll see."

"Check, will you?" Marcus' gaze was intense. "Check and see how bad his injuries are. Do it now."

She hesitated, reluctant to have her fears confirmed. What if their hurts were too severe? What if she didn't have the magical or physical strength left to heal them? What then?

"Do it!" he ordered.

Jade jumped at his forceful tone. Closing her eyes, she ran her hands over Phoenix from head to toe, feeling, sensing, mapping out the worst of his wounds. It wasn't as bad as she'd expected but not good, either. Not immediately fatal but bad enough that he would die within a day if she couldn't get help or heal him herself. If she had enough energy right now, it wouldn't be too difficult – there were a few sluggishly-bleeding bolt-injuries, but more concerning was the internal damage and a head contusion causing swelling in his brain. He would to stay unconscious for a long time unless she could reduce that pressure soon.

She turned back to Marcus, biting her lip. "I could heal him, if I had my herbs maybe. But I don't, Marcus; and there's your injuries, too." She raised a hand to assess him but he grabbed her wrist with feeble strength and held it away.

With a shake of his head, he looked at her. "No. There's nothing you can do. You and Phoenix are the important ones. He's the one you have to restore, not me."

"What do you mean?" She pulled her hand free, frightened. "I can fix you. I've done it before."

"No," he repeated, closing his eyes briefly and pausing to take a long, slow breath. "I know you. You'll try so hard to save both of us that you'll lose your last life and ruin everything." He opened his eyes and stared hard at her. "You can't save both of us, Jade. I'm dying and I know it. Let me go. Save Phoenix. You two have a job to do here. It's essential to the whole world that you finish it. I'm not important. He is."

"Marcus, no." She cupped a hand around his face,

tears blinding her. She brushed them away impatiently. "You can't just expect me to just let you die. I *can* save you. I have to. You *are* important. I can't..."

"Jade," he interrupted her. "Do you remember, in Egypt, when I told you that, if you had to, I wanted you to take my life force to save yourself or Phoenix?"

"Yes." Tears thickened her throat and made it hard to talk. "I also remember I said I couldn't promise something like that. I won't do it, Marcus. I won't sacrifice you to save either of us. I won't choose him over you."

"It's not your choice to make." His lips twisted. "It's mine. Now do it, before it's too late." Taking her hand again, he placed it over his faintly-beating heart.

"No!" Jade shook her head. "I can't, Marcus. Don't make me do this. Please? I'm sure I'm strong enough to heal him. Really."

"You're a bad liar, Jade." Marcus gazed fondly at her. "It's one of the many reasons I love you."

There was a long silence as Jade gazed, open-mouthed at him. Water dripped. The little witch-light hovered overhead, lighting the whole scene in an eerie, greenish half-glow.

"You...love me?" she finally asked.

He gave an ironic half-laugh at her stunned expression. "Since we first met."

She shifted uncomfortably, not sure what to say. "What, when I looked like a hag from running through the forest all day?"

Marcus managed a small shake of his head. "It's not how you look, Jade. It's always been about who you are, inside." He coughed once more. Blood tinged his lips red.

Jade's heart contracted with fear. She couldn't lose him. Not now.

"Save your strength. Don't talk," she whispered, holding his hand.

"I won't get another chance to say this," he replied

wryly. "You worry too much about what other people think of you. You are the most incredible girl: you're smart, funny, wise, strong, kind and honourable. I've never cared how you look or whether you are perfect. I know you're not but you always try your hardest and you do the right thing, even when it's difficult. It's who you *are* that makes you special. If you'd just believe in yourself, you'd find you are capable of great things."

Jade hung her head, an odd mix of breathless joy, denial and overwhelming fear churning in her stomach. He was dying because she *had* made the wrong choice this time. Surely he saw that? She wasn't special and she certainly wasn't capable of anything great.

Marcus coughed again, his breath rattling in his throat. "There's not much time. You *must* do the right thing now. Take my remaining life force and use it to cure Phoenix. Don't wear yourself out, though. Promise. You and he *have* to finish your Quest or my whole world is in danger. Do it Jade. Now."

He placed her hand once more over his heart.

Seeing the determination in him, she nodded, slowly, reluctantly; her heart heavy. It took a moment to remember exactly how she had drawn power from Phoenix to strengthen her shield in Egypt but finally she felt it pulsing faintly through Marcus' battered body. His life energy tasted cool, blue-green, almost like that of the forests she knew so well. Slowly, she drew it from him, storing it inside her own body until she could use it on Phoenix.

His heart slowed, his breathing eased. His dark eyes lost focus. His eyelids flickered as he smiled at Jade one, last time.

Then, with the faintest sigh of relief, Marcus Gnaeus Agricola, died.

CHAPTER TWELVE

Phoenix awoke to a throbbing pain in his head and another in his left hand. For a moment, he simply lay still, utterly astonished that he was actually able to *be* awake. When Zhudai gave the command to fire, he'd been certain his final life was about to be wiped out. Jade threw her arms and a Shield around them but even he could tell it was a feeble effort at magic. The three of them fell together and Phoenix smacked his head hard on the ground. His last thought before succumbing to unconsciousness was to wonder if he'd wake up back home in England, or not at all…ever.

He had certainly not expected to wake up in his digital body, obviously still somewhere in 80AD China…maybe. It was a bit dark to tell where, exactly, though.

Slowly, the sounds, smells and sensations of the place filtered in through a haze of pain: water trickling; the scent of damp, rotting things; wet stone beneath his fingers; a greenish glow off to his left somewhere; the sound of someone crying, quietly, forlornly.

With an effort, he turned his head that way, wincing as the hard stone pushed on his bruised skull. Dimly outlined in a familiar greenish light were Jade and Marcus. Jade's back was to him, her head and arms resting on Marcus' chest. He could tell it was her by the long, white-blonde hair lying loose across her face. Phoenix could only see Marcus' profile. His eyes were closed.

It took a few moments for the pieces to fit together in his aching head: Jade crying; Marcus lying still; Phoenix's left hand hurting like someone had stabbed it; a strange sense of emptiness somewhere near his heart. He'd felt it before – when Brynn had been killed and the Binding spell broke.

No. It couldn't be true. Marcus couldn't be dead. It wasn't possible.

Phoenix rolled over onto his knees, gagging as the pain in his head caused a wave of nausea. Jade appeared at his side, running her hands over his head.

"Don't move yet. I've healed the worst of it but you'll have an awful headache for awhile. I'm sorry…" She stopped to wipe away tears and clear her throat. "I didn't have enough energy to do more. I p...promised M…Marcus I wouldn't overdo it."

Fresh tears streamed down her face as she looked again at Marcus' still form.

"He…he's gone. I couldn't save him. I couldn't save both of you. He made me save you and now he's gone."

Phoenix shook off her hands and crawled over to his friend, touching the still-warm skin on his throat. There was no pulse. He shook his head in disbelief.

"Don't be stupid. He can't be dead." He gripped the boy's shoulder. "C'mon Marcus, quit playing around. Get up!"

Nothing happened.

This wasn't possible. How could it be? Marcus had no right to die now. He needed him. He trusted him. He relied on the Roman like family. Phoenix felt the old, helpless anger born of loss build in his guts.

He turned on Jade. "How could you let him die? It's your job to heal him. What were you doing?"

She shrank back. "It's not my fault. I couldn't save both of you. I tried. I really did."

"Well you didn't try hard enough," he snarled. "It *is*

your fault. If you'd never been stupid enough to fall for Zhudai's tricks, we wouldn't be here in the first place. First Cadoc then you let yourself get kidnapped by Yajat; then you actually *believe* Zhudai. God, Jade. Can't you do anything right?"

Instead of fighting back, Jade pulled her knees up to her chest and hid her face, crying harder. She wrapped her arms around herself, her sobs becoming wilder until Phoenix couldn't stand it any longer. His head throbbed with blinding pain. A sense of hopelessness swept through him as he looked again at Marcus. It was like losing his father, all over again.

With that realisation, he understood his own reactions and all the anger drained away. He collapsed next to Jade and put an arm around her shoulders.

"Oh man, I'm sorry." He squeezed awkwardly. "I shouldn't have said that. It's not true. I'm an idiot. You didn't do anything wrong. It's not your fault. I know you must have tried your best to save him."

She shook her head. "No! I didn't. He made me take out the last of his life force to save *you*. I couldn't heal either of you on my own, so he made me promise to save you. *I* killed Marcus. *I* did! You were right. It *is* my fault!"

She shoved his arm off and scrambled away into a corner of the dank prison, huddling there, crying harder than ever.

Phoenix stayed where he was, dumbfounded. Guilt and bile rose in his throat. He didn't know what to think. He looked at Marcus' peaceful expression. Marcus had deliberately given up his life to save him? What sort of person made that kind of sacrifice willingly?

The answer came: a truly selfless one who could see what had to be done in the greater scheme of things - and actually do it. A better man than he was: a hero.

Torchlight flared.

Startled from his thoughts, Phoenix flung up a hand to protect his eyes. The prison door swung open to admit Zhudai. The sorcerer strode into the room, looking around.

"So you two you survived, did you?" He sneered. "Good. That gives me two hostages to bargain with. Guards!"

Two liveried soldiers bowed into the room.

"Take that carcass out and throw it in the rubbish heap. The cleaners can deal with it."

"No!" "No!" Phoenix and Jade spoke together, stumbling over to their friend's body.

More guards came in, holding them at bay with spears. Phoenix grabbed Jade as she tried to get to Marcus, holding her back as she struggled. He watched, heart hardening to stone, as they dragged his friend from the room.

Looking at their faces, Zhudai laughed callously. "Now we wait and see exactly how much your friend, Brynn, wants you alive. He has a few little things I need: the Hyllion Bagia's contents: the Horn of Aurfanon, your daggers and amulets. It was most inconvenient of you to hide them from me, Jade. If he co-operates and tells me the names to use to retrieve them, I'll consider letting one of you go. Which one, I'm not sure. We'll have to see. Maybe I'll make him choose."

"Brynn will *never* give the Bag to you," Jade cried, her voice choked.

Zhudai laughed again. "But I already *have* the Bag, my dear. I just need him to Gift the Horn, daggers and amulets inside it to me. While you two may have nothing to lose," he paused and glanced ironically at where Marcus had lain, "your young friend still does - you. Of course, you could always save him by Gifting it to me yourselves?" He waited, giving them a chance to respond. When they stayed stubbornly silent, he chuckled again and turned to leave.

Pausing in the door, he held up his long robe

fastidiously. "Perhaps you can commiserate with your fellow prisoner next door – Long Baiyu." He raised his voice. "You have lost, old friend. Tomorrow at midday, you die. With the daggers, amulets, Bag, Blódbál, the Horn and the immortality I will gain at the *ri shi*, I will be invincible. I will conquer two worlds and rule uncontested." He glanced back over his shoulder. "Our young friends here can watch the ceremony and see what they had the audacity to think they could prevent."

The door slammed shut, leaving them in almost-darkness again. Jade's green witchlight hovered over her head, showing her stricken face, shadowed with grief and failure.

Phoenix drew her down to sit on the hard, slippery floor. He kept an arm around her shoulder this time, misliking the empty, hopeless look in her green eyes. She stayed silent for a long time, just staring at the place where Marcus had lain. The withered remains of the vine she had used for the Binding Spell marked his place, a reminder of what had been lost.

Finally, she spoke in a broken, soft little voice that tore at his heart.

"We failed, Phoenix. We tried so hard but we failed. *I* failed." She sighed and drew her knees up again, resting her chin on them and closing her eyes. "Marcus died for nothing and now we'll never get home. It's impossible."

Phoenix dug deep inside himself, trying to find reserves of hope.

"You don't know that for sure." He pulled her closer. "Maybe...maybe Zhudai was lying about having the Bag. I mean, why would he need Brynn to gift it to him when he could get us to do it if he really tried? He obviously doesn't know the knives and amulets aren't in the Bag. Maybe it was all just a bluff. Maybe...we'll find a way to escape and stop Zhudai after all. You can't give up now."

Jade sighed again. "The Horn can't be taken under any

sort of duress. If we're in prison or tortured then we can't gift it to him. Aurfanon said it had to be freely given. If Brynn is still free then only he can Gift it and Zhudai must know that. Plus, when he can't find the daggers in the bag, he can just use your life as leverage to get me to tell him where they are."

She turned her face away. "Anyway, what's the point? Even if he survived, Brynn will think we're dead because the Binding Spell is broken. We can't escape without outside help. Tomorrow Zhudai will kill Baiyu and become immortal. He'll torture the daggers and the amulets out of us and he'll use them to take over our world as well. Face it, we're stuck here. We're never going home."

*****

Brynn sat, staring at his left hand in disbelief. It was early evening and he had finally made it back to Zhi Hui's house. The guard who took the Bag at swordpoint was quick enough to snatch it but not quite quick enough to catch Brynn when he took advantage of the momentary distraction to bolt for freedom. As much as he hated giving up the Bag and the Horn in it, being free was his only hope of saving the others.

Guards still patrolled every street, searching randomly for him, he assumed. Twice he'd hidden in piles of rubbish to avoid them. Stinking and tired, he'd climbed over a wall so as not to disturb Zhi Hui's servants or cause suspicion in the neighbourhood. He didn't want to get Zhi Hui in trouble, so he'd snuck in to get the rest of the weapons and gear and mount a rescue on his own.

Now, it was too late.

No sooner had he collected everything useful he could carry, than his breath was stolen by a sharp pain in his left hand and a strange, forlorn feeling of solitude in his soul. He knew immediately what had happened: his friends were dead. There was no other explanation. He had left them in the hopes that he could save them but he hadn't been fast enough. They were dead and he was alone again.

Hours later, Zhi Hui found him, curled into a small, pitiful ball in a corner of her guest bedroom. He had long since stopped crying and simply stared silently at the wall with his arms wrapped around his chest.

Zhi Hui bustled in and stopped on the threshold, pursing her lips. "Come on, boy. There's work to do. Get up."

"Go away," Brynn muttered. "We've failed. Zhudai wins."

The old woman came into the room instead, standing over him with her hands on her hips. "Fall seven times, get up eight. Then you have not failed."

"Oh stop it with the stupid sayings, I don't care." Brynn hunched a shoulder, dashing fresh tears away.

Grabbing him by the elbow, Zhi Hui hauled him to his feet with surprising strength. "Don't be silly. You have a job to do. Now take a bath and get dressed in clean clothes. Something dark."

"Why?" He defiantly shook free of her grip. "There's no point. I can go home now. It's over."

"Over?" She raised thin eyebrows at him. "So you're going to leave Marcus unburied and your companions to rot in Zhudai's prison, are you? Well, some friend you are." She huffed and turned away.

"Jade and Phoenix are alive?" Brynn ran around in front of her, his heart pounding. "Are you sure?"

Zhi Hui nodded. "I overheard Zhudai speaking with them just a little while ago. I have Marcus' body, too." She grimaced and spat. "Zhudai had his guards throw him onto the rubbish pit like carrion. He has no respect. Come. We must prepare him for a proper burial and find a way to save your friends and my son."

When Brynn did not follow her, Zhi Hui frowned at him. "Come on, boy. There's no time to be lost. We have only this night and the morning before the *ri shi*. We must stop Zhudai or Marcus' sacrifice is for nought."

"Yes…" Brynn replied, thinking hard. He nodded sharply at the old woman. "Let me see his body first then I'll take that bath."

*****

"Marcus knew this was coming, you know." Phoenix finally broke the long silence between them.

Jade turned to stare at him in vague astonishment. "How could he? How do you know?"

He shrugged, glad she was showing at least a little interest again. "We met an old Buddhist monk in India after you'd been kidnapped. He talked to Marcus for ages in private. Afterward, Marcus got very quiet." He stopped when he saw her upraised eyebrows. "OK, quieter than normal."

"And?" she prompted.

"And when we got to China, he said something about having to help you make the 'right choice' sometime soon." Phoenix shook his head. "I didn't understand what he meant. I thought he was talking about something like when you chose to come with us instead of living with Arawn as an Elven princess – y'know, some sort of moral choice. Not this."

Jade looked again at the spot where their friend had died. "So you think he *knew* he was going to die? That I would have to choose between the two of you?"

Phoenix frowned. "Yeah, he did. And he also knew that you would find it hard to let him go. Did he…did he *say* anything to you?"

She turned away, hiding her face. "I don't really want to talk about it."

"Right." He gave up, not really knowing what else he could do to bring her out of her depression.

Silence fell between them again, broken only by the continuous trickle of water and scurry of unseen, small animals. Jade allowed her witchlight to fade until they were left in complete darkness.

Phoenix shivered. The chill intensified, making his head ache worse than ever. Despondently, he drew up his own knees and rested it on his folded arms, wishing the dull thud in his skull would go away.

Now would be the time, he thought, for one of their god-acquaintances to turn up and miraculously free them. He looked up hopefully. The darkness pressed in unchanged. No gods, no miracles. Maybe Jade had been right. Maybe they were stuck here.

"Do not anxiously hope for that which is not yet come. Do not vainly regret that which is already past."

One of Jade's lights popped into being and Phoenix looked at her. She was as startled as he by a seemingly disembodied voice in the cell with them. They peered into the shadows.

"Hello?" She sent the light skittering off into the darkest corners of the room. There was no-one visible. Still, in this world, that didn't necessarily mean anything.

"My mentor always said that," the voice came again, "but I was never very good at following it."

The light flitted in a different direction, toward the stone wall opposite where they sat. There, in the wall, a piece of mortar between the stones had fallen out and an eye now blinked through the gap at them. A single, dark, narrow eye.

They crept closer.

"Are you Long Baiyu?" Phoenix ventured.

"Yes, and you are Phoenix Carter and Jade Lockyer of England." Their neighbouring prisoner stumbled over the unfamiliar names.

Jade and Phoenix exchanged puzzled glances.

"How do you know us?" Jade finally asked.

There was a faint sigh from the other side. "I brought you here. It's my fault you are in this place. My fault your friend died. I am so very sorry."

CHAPTER THIRTEEN

"*You?*" Phoenix and Jade said it at the same time but Jade was the one who continued. "

You brought us here? To this world you mean? How? Why? Can you send us back?" She leaned forward, fighting against the hope that rose in her chest.

There was a long silence and the eye disappeared for a moment then returned. "I sent out a Seeker Spell to find those who could free me from this prison. I am no longer strong enough to escape on my own. I just did not expect the spell to Seek so far from my own world. I did not know it would draw you from so far away in time and space. You are both so young, too. I am sorry."

"Enough of the apologising," Phoenix broke in, sounding irritated. "Just answer the question. Can you send us back?"

"When your horse is at the edge of a precipice, it is too late to pull on the reins," came the regretful, cryptic reply.

"Not you, too," he groaned. "What does that mean?"

There was a faint laugh from the other side. "It means I can't send you home. Not until you have completed your last Quest."

"So we really are stuck here unless we can master the Yu dragon and defeat Zhudai, huh?" Phoenix slumped against the stone wall. He pushed slimy fingers through matted, dirty hair, wincing as they must have brushed the bruise on his head.

"I am afraid so," Baiyu agreed.

"Pretty bloody tough to do from inside a prison," Phoenix growled.

Jade flicked him a glance, wondering how much he blamed her for their imprisonment. It was her fault, after all. Cold depression settled in her stomach again, clouding her mind. Her heart ached. Hope faded.

There was a long silence.

"Well, it's nice to finally know who's to blame for getting us into this mess," Phoenix finally said, "but I don't see how it helps us get *out* of here. I'm assuming you don't have any bright ideas, or you wouldn't have sent for us in the first place."

There was a faint sigh from beyond the stone wall. "You are right. My poor old mother is a cleaner here but she has not been able to do more than occasionally bring me food. She cannot open the locks nor clear the spells placed upon them by Zhudai. If I were stronger, I could but Zhudai has been very careful about keeping me in the dark."

Jade sent a questioning look at Phoenix when he nodded like he knew something about Long Baiyu's conversation that she didn't.

"Yes," Phoenix must have caught her expression, "I've met your mother, Zhi Hui. She's the one who told us we had to complete these quests, right at the beginning, back in Albion. Very interesting lady. She told us you need light to regain your powers."

Jade gaped at him. Long Baiyu's *mother* was the lady in the grey limbo world? She shook herself, trying to see if this could help them. Light.

"Will my little lights help?"

"No," Baiyu said regretfully. "They are simply not strong enough and I would draw the last of your power trying to harness them."

"So we aren't going anywhere." The brief flicker of

hope again died in her and misery crowded back.

"When you fall into a pit, you either die or get out," Baiyu replied.

"Oh, please." Phoenix scowled. "I'm really over the mystical sayings. Fine then... how about *a bird in the hand is worth two in the bush?*"

There was a pause then Baiyu's voice came back, faintly amused. "A journey of a thousand miles begins with a single step."

Phoenix grinned. Jade rolled her eyes at him.

"Waste not, want not," he returned.

"Do not remove a fly from a friends' forehead with a hatchet," came the answer.

"Ummm... a stitch in time saves nine." Phoenix scratched his head, looking at her for inspiration.

Jade folded her arms and glared at him. This was not the time for silliness.

"The beginning of wisdom is calling things by their right names."

"Hey!" Phoenix sat up straight. "I've heard that one before. The old Buddhist monk in Karla caves said it just before we came through to China."

"Then perhaps it is something important for you to know," Baiyu said mildly.

Phoenix frowned. Jade wondered what it meant. She was about to ask when she caught the faintest sound outside the cell. It was the sound of someone trying to be stealthy and doing a reasonable job of it. Only her keen Elven hearing made it possible for her to catch the soft brush of cloth against stone.

Jade grabbed Phoenix's arm as he opened his mouth to speak. Putting a finger to her lips, she pointed at the door. With no more than a head jerk and a mutual nod of understanding, they crept over to stand on either side of the opening. She doused the light and they waited in breathless, dark, silence.

There was a scuff of soft-shod feet on stone; the brief flare of a dark lantern; a dull thud quickly followed by a muffled curse.

"Don't step on my heels!" It was a familiar voice. "I knew I should have left you behind."

"Some roads are not meant to be travelled alone," a quavering, older voice replied.

"Oh, be quiet and let me concentrate. Hold the lantern still. This lock is being stubborn and I can hardly see a thing."

"Brynn?" Jade hissed. "Is that you?" She lit a witchlight and with it came a fresh spark of hope. Was he alive?

"Who else would it be?" The boy's cross reply came through the door. "Now all of you shut up and let me work."

"We're glad to hear you, too," Phoenix replied.

"Look," Brynn's tone was impatient, "Zhi Hui gave the guards a drink that makes them sleep but it will only last a few minutes. Are we going to stand around and chat, or are you going to let me get on with it?"

"You won't be able to open the door by picking the lock," Baiyu chimed in from next door.

"Says who?" Brynn's indignant reply made Phoenix grin.

"There's a magic component, too," Jade explained.

There was a short silence, followed by the sounds of cloth rustling. A hinged flap in the bottom of the door was pushed open. A wrinkled hand came through, holding a small, parcel wrapped in cloth. The hand waggled.

"It's herbs, girl. There is ginseng and some *ma huang*. Use them now. Release the locks."

Jade snatched the little bag and opened it quickly. Several of the distinctive, needle-like leaves of the ma huang fell into her palm.

"It *is* the Ephedra plant," she showed Phoenix, awed.

"This is banned in a lot of places. It's considered too dangerous."

Carefully, she picked up one, small needle-leaf and looked at it. Then she handed it to Phoenix. "Maybe you should have some, too."

Err..." He eyed it with misgiving. "What's it meant to do?"

"It's been used for thousands of years for treating asthma, colds and generally giving you more energy," she explained. "It increases your bloodpressure and opens up your lungs. Too much can cause nasty side effects but it is the basis of modern cold medicines. You know: pseudo*ephed*rine drugs."

"So why give it to me then? Why don't you just take it?" He stopped with the leaf halfway to his mouth.

Jade shrugged. "You need the energy, too. Besides, you know how much these herbs seem to affect me. We should see what it does to you, first. If you're fine with one then I'll take it, too."

"Oh. Nice – make me your guinea pig," he returned sarcastically but he did put the herb in his mouth and chew. Jade watched him.

"OK?" she prompted.

He nodded. "Sure. I don't feel much different. A little warmer, maybe."

"Good. If one doesn't affect you much then it should be about right for me." Without further ado, she put a needle in her mouth, chewed and swallowed. A few seconds later, she blinked rapidly, feeling a flush in her cheeks.

"Wow," she breathed. "I'm glad I didn't take more." Turning back to the door, she whispered through it. "You done yet, Brynn?"

There was a grunt and a click then a sound of satisfaction. "Done and ready. I'll go work on Baiyu's door while you do your thing."

"The lock mechanism is iron," Phoenix warned. "Can you still deal with it?"

Jade waved him back, frowning in concentration. She laid her hands on the wooden door and closed her eyes. There, wrapped around wood and sunk into stone – an invisible net of purple-blue energy.

"The magic element is nowhere near the iron. Give me a second to figure out what he's done."

There was another click and Brynn called softly to tell them he had done his part with Baiyu's door. Jade said nothing, chewing on her lower lip. Whatever Zhudai had done, it was hideously complex magic. Phoenix began to shift from foot to foot beside her.

"Come on-" he began.

"Shut *up*, will you," Jade snapped, glaring at him. She 'looked' again at the weave of the spell and shook her head in despair. "It's no use. I can't do it. I don't know what he's done."

"It will be something similar to your Binding spell," Baiyu's voice drifted to them, "but with a component not unlike a Shield spell thrown in. It was his favourite method of keeping me out of his cupboard as a child."

Jade reached out again, feeling through her skin the magic that encased the door. *Ahh.* Yes, now it made sense. Muttering counter-spells under her breath, Jade slipped her own enchantment inside Zhudai's and twisted, breaking his wards apart deftly. Invisible bonds fell free and the door swung inward.

Brynn threw himself into her arms and hugged her tightly. His small face was pinched with worry. "I thought you were all dead."

Jade hugged him back. "Marcus..." she began but choked on the words

"I know," he murmured. "Zhi Hui brought him to me. It was all my fault. I shouldn't have left you behind. I shouldn't have let the guard take the Bag. But..."

"It wasn't your fault, Brynn," she interrupted him, trying to stem the flow of grief that threatened to swamp her mind with blackness again. She leaned her cheek on the top of the boy's head briefly then put him aside. "It was mine. We can talk about it later. We have to get Baiyu free. Let me go now."

She made quick work of the wards on the second door and it opened smoothly. Baiyu was still inside. "Brynn," she called out. "We need your help again. Hurry."

The boy was by her side in an instant, working on the thick, iron manacles around Baiyu's wrists and ankles. It took only a few moments for him to release each one but the sound of iron clattering on stone seemed frighteningly loud.

Brynn re-locked the mechanical parts of the doors behind them. Jade, Phoenix, and Long Baiyu followed Zhi Hui back to where the guards were stationed. They slept on but twitches and groans showed they were not far from recovering.

Jade caught a glimpse of herself in the warped shine of a bronze shield hanging on the wall. She looked ghastly in the torchlit guardroom – ghostly, in fact. Blood smeared her skin and her white hair and pale silken clothing hung in tatters.

Baiyu looked far worse. Thin and haggard; his long, dark hair tied back with a strip of cloth torn from the remains of a dark red robe that now hung like a sack from his wasted frame. He would have been handsome, once. Now, sallow skin and dark shadows framed sunken eyes. Those eyes were the only alive part of him. They sparkled with intelligence, wisdom and humour. They were the eyes of a Master.

Knowing his martial arts background, she was not surprised when Phoenix bowed as he would have to his Sensei in his dojo back home.

Baiyu smiled, laying on hand on his shoulder. "No,

son, it is I who should honour you for your bravery and persistence. Now let us go. We need to get away from here quickly. Well," he swayed slightly on his feet, "as quickly as we can."

Phoenix reached down to grab a sword from a sleeping guard.

Zhi Hui stayed his hand. "If we can slip past, they may not notice we're gone for many hours. If we are very lucky, your escape may not be discovered until just before the *ri shi*. We will get you a weapon elsewhere."

He hesitated, staring at the sword with longing in his eyes. "I hate feeling defenceless."

Long Baiyu chuckled. "In your world, had you ever before used a true sword in a real battle for your life?"

Phoenix shook his head slowly, his expression bemused. "No. Aikido is about the empty-handed swordsman."

"So why do you feel defenceless now?" Baiyu smiled. "Your skills are the same - better even."

Phoenix blinked and looked now at his own empty hands. Jade saw him turning the idea over. Maybe it was just what he needed to break his dependence on Blódbál.

One of the guards groaned and shifted in his sleep.

"Here." Wanting to get moving but not liking the weakness she could sense in Baiyu's life-energy, Jade handed him two needles of the ma huang herb. "We have to move but you need this, too."

Baiyu nodded and ate it. Soon the flush of false energy sprang into his cheeks and he waved at Brynn to lead the way out. Zhi Hui and Jade draped his arms around their shoulders. Phoenix followed, watching the stirring guards for signs of alertness.

Jade only breathed again when they left the guard room and stumbled through darkened corridors toward the servants' wing. With Brynn scouting ahead and Zhi Hui giving directions in whispers, it took only minutes to reach a low door leading to the outside world.

It seemed like a week.

Three times they took refuge in darkened doorways to avoid being seen by scurrying servants or patrolling guards. Each time, Jade awaited the inevitable outcry with dread and anticipation. Each time, they passed undetected, somehow.

Brynn laid his hand on the last door handle.

"Wait," she whispered.

Brynn snatched his hand back, looking around fearfully. She slipped out from beneath Baiyu's arm and squinted at the door.

"There's a magic ward around the whole palace. I wouldn't be surprised if it were set to detect the passage of Baiyu himself," she explained, as the moment stretched tensely out and Phoenix twitched with impatience.

Baiyu laughed painfully. "You are wise beyond your years, child. I had not thought of that but you are probably right. It would be very much in keeping with Zhudai's character."

She held her hands out and closed her eyes again, feeling the unbelievable power of Zhudai's magic pulsing just inches away. She reached behind, touching Baiyu lightly – just enough to get an image of his unique aura. Even in his diminished state, his energy tasted a white so brilliant it was almost shocking. That very brilliance should make it easier to find any trap in the shields.

Yes, there it was. Interwoven in Zhudai's shields was a trigger spell. Set to detect Baiyu's individuality, it would immediately activate a magical snare and hold him prisoner until Zhudai came. It was a magic way beyond her ability to break or change. She wasn't sure she even understood it.

Jade opened her eyes, biting her lip in consternation. "There's no way I can break down these wards without Zhudai noticing, even if I had the power. We can't take Baiyu through, either, because it will set off the alarms. Is there another way out? Some way that *isn't* magically guarded?" she asked Zhi Hui.

The old woman shook her head. "Zhudai spent many hours finding every tunnel and door. He knows and has warded all of the entrances, secret or not. This is the only entrance servants are allowed to use and it is the only one so lightly guarded." She nodded toward a sleeping soldier, slumped in the shadows.

"Can't we disguise him somehow?" Phoenix suggested. "We have to get him out. We need him to defeat Zhudai."

"Really?" Jade said, surprised. "You didn't tell me that before."

"Sorry. We had other things to worry about, remember?" Phoenix grimaced.

She closed her eyes briefly against the surge of pain. Marcus' death was still fresh in her heart, too. Now was not the time. She could grieve later. Now she had to think of a way to get them out. What was it Phoenix had said? Disguise...

"Hang on…" She held up a hand as he opened his mouth to speak again. "Disguise him. Yes. Good idea."

"But," Brynn protested, "just changing his clothes won't stop Zhudai's magic from sensing him, will it?"

"No, but changing his energy signature will. Hold still." She took Baiyu's hand in one of her own, and Zhi Hui's in the other. "You two will have the most similar aura's, being family. I'm going to try and mask Baiyu with yours."

"Whatever you do," Phoenix said in a low voice, "do it soon. I hear people stirring in the palace."

"Yes, the slaves and eunuchs begin work at midnight. We must hurry," Zhi Hui agreed.

Trying to put aside worry and fear, Jade extended herself, reaching out to feel the aura of both Zhi Hui and her son. She was right, their magical fingerprint was very similar, although Baiyu's clearly had the potential to be vastly stronger than his mother's – once his strength returned. Slowly, Jade drew the two closer together, using herself as a conduit to mingle their energies until Baiyu's unique luminosity was dulled, merged with his mother's yellow-white and a hint of Jade's own green-gold.

Finally, she released their hands and drew a deep breath. Phoenix was there, holding her as weakness swept through her once more and her knees sagged.

"I'm ok," she managed. "It's done. The effect is only temporary but it should be enough to fool Zhudai's wards."

"Let's hope so," Brynn muttered, "or this will be a very short excursion." With a quick glance around, he squared his shoulders and opened the door to the outside world.

CHAPTER FOURTEEN

One by one, they passed beneath the stone arch, holding their breath. Baiyu came last – at his own insistence. The others waited tensely as he stepped beyond his prison walls for the first time in many months. He moved through, pausing in the darkness beyond the stone wall, waiting for an outcry, a bolt of magic...anything.

Nothing happened.

Baiyu's thin face broke into a broad smile. He turned to look up at the stars and closed his eyes. His chest rose as he drew his first breath of freedom. The half-light hid many of the marks and scars of imprisonment, transforming his face until it seemed as though he, himself was glowing; reflecting the starlight. When he looked down at them again, Jade saw it wasn't entirely an illusion. He really did look a little better.

"Even the rays of distant suns are better than none at all," he murmured. "Come. Let us continue our journey in all haste before Zhudai discovers our absence."

Brynn nodded and began to lead the way along darkened, silent streets. The boy slipped soundlessly from shadow to shadow with skilled invisibility. The others followed as best they could but Jade was conscious that her pale hair and clothing made her more visible than the rest. Her heart raced.

After several blocks, Baiyu touched her lightly on the arm. She jumped then nodded as he held up a hand to indicate they needed to stop. Quickly, she passed on the message. They huddled in a narrow alley between a fish market and a fruit stall.

"Where are you taking us, little one?" Baiyu whispered.

"Back to Zhi Hui's house, of course." Brynn raised his brows in surprise.

"Do you think that's wise?"

"We're not exactly swamped with choices," the boy returned acerbically. Jade laid a calming hand on his arm and he closed his mouth with a resentful glare.

"I meant that, should our absence be discovered," Baiyu said gently, "the first place they will look will be my family home."

Brynn frowned, glanced at Zhi Hui, who nodded back.

He shrugged. "Where then?"

Zhi Hui chuckled, plucking at Jade's loose, tattered clothing. "How about a bathhouse?"

Baiyu smiled. "The Red Lotus?"

His mother pursed her lips, a wise, wicked gleam in her eyes. "Hua Mei-Lien will be glad to see you again. She has little enough reason to trust Zhudai and he has found no reason to suspect her. It should be safe for the night. This way."

The woman slipped further into the alley, vanishing with astonishing spryness and skill for one so old. Brynn raised an eyebrow at Baiyu, who shrugged and nodded for him to follow.

Less than twenty minutes and considerably more than twenty twists and turns later, the tired group emerged into a noisome courtyard behind a three-story wooden building. Every window glowed warm with red-shaded lanterns. Steam escaped in long, thin trails from gaps between doors. The sound of laughter, music and the chink of plates drifted out into the night. The mouthwatering scent of food enticed them closer to the back door.

Zhi Hui scurried across the open, starlit square and knocked on the plain back door. After a few moments, it opened slightly. A whispered conversation ensued then the door opened further. Golden light spilled into the courtyard, welcoming and warm. Zhi Hui waved them over.

"Come in, quickly," a pretty girl of about seventeen or eighteen urged.

She bowed the group in and closed the door behind them with a quick, searching look outside to make sure no-one spied. She looked at her unexpected guests. Her almond-shaped dark eyes widened in surprise as she took in their bedraggled appearance and Western looks. She smiled shyly. Her porcelain skin flushed, matching the delicate pink-embroidered flowers on her cream silk robe. Long, shining black hair was pulled back into an elaborate hairdo that made Jade's head ache in remembrance.

"My mother is in the front room with guests but I will send her a message and make the baths ready for you, too."

"Wait, Hua Xinyu." Baiyu laid a hand on her silk-clad arm. "Your mother – and you – are you both well?"

Xinyu bowed again, more deeply this time. "Yes Father, Zhudai has not harmed us since your capture. Mother believes he still does not know."

A look of relief flickered across Baiyu's face and he returned her bow before waving her away. Xinyu shot a quick look beneath her lashes at Phoenix then ran with tiny, elegant steps, through a beaded curtain toward the front of the house.

His young companions stared at him as Baiyu turned back toward them. He raised a shoulder deprecatingly. "I was worried Zhudai might have discovered my family and used them against me."

"Er..." Jade searched for something to say. "You don't look old enough to have a daughter. I'm glad she's ok. She's beautiful." She glanced across at Phoenix, only to find him staring blankly at the exit through which Xinyu had vanished. A nudge in her ribs drew her attention. Brynn jerked his head toward Phoenix, made a face like a dog panting then rolled his eyes. Jade elbowed him back, frowning.

"Come then," Zhi Hui said briskly. "My granddaughter has had two of the bath rooms emptied so we may have some privacy. Jade, come with me. You boys go that way and make yourselves tidy. Baiyu, Xinyu will have given you the Lantern Room in the hopes that it will add to your strength. You know where it is. Go now. We have much to do before morning and little time to achieve it."

Jade tried to catch Phoenix's eye but he still stared after Xinyu like a bewildered puppy. She allowed Zhi Hui to lead her away, trying hard to ignore the rush of pain that made her chest and throat hurt. She missed Marcus. She tried to focus on what Zhi Hui was muttering but could not make the words out – only that the woman seemed unusually worried.

"Ah." The old woman's wrinkled face lit up as Xinyu reappeared. "Granddaughter. You must send a message to my house. If, as Baiyu suspects, Zhudai attacks my house, the servants will be in danger. Also, I need someone to bring *all* of the things belonging to the Westerners. *All* of them, do you understand? Is there somewhere their horses can be stabled without arousing suspicion?"

Xinyu gave her grandmother a knowing look. "Of course. Mother is the best at helping her guests to be discrete, Grandmother. I will arrange it – and some new clothes to replace yours." She nodded at Jade's shredded garments.

"Can I have something like the loose pants and tops that men wear?" Jade asked quickly. Xinyu blinked at her, apparently shocked by the suggestion, so Jade hurried to explain. "I can't stand tripping over flimsy skirts and long sleeves again."

"Of course." Xinyu bowed, casting a sidelong, speculative look from beneath long black lashes.

"Thankyou." Jade bowed awkwardly. "I'm Jade, by the way. My friends are Brynn, the boy and Phoenix, the warrior."

Xinyu smiled and Jade managed a tentative one in return. Her smile faded as she remembered Li Lei's false friendship. Could this girl be trusted? Could any of them, here? They didn't really know Zhi Hui, Baiyu or his family at all. They had only his word that he was the one who brought them here; that he was needed to kill Zhudai; that he was the one who could return them home.

She followed Zhi Hui into a steaming bath room in thoughtful silence, determined not to trust so easily this time. She would not make the same mistake a third time.

*****

Phoenix was startled out of his bemusement by a blaze of lights. The room they entered glowed with the light of dozens of lanterns in white, red and gold paper frames. It was hot, too, from the candlelight and steam. In the centre rippled a deep plungepool on which floated lily-shaped candles. Standing beside this stood three, large, wooden bathtubs, filled with scented, steaming water. An array of soaps, oils and scrubbing brushes were carefully laid out nearby.

Brynn took one look and backed away to sit on a bench. "Oh no! Zhi Hui made me take one bath already today. I'm not taking another. I've had four baths in the last three weeks – that's more than I usually have in a year. I'm *clean*."

Phoenix was too tired to argue or care. He shucked his filthy clothing and climbed readily into the warm water, wincing as it connected with scrapes and bruises he didn't even know existed. "You keep watch then. I'm going to enjoy this."

"And I," Baiyu sighed, easing into a bathtub with an expression of bliss.

For several long minutes nothing could be heard except the occasional splash as Phoenix and Baiyu scrubbed the grime of imprisonment from their skins. At last, when Brynn began to fidget with impatience, they both clambered out. Phoenix reached for a towel. Baiyu stayed his hand and waved toward the plungepool.

"Come, it is better if you follow with a cool bath. The body is invigorated and you will think more clearly."

Phoenix eyed the water dubiously. He was nicely warm and more than a little sleepy. The last thing he wanted was to be awake again. Still, he conceded, they did have a lot of thinking and planning to do tonight if they wanted to defeat Zhudai in the morning.

Clenching his teeth, fists and a few other bits, he slid into the water, yelping as his missed his footing and cold water closed over his head. He shoved off and floundered back to the edge, gasping and sputtering. Baiyu was already out again, drying off and watching him with amusement.

Teeth chattering, Phoenix snatched at the square of linen Brynn laughingly threw at him. "Th...that's insane."

Baiyu smiled then sobered and shook his head. Drops of water flew from his long hair, sparkling in the lantern light as he swiftly braided it away from his face. He already looked more muscular and healthy than they had when he had first emerged from prison.

"No, a cold bath is not insane. What we will attempt tomorrow, however, probably is. Come. We must make plans."

A short while later they joined Jade and Zhi Hui in a small room laid out for dining. A long, low wooden table dominated the centre of the room, surrounded by cushions of gold and red silk. The table was tastefully set with white and black plates and chopsticks. Again, numerous lanterns hung from the white and black paper-thin walls.

An elegant woman, dressed in a beautiful, royal blue robe embroidered with silver dragons, sat straightbacked and cool at the head of the table. Her strong resemblance to Xinyu, seated to her right, told him she must be Hua Mei-Lien. Xinyu did not look up. She sat with hands folded in her lap, eyes downcast.

Jade was across the table but she had left two spare seats between herself and the two Chinese women. Phoenix saw she had chosen to dress in a plain black, loose outfit much like what he and Brynn had been given. Not a jewel or bit of embroidery to be seen. Her pale hair was pulled back into a severe ponytail. He wondered why.

She raised troubled green eyes to his as they entered and he thought he had some idea: she felt guilty about Marcus' death and was trying to show she would not again be influenced by the promise of finery and ease. He sighed internally. He'd never understand girls. Then he caught a quick, sidelong look from Xinyu and wished fervently that he did. He couldn't speak. The breath caught in his throat. She was so beautiful.

Beside him, Baiyu cleared his throat significantly. Phoenix jumped, flushed and hurried to sit. He chose the seat next to Xinyu and tried to think of something intelligent and witty to say.

"Hi," was what came out. He kicked himself mentally. C'mon, there had to be something cool he could tell her that would make her pay attention.

Luckily, before he could make a complete fool of himself, a section of the wall slid open and servants began serving food. His stomach rumbled and he couldn't help but see the tiny smile on Xinyu's lips. Oh man. Now she thought he was a boorish barbarian. Glumly, he ate. At least he was good with chopsticks.

"When you have eaten, you must sleep and regain your strength." Mei-Lein's cultured voice broke the long silence. "You have a difficult task in the morning. Defeating Zhudai will take all of your skill and power."

Jade laid down her chopsticks, biting her lip. "But *how?*" She sent a worried look at Zhi Hui and Baiyu. "How are we supposed to defeat him? We don't have Blódbál, I've already proven I'm not strong enough to beat him with magic. I couldn't even protect..." Her voice broke and she looked away.

"Count not what is lost but what is left." Zhi Hui patted her hand.

Jade's laugh had a hysterical tinge. "What, two people who have barely enough magic between us to cook a chicken, a warrior with no sword and a boy-thief. We don't even have the Horn any more. Great. Now I'm reassured. We'll win for certain. C'mon - we don't have a hope of defeating Zhudai, and you know it."

An uneasy silence fell over the group. Phoenix picked at his food, trying not to believe Jade was right. He was almost angry at her for voicing what they had all, secretly, been thinking. Somehow, saying it aloud made it more real, more depressing. He suddenly felt young and inexperienced again in a room full of older adults.

Baiyu's calm voice intruded on his thoughts. "The question is not if you have failed, it is whether you are content with failure. There will be a way to defeat him."

"Ah ha!" Zhi Hui cackled. "I am glad to see you did listen to your old mother sometimes."

"Indeed, mother," Baiyu replied, though his gaze was locked on Mei-Lien. "Although perhaps it has only been the last few years that I have understood much of what you said."

"Maybe you can translate for us then," Phoenix murmured. Brynn grinned at him.

Jade pushed abruptly back from the table. "I'm sorry. I can't do this. I... I'm tired and I ... I need some time alone. Maybe we can plan in the morning. I'm going to bed.”

Annoyed at Jade’s dramatics and a little worried about what she might do, Phoenix went to go after her as she hurried from the room. Xinyu laid a hand on his leg.

“She is afraid she is not good enough. She misses her friend and her home. Do not be too hard on her.”

“How do you know that?” Phoenix frowned at her.

Xinyu cast a quick glance at her father. “My father has shared your story with me. I am sorry if I have offended. I only want to help.”

“Oh…well, thanks.” He felt like a fool for being suspicious. “I’d better go see if I can calm her down and get her back here. We need her ideas.”

Baiyu sighed and laid his hands on the table. “No, I think she has the right idea. We all need sleep. It will be morning soon enough. The *ri shi* is at midday. We will have time to make plans after breakfast.” He stood and reached down a hand to Mei-Lien. His expression was gentle. “Will you retire with me, my love?”

Phoenix saw a fleeting look of what appeared to be guilt and worry as the woman took his hand and rose to leave with her lover. He stared thoughtfully after the couple for a moment then shrugged. They hadn’t seen each other for months and Mei-Lien had thought her lover was doomed. It was quite possible she had cheated on Baiyu and felt guilty about it. Whatever the reason, it was none of his business.

He looked at Brynn. The boy drooped, half-asleep where he sat. “Xinyu, can you make sure Brynn gets to bed? I’ll check on Jade first.”

“Of course.” The girl bowed and smiled sweetly at Phoenix. He tried hard to ignore a sudden thrill of delight. This was hardly the time.

He pushed an annoying lock of hair back from his face as he walked through the halls toward Jade’s quarters. The sound of distant laughter and splashing told that Mei-Lien’s customers were still enjoying their night out. He envied them their lack of care, whoever they were. Sternly, he spoke to his tired, wandering thoughts. Right now, he somehow had to get inside Jade's head and work out how to get her back on track. Man, where was Marcus when you needed him? Pushing the thought of his lost friend aside, he reached Jade's quarters and hesitated outside, wondering what he could possibly say to comfort her.

The door shot open. Jade's hand reached out and grabbed him by the shirtfront. She hauled him inside and closed the door again. Her startling green eyes mere inches away, she glared at him intensely.

"Someone in that room has betrayed us."

CHAPTER FIFTEEN

"Wha…?" Phoenix staggered back as Jade released him. She paced the room. There were two sleeping mats unrolled on the floor with a small, hard, wooden pillow at the end of each. They looked hideously uncomfortable and made Phoenix briefly homesick for his feather pillow and cotton sheets.

Jade continued to pace, frowning blackly. "Either Mei-Lien or Xinyu, I think. I couldn't quite tell which one but one of them was feeling incredibly guilty about something; something to do with Baiyu and Zhudai."

He shook his head, trying to think straight through a haze of exhaustion. "Maybe Mei-Lien had something to do with Baiyu's original capture and she feels bad about how long he's been in prison. Maybe she's had an affair while he's been in there. Could be anything."

She gave him a scornful look. "You're just saying that because you like Xinyu."

Phoenix swallowed a rush of annoyance and managed to keep his voice even. "No, actually I'm saying it because I saw her look guilty as they left the room. You can't condemn someone just for feeling guilty. If you did," he raised an eyebrow at her, "you'd really have to hate yourself, wouldn't you? You're always feeling guilty about all sorts of stuff that wasn't really your fault."

Jade stopped in mid-step and stared at him, her green eyes wide with startled hurt and dawning understanding of something. Her mouth gaped open for a second as she looked completely through him into nothing.

"Goodness," she murmured, blinking. "I think I understand something Zhi Hui said to me in the baths."

"Is it another one of those cryptic sayings?" he asked uneasily.

She smiled the first real smile he'd seen on her face for awhile. "*A man must despise himself before others will.* I thought she meant Zhudai – and she probably did – but maybe she meant me, too."

Phoenix kept quiet, not really knowing what to say to that. No-one despised her but she was too hard on herself.

Eventually, she flapped her hands dismissively and resumed walking around the room. "Anyway, I'm sure there's something going on with either Mei-Lien or Xinyu. I didn't want to make plans in front of them, in case one of them was a spy."

"Is *that* was what that little scene was about?" He was annoyed. "You could have just mind-talked me."

Jade shook her head. "Baiyu might have heard and I don't know if the others have magical abilities of any sort. I couldn't risk it. We can't afford to trust these people, Phoenix, we don't even know them."

Phoenix sank to the floor, wishing for couches. "Look, let me fill you in on who Baiyu is, at least." Jade listened as he sketched out the encounters he'd had with the old Buddhist monk and with Zhi Hui. When he finished, she frowned and slid down the wall to sit beside him.

"You can't take their word for it. The monk was Baiyu's friend and Zhi Hui is his mother, for goodness sake. Of course they would want us to save him."

"Don't forget, though," he reminded her, "Baiyu did know exactly who we were and how we got here. Who else would know that? Plus it was his mother who contacted us when we first came into the game and told us what to do. What would he have to gain by that?"

"Zhudai knew who we were and by contacting us Zhi Hui got us to come here and release Baiyu, didn't she? Baiyu had everything to gain by drawing us here but there's no guarantee he can actually get us home," she retorted acerbically. "I'm just not willing to trust so easily again. This is getting too complicated. It was easier when it was just the…four of us." Her shoulders slumped and she sighed. "I miss him so much."

"Me too. We made a good team." Phoenix sagged against the wall. "I don't much like the way Zhi Hui and Baiyu make me feel like a kid again, either."

"I know what you mean. So what do you think we should do? About the others, I mean." Jade rested her chin on her knees.

He yawned. "Personally, I think you're just picking up on ordinary relationship stuff between Mei-Lien and Baiyu. He's the father of her daughter. Zhi Hui said Xinyu and hundreds of others of the Light were in danger from Zhudai. Mei-Lien's not going to betray Baiyu or her own daughter to Zhudai. We're safe enough until morning. I vote we get some sleep."

Jade rubbed her face with the palms of her hands and yawned as well. "I'm sure there's something wrong. I just can't tell what. Maybe I'm a little hyper-sensitive about the whole 'trust' thing right now. You might be right. G'night then."

Phoenix struggled to his feet. "Hey, in the morning…"

She looked up at him expectantly.

"Whaddya think we go kick some badguy butt?" He finished with a grin.

She gave him a worried little smile and nodded, obviously trying to appear blase. "I'll have your people call mine and we'll book it in for around midday. I hear Zhi Hui coming. Go away."

Phoenix found his room and collapsed gratefully onto the bed. It felt so good to lie down. He fell into sleep without even bothering to remove his clothing.

Too short a time later, just as the first grey of dawn lightened the sky, he sat bolt upright on the hard bed, wide awake. Something was wrong. He could sense it. But what? Nearby, Brynn slumbered peacefully. The vast house was quiet and dark at last. So what had woken him with such a strong feeling of impending trouble?

A faint noise reached his ears: near-silent footsteps on a wooden floor; the sliding of a door. He pulled out one of his throwing knives. Zhi Hui had thoughtfully requested her servants bring them. They were the only weapons they had left, apart from Brynn's sling and dagger and Jade's staff.

"Phoenix! Brynn!" Xinyu's faint whisper drifted into the room. "You must get up. Quickly. You have been betrayed. You must flee." The Chinese girl's dark shape moved against grey walls as she came to crouch beside Phoenix's bed.

"I'm awake. What's going on?"

Xinyu opened the shutter on a dark lantern just a fraction, allowing a thin beam of golden light to escape. She bowed her head. "I am deeply ashamed. My mother has traded our safety for my fathers' and yours. She sent a messenger to Zhudai. His men will be here within minutes. You and your friends must go now."

Phoenix sprang up with an angry growl. "Dammit! I should have listened to Jade. She suspected something was wrong and I didn't believe her."

"Please," Xinyu laid a delicate hand on his arm, "do not blame my mother. She is just trying to protect me. Zhudai does not know I am Baiyu's daughter. She knows she *must* keep me safe. If he knew..." She shuddered and looked away.

He pressed his lips together in scorn but he got it. "You're right. We can't waste time on blame, anyway. Go wake the others. I'll wake Brynn and we'll meet you at the back door."

"I can show you where the horses are but I can't come with you," Xinyu protested. "Zhudai would suspect. I must stay with my mother."

Phoenix nodded reluctantly and the Chinese girl slipped out.

Several long, tense minutes later, a very worried-looking Jade and Zhi Hui joined them at the back door. Jade pushed open the door and peered out cautiously. She cast a listening spell but shook her head to indicate there was nothing out there yet. Phoenix nodded, looking back over his shoulder toward the interior of the house. Xinyu had not come.

From the front of the house came the crashing, tearing sounds of the front door being broken down. Screams followed. Men yelled, swords clashed and more timber splintered. The first faint flickerings of orange glowed as soldiers set fire to the building. The scent of smoke caught in the back of his throat.

"We must go now," Zhi Hui whispered, "before they surround the house."

"But what about Xinyu and Baiyu?" Phoenix half-turned to go back inside.

As he did, the noise of hurried footfalls brought them all to alert. Someone plunged around the corner, sliding on the wooden floor to collide with Phoenix. Instinctively, he grabbed and discovered Xinyu, soft in his arms. She smelled of smoke and blood.

"Thankyou," she panted, showing him a face wide-eyed with fear. "Zhudai's men have taken my father."

He released her, taking a step back the way she'd come. "We have to get him. We can't beat Zhudai without him!"

The girl grabbed his arm. "No! There are too many men and Zhudai himself is coming. The house is burning. We must go, now. Our only hope is to keep you safe. My father will be kept alive until tomorrow. Please!"

"But what about your mother?" Jade broke in. "Will she be alright?"

Xinyu dropped her head, long hair spilling loose to her waist and hiding her face. "One of Zhudai's men tried to kill my father when he resisted. My mother threw herself in the path of the sword to save him. She is dead. Zhudai will not keep his word now. He once loved her, too and it will not take him long to realise she was with his enemy; and who I am. I cannot be taken or he will have a tool to force my father to co-operate." She raised stricken eyes to Phoenix's. "Please. I have always known this day might come. It breaks my heart to leave him but we cannot save him now. We must go and find another way to stop Zhudai."

Phoenix glanced at Jade and Brynn. They both shrugged and nodded. He couldn't see any other options, either, with few weapons and Jade still too weak to take on Zhudai. They were more likely to be able to help in some way if they regrouped and were *not* back in that dungeon.

"OK," he agreed reluctantly. "Take us to the horses. Then we need to find somewhere else to hide until midday." Peering out into the grey morning light, he nodded the all clear and opened the door. Together the group slipped out, into the empty courtyard.

"I must go see my servants are unharmed," Zhi Hui whispered. With a nod, she scurried off, vanishing through a half-concealed exit in the brick walls which enclosed the courtyard.

"The horses are this way." Xinyu pointed in the opposite direction and took Phoenix's hand.

Just as they reached a low, arched doorway, it flew open and a dozen or so soldiers marched through. They wore the black and red bird insignia of Zhudai's personal guard.

"Oh man!" Phoenix muttered.

Beside him, Jade took a tighter grip on her staff. Brynn snatched out his dagger and Xinyu raised her hands defensively. Phoenix glanced at her, wondering if she would be alright. He was answered almost immediately. One of the guards yelled something incomprehensible and ran at her. Her hands flashed, moving so quickly Phoenix couldn't even see what she'd done. All he saw was the limp body of the guard fly past and sprawl on the hard earth beyond.

"Sweet," he admired, grinning at her.

The Chinese girl sent him a small, shy smile. "We must take care of these quickly, before they send more men and we are caught."

En masse, the rest of the guards ran at the small group. Phoenix had little time to admire Xinyu's kung fu after that. He was too busy coping with the four men attacking him all at once. Without Blódbál to cloud his mind with berserker bloodlust, Phoenix found himself a whole lot more clear-headed – and a whole lot more wary of jumping into battle.

The first guard lunged, thrusting with an iron-tipped spear. Aikido training took over. Phoenix turned aside. He grabbed the wooden shaft and pulled its owner forward, overbalancing him. When the guard didn't let go, Phoenix continued the motion – down...around... up and then sharply down again. Apparently too surprised to let go, the guard flipped upside down. His head hit the ground and he collapsed in an unconscious heap.

Phoenix now had a spear in his possession. He flipped it over so the pointy end was in the right direction. Two guards hesitated, eyeing the spear. Phoenix jabbed it at them. They flinched back. The third began to circle around, aiming to get behind him. Phoenix started to circle as well, trying to keep all three in sight. In the uncertain half-light of dawn, it would be easy to miss seeing an opponent. Easy and fatal.

Somewhere, off to his left, Jade busily whacked anyone who came too close. Brynn ran out of stones for his sling but stayed beside her, holding the guards at bay with his little dagger. Xinyu had her back to both of them. She was engaged in hand to hand combat with two guards, her hands and feet a blur of motion. They seemed to be holding their own but Phoenix was desperately aware that it was only a matter of time before more guards arrived and they were outnumbered. Time to put an end to this.

He stood up straight and threw the spear. He wasn't great with a staff anyway. The guard he'd aimed at jumped aside, grinning. Confident now, the man ran forward, his companion close behind. The third again moved around behind.

Phoenix put himself back in the dojo. He'd practiced two-on-one before but three-on-one was different. What had his aikido sensei said? Ah! Keep circling. Keep moving. Don't stop. Don't let them corner you. Let them get in each others' way.

Two came at him at once. He waited until the last second then dodged to one side. He caught an outstretched hand. Two quick steps, a deft twist of the wrist and the guard flew through the air to land in a twisted, motionless mound up against a wall. Only two left.

They came at him from two directions at once. One had a sword, the other a short dagger. Phoenix moved, running at right angles to his attackers to keep them both in sight. They paired up and came at him together. Perfect. Again he waited until the last moment before moving. This time he dodged left, putting the sword-wielding man between himself and the dagger. Turning fractionally, he deflected the downswinging sword arm with his own forearm, redirecting the guard's momentum just enough so the sword swished harmlessly past.

The soldier staggered on, turning to look back in confusion. Phoenix caught the second man under the chin with the palm of a hand. He arced his hand up, controlling the head, then drove back down, dropping to one knee. The guard's feet flew out from beneath him. His head and shoulders hit the hard ground with a sickening thud. Out cold, his arms and legs flopped and the dagger skittered away in the dust.

Phoenix stood quickly, facing his final opponent again. The guard with the sword looked frantically about for help. All around, the black and red insignia of Zhudai's men lay scattered, unmoving on the ground. Not far away, Jade, Xinyu and Brynn clustered together, watching. The soldier swallowed hard.

Then, unexpectedly, his eyes flicked back over Phoenix's shoulder and widened in surprise. Phoenix shook his head.

"Oh no, I'm not falling for that old routine. There's no-one behind me. It's just you and me."

There was a soft chuckle that sent chills down Phoenix's spine.

"But you are wrong. There *is* someone behind you."

Phoenix froze. He knew that voice. Jade gasped and he saw a look of fearful surprise on her face. OK. Not his imagination then. He turned, backing away from both opponents, not wanting to stand directly between them. He halted near to his friends. He risked a look at his newest, old enemy.

A familiar, dark-skinned, grinning face greeted him.

"Oh man," Phoenix groaned, "not you again."

Yajat, the Indian assassin, smiled more broadly, his white teeth almost glowing in his dark face. He inclined his head gracefully and drew a long, curved blade from a sheath at his belt. It made a whining noise as it sliced through the air around his head. He wore black, flared pants, tight at the ankles and waist; coupled with a black, longsleeved shirt, open at the chest. He looked like a pirate.

"The moment is finally here," Yajat swished his sword again, slicing dramatic figure-eights in the air. "The moment when I kill you for the last time."

The two stood, facing each other like a standoff in a bad Western movie

Phoenix rubbed his forehead wearily. "I really don't have time for this, you know."

"Correction," Yajat replied, "you no longer have time for anything."

"Oh please," Phoenix shifted his balance and rolled his eyes, "spare me the bad-guy talk. I've had enough of that from your boss. I really don't care, you know."

"When I am through with you," the Indian moved to the left with smooth, tigerish steps, "you will not care about anything."

"Get a decent script writer, would you?" Phoenix taunted. "Or better yet, just come here so I can kill you and get on with more important things."

Yajat bowed slightly. "As you wish but I expect a good fight before you die." He advanced, murder in his eyes. "But perhaps you are not the warrior I thought you were. Perhaps you are too weak to fight the best of the best." He thumped his bare chest, grinning arrogantly.

Phoenix gritted his teeth, allowing a surge of anger that followed Yajat's mocking words to wash through him and slip away. Behind the assassin, Phoenix saw a flicker of movement as more of Zhudai's troops advanced through the neighbourhood. Taking a deep breath, he straightened up, made a quick decision and shook his head.

"I really don't have time and if you think goading me into fighting you will work, then think again. I've learned a few things. And y'know what one of the best things about being here is?" Phoenix half turned away and slipped one of Cadoc's throwing knives from its sheath across his shirt. It nestled neatly in the palm of his hand, hidden from view.

Yajat frowned at him. "What are you talking about? Fight!" He swept his sword in another series of flashy moves, the blade glinting hypnotically.

Phoenix grinned at him, continuing as though he hadn't been interrupted. "The best thing is: you haven't seen *Raiders of the Lost Ark.*"

The Indian straightened slightly, his expression puzzled and annoyed. Seeing the perfect moment, Phoenix drew his arm back and flipped the knife expertly toward the assassin.

Yajat paused in mid-step, his eyes widening in shock. He looked down. The knife was buried up to the hilt in the left side of his chest. He stared at Phoenix, his mouth opening and closing like a beached fish's. Abruptly, his face slackened and he slumped to the ground, dead.

Phoenix grinned, satisfied. "Told you - I really don't have time."

The sound of many male voices reached his ears. Behind him, the Red Lotus blazed, sending a huge column of black smoke and sparks high into the paling sky. Brynn appeared at his elbow, looking apprehensively around. He tugged at Phoenix's sleeve.

"I think *now* would be a good time to run away and hide."

CHAPTER SIXTEEN

"Are you *sure* this is the right place, Brynn?" Phoenix grumbled, pushing the half-rotted remains of a withered fruit from his arm.

The boy smirked over his shoulder and nodded. "It's an abandoned warehouse. I spotted it yesterday when the guards were after me. I don't think anyone's been here for years."

"I can see why," Phoenix sniffed his clothing. "Having to dig through a mound of rubbish to get in would discourage most people."

He peered into the gloom. Dust danced in shafts of morning sunlight streaming in through cracked roof tiles. Pigeons roosted on rotting ceiling beams, making soft cooing noises and leaving unpleasant mounds of pigeon-poo on the packed-earth floor. Here and there, piles of timber and scraps of furniture attested to a once-thriving business. Now it waited, silent, cool and musty.

Brynn brushed away a cobweb. "As long as we can keep the horses quiet once they get here, we should be safe enough. There's water in a trough in the corner but no feed. If we wrap their hooves in those old sacks over there it should stop any noise."

"Good thinking," Phoenix approved.

"Well," Jade murmured, "it's time we did some more. With Baiyu captured and Zhudai planning to start his immortality scheme in less than six hours, we don't have a lot to work with. Are you sure no-one followed us, Brynn?" she asked for the third time.

Brynn gave a one-shoulder shrug. "Once you'd put that last guard to sleep, who was to see us leave?" He caught Jade's glare and flapped his hands at her. "I checked, I checked. We weren't followed."

Jade jerked her head and' sat down on a rickety chair, only to jump back up and pace restlessly. "I hate sitting around waiting like this. Where are Zhi Hui and Xinyu with the horses, anyway?"

Phoenix sank onto the heap of sacks. "They'll be here. It would have been too suspicious for us Westerners to traipse through town with the horses."

"Yeah," Jade replied, her tone sour, "that's what Xinyu said. I do think it's interesting how quickly you agree with everything she says."

"Hey!" Phoenix felt himself flushing. "You're just jealous because you didn't think of it."

Jade curled a scornful lip. "As if. You act like a brainless idiot around her, Phoenix. Don't let a pretty face turn your head. We need to think straight now."

Phoenix sputtered in indignation. "Me? Talk about letting a pretty face turn your head – what about you and Cadoc?"

"Hey." Brynn stepped between them as Jade opened her mouth to retaliate. "Enough. You've both made mistakes." He looked meaningfully between them. "*Dumb* mistakes. *Both* of you. *All* of us. Forget it and move on."

Jade and Phoenix glared at each other a moment longer then turned away. Jade sighed and sat down on a stack of timber.

"I'm sorry, Phoenix. Brynn's right. I..." She raised her hands and let them fall again. "I just don't know what to do next. I honestly thought we'd actually have a chance, with Baiyu on our side. If what you've said about him is true then without him, we don't."

"There has to be *something* we can do, or we wouldn't have got this far," he argued, trying to remind Jade of their real situation. "Remember where we are? There has to be a way to *win.*"

"I suppose so," she shrugged. "I just can't think of it. I mean," she began to tick off points on her fingers, "we have no significant weapons any more, I have limited magical ability and we have three women, a boy and one warrior against Zhudai and his thousands of soldiers."

"Hey, don't forget that I've already killed off the sub-badguy," Phoenix pointed out. "That has to count for something."

She managed a small smile. "I have to admit that I'm kind of glad not to be looking over my shoulder for Yajat any more." She sighed. "But we still need to come up with a plan. We have to think of some way to get to Baiyu, get back the Horn and stop Zhudai from taking over. Last time I looked at our Life-daggers, we were out of spare lives to risk, so it will have to be a pretty foolproof plan."

The three were silent a moment. Phoenix frowned.

"Hey, what did happen to our Life daggers and amulets? You said you'd tell me if we had time later. Well," he gestured around the empty warehouse, "we do."

Jade shrugged. "I didn't want them falling into Zhudai's hands, so I put them in a twenty-four hour time-pocket. It's a variation on that speed-up spell I did on us but it has to be stationery. If you happen to be out on the courtyard today at about the same moment, our stuff will appear at the same spot. Retrieving them is one thing we have to plan for, too. I'm pretty sure we will need them to get home, somehow. If we make it that far."

Phoenix and Brynn stared at her, slackjawed.

"What?"

Brynn grinned. "That is *so* awesome!"

"Could you do it with people?" Phoenix gazed absently through both of them, turning over the possibilities.

She shook her head. "I don't think so. I used the spell because I was desperate. I don't know what's inside a time-pocket. There might not be any air. It might take way too much energy from me to create and maintain it. You might come out at the wrong time or end up inside a person standing in the wrong place when you rejoined the normal timestream. There are just too many unknowns."

"But it could be worth a try, don't you think?" he persisted. "It's the best idea we've got so far, anyway. We just need to find out where Zhudai is going to hold the ritual to sacrifice Baiyu. If we can get there early and if you can put one or all of us into a time-pocket-thingie or your speed-up thing then we can break out at the right moment, kill Zhudai and rescue Baiyu all at once."

"There are a lot of 'ifs' in that plan," Jade sounded doubtful. "I can't do the speed-up one for long enough to get us across the whole courtyard. It takes way too much energy. So are you willing to risk your last life on a new spell?"

"What else have we got?" Phoenix said fatalistically. "Besides, if it goes wrong, it'll at least give you a good reason to blow the Horn."

"Not helpful," she grimaced, "especially if you're dead and I'm stuck here with a megalomaniac running the world and no way to get home. Besides, we don't have the Horn, remember?"

"So I repeat," he tried to be patient. "What other options have we got?"

She closed her eyes. "None that I can think of right now."

"Right then let's test it, huh?" He jumped up, galvanised by the thought of action again.

Jade eyed him wearily. "So who am I supposed to test this little plan of yours on? Do you want to sacrifice yourself, or Brynn? I can't cast the time-pocket one on myself, or I would, so who's it going to be: the one person who *has* to survive with me if I want to get out of this world, or a ten year old boy?"

There was a long, significant pause as Phoenix and Brynn exchanged looks. Brynn shrugged and stepped forward. He opened his mouth.

"What about me?" A new voice echoed in the vaulted room; a deep, masculine voice.

As one, the three companions turned slowly toward the source. A figure stepped out of the gloom, into a shaft of sunlight. It haloed his dark hair and handsome, faintly-smiling face.

Phoenix's mouth fell open. He couldn't find the words to say anything at all. Brynn laughed.

Jade's astonished whisper came out as a choked gasp. *"Marcus?"*

"Whoo hooo! It worked!"

Brynn's exclamation caused the horses Marcus led to roll their eyes and throw their heads back. Bridles jingled and hooves stomped. Brynn clapped his hand over his mouth but his eyes sparkled with excitement. He did a little jig on the spot. Behind Marcus, Xinyu took the horses, giggling as she led them to the water trough.

Jade was the first to unfreeze. She took three hesitant steps to bridge the gap. With a wondering expression, she reached out and traced the familiar features of their friend.

"You're alive?"

He smiled and nodded. Seemingly unable to speak further, she threw her arms around his waist and buried her face in his broad shoulder. He returned her embrace briefly, before Phoenix broke them apart so he could thump Marcus on the back and give him a quick, rough hug. The Roman gripped his forearm with both hands, smiling more widely than they had ever seen him do before.

Phoenix swore and shook his head, awestruck. "Dude, you have no idea how glad we are to see you. I really thought I'd seen everything here, but this takes the cake. Man!"

Jade nodded, apparently still unable to find her voice.

Phoenix cleared his throat, suddenly aware of the charged atmosphere between the two of them. He stepped back, feeling awkward. Marcus went back to her side and smiled gently down at her, his fingers intertwining with hers. Her cheeks flushed bright pink. She leaned her head on his shoulder, a hint of tears glittering in her green eyes.

"I think explanations are called for." Phoenix cleared his throat again, glancing back and forth between Marcus and Brynn. The latter grinned manically at him.

"I gave him a Life Potion," the boy explained, as though it were an everyday occurrence.

Jade raised her eyebrows. "Where did you get a Life Potion from?"

Brynn tried to look casual but was clearly proud of himself. "Back in India, when Cadoc got killed, he said he'd drunk a 'pretty blue potion that restored a life'."

"So?"

"So in Egypt," he explained patiently, "one of the pieces of treasure I ended up with was a little glass bottle of blue liquid. It was in my pocket."

Phoenix, Jade and Marcus all stared at the boy incredulously. Jade shut her mouth with a snap and glared at him.

"You used a completely unknown potion on Marcus because it was *blue*? What if it was meant to turn someone into a werewolf, or…or to grow really big potatoes?"

Brynn scowled. "It wasn't, was it? Marcus didn't exactly have much to lose. He *was* dead. Now he isn't. Can't you just say 'thanks'?"

Jade looked as though she regretted her critical words and caught the boy to her side in a quick hug. "I'm sorry. You're right. It was worth the risk and I'm glad you did it." She looked again with amazement at the Roman. "I still can't believe you're here."

Marcus nodded. "I too. Thankyou Brynn." He bowed to the boy, took Jade's hand again and pulled her close. "Now, I think we have an evil Grand Vizier to defeat, don't we?"

Phoenix shouted a laugh and slapped his friend on the shoulder. Marcus remained unmoved.

Xinyu returned to the group and they dragged pieces of half-made old furniture into a circle. She brought out food and water and they shared an impromptu celebratory picnic on the remains of a once-grand dining table. Jade sat close to Marcus, her cheeks flushing every time he smiled at her; her expression starry-eyed and dreamy. Phoenix looked away, uncomfortable with their obvious affection for each other. It was about time, of course, but it did complicate things. He focused on eating instead. Finally, replete, he leaned back with a sigh of contentment – until he realised they were down one person.

"Hey, where's Zhi Hui?"

Xinyu cast down her eyes. "Grandmother felt she could not be of much assistance to our cause and would only slow us down. She stayed to take care of an old servant who was injured when Zhudai's men came to her house."

"Will they be ok?" Jade asked.

The girl nodded. "They will stay in hiding. Grandmother gave us what few weapons she could find."

She produced a dagger for Phoenix and a beautifully carved bow and arrows for Marcus. He accepted it gravely, stringing it and testing its draw with a faintly pleased expression.

Xinyu swallowed hard. "Grandmother also asked me to tell you one thing. She said that, if you cannot free my father before the ceremony, at the height of the *ri shi*, then you must kill him. Zhudai *must* not be allowed to use his living blood for the rite."

The four travellers exchanged uncomfortable looks. Phoenix grimaced.

"What is it about his blood that's so important, anyway? How is it supposed to make Zhudai immortal?"

"To attain immortality, Zhudai must say the Rite and drink the blood of Long Baiyu at the right time," Xinyu explained.

"*Drink* it?" Jade sat up straight, her face pale, eyes wide. Xinyu nodded. Jade's hand stole to her cheek. She stared off into the distance.

"What?" Phoenix prompted.

She snapped back into focus. "What did that old Buddhist monk say to you – something about names?"

Phoenix thought for a moment. *"The beginning of wisdom is calling things by their right names."*

Jade mouthed it back to herself silently then her green eyes lit with amazement and her jaw dropped open.

"*What?*" Phoenix almost yelled at her. "What is it?"

"The meaning of names," she repeated, as though it should now be obvious.

He grabbed two handfuls of his own hair and pulled it with a low groan of frustration. "Just *tell* us, would you?"

"If you stop thinking of names as peoples' *names* and translate them into what they actually *mean*," her tone was tinged with impatient excitement, "it will start to make sense."

Marcus looked at the Chinese girl. "I see. So Hua Xinyu becomes 'Flower, precious jade'."

Xinyu nodded, a small, secret smile on her lips as she watched them work it out. "Hua is my mother's family name. It means 'Flower'. My mothers' name is…was Hua Mei-Lien, which means 'Beautiful Lotus flower'."

Enlightenment changed Phoenix's irritation to comprehension. "I get it. So 'Long' is umm…. 'dragon' and your grandmother, Long Zhi Hui is… 'wise dragon trainer'."

Xinyu stifled a giggle, nodding again.

"Which means," Jade continued triumphantly, "Long Baiyu translates to 'White Jade Dragon'. One of the ways to attain immortality is to drink the blood of a white dragon." She stopped and frowned at Xinyu. "But surely it has to be the blood of an actual dragon, not just someone whose name is 'white dragon'?"

Xinyu inclined her head. "He *is* the White Jade Dragon. It is in his bloodline, passed down through three hundred years from our ancestor, the Dragon Emperor, Qinshihuan. When the need arises, my father transforms into the White Jade Dragon to protect the people of the Empire. Only now, he is weak from lack of sunlight. He draws strength from the sun, the Light."

"And you?" Phoenix shifted on his seat, made uneasy by her words. Liking a girl was one thing, liking a dragon-girl another entirely. "Do you go Dragon, too?"

Xinyu shook her head. "Only one at a time can have the power. Grandfather passed the ability on to my father seven years ago. I will inherit it when the time is right...or when he is...dead."

"So *that's* what caused the big falling out between Zhudai and Baiyu then?" Brynn concluded. "Not just your mother?"

Xinyu nodded. "Zhudai could not stand the thought that Baiyu was somehow more; somehow stronger. He thought my mother only loved my father because of his powers. He was angry and went to find a way to become his equal again." Xinyu looked at them all, solemn and wide-eyed. "I fear he has found it and, once he is immortal, he will be impossible to defeat."

"Wait," Jade held up a hand, frowning again. "That's not all. Phoenix, remember what our last Quest is?"

"Sure. Master the Yu Dragon and defeat Zhudai. How could I forget?"

"And if 'Yu' translates to 'Jade' and 'Long' is

'Dragon'," Jade said patiently, "then the Yu Dragon *is* Long Bai *Yu*."

There was a dumbfounded silence as they digested this news. Then the babble started – mostly between Brynn and Phoenix. *How* did they master him? What did it mean? How did you master a person? Did they have to make him their slave? Did they have to control him somehow? Did they have to kill him? Finally, Jade slapped her hands over her ears.

"Enough!" They subsided and she dropped her hands, looking relieved. "I think it's safe to say none of us have any idea what we have to do to 'master' him. We're running out of time, so, at least we can work on a plan to *rescue* him. Then we'll get a chance to do any mastering *after* Zhudai's been stopped. Agreed?"

The others nodded reluctantly. Phoenix leaned back in his chair, tucking his hands behind his head and staring at the ceiling as ideas collided with each other in his tired brain.

"The first thing we need to know," Marcus advised, "is *where* this *ri shi* ritual will take place. If it's inside the palace walls, we could have a problem."

"It will be held in the great courtyard in front of the palace gates," Xinyu said, quietly confident.

"You sure?" Phoenix asked.

"Grandmother said the servants have been ordered to set up a dais in the very centre of the courtyard; with an altar and blood-bowl to be placed on it in preparation." Shuddering, she looked away. Phoenix edged closer, putting an arm around her shoulder. She leaned into him.

"It'll be ok. We'll save him somehow," he assured her. She smiled gratefully.

"If the place is full of servants and soldiers now," Jade mused, "then your idea with the time pocket spell won't work, Phoenix. We won't be able to get close enough to the dais to place anyone in a time pocket without being seen. Besides, I just can't be that accurate with *when* you'd come out of the pocket anyway."

"What about our daggers and amulets," he asked, feeling very self-conscious about having his arm around Xinyu's shoulders. He wasn't quite sure how to remove it. Xinyu solved his dilemma by sitting up and moving slightly away.

"We need to get them back but I don't really see how they're going to help in rescuing Long Baiyu." Jade screwed up her nose. "If I'm right, they'll appear at almost exactly the same time as the eclipse – maybe a little after - but they'll be about…umm," she closed her eyes, "ten or fifteen metres west of the dais."

"OK." Phoenix leaned forward, elbows on his knees, fingers intertwined. "So we need to free Baiyu, get our stuff *and* defeat Zhudai – all in front of a few thousand soldiers and peasants, I'm betting."

Xinyu confirmed his guess with a silent nod.

Jade gazed off into the distance, her head characteristically tilted, one finger tapping her front teeth, deep in thought. Phoenix clamped down on his own impatience. He had to let her think.

Finally she glanced over at the Chinese girl. "Xinyu, if we could free your father *before* the *ri shi*, how long would it take for him to absorb enough light to be strong enough to take on Zhudai himself?"

"Maybe five minutes," she replied. "I'm not really sure. He was very weak."

"So…" Jade drummed her fingers on the tabletop, looking intently at all her companions as though assessing their abilities. "What we need is some way to get close to him, and a diversion to keep Zhudai distracted long enough for Baiyu to recover his strength."

Phoenix leaned over and murmured into Brynn's ear. "I think I sense a plan coming."

Jade sat up straight. "You do but it will only work if

we can get the Bag back. I don't imagine Zhudai will let it out of his sight, so we'll have to take it off him before the eclipse."

"Oh good." Phoenix closed his eyes momentarily. "For a moment I thought you were going to ask us to do something hard."

CHAPTER SEVENTEEN

"This has to be your most insane idea yet," Phoenix whispered hoarsely. Jade put a finger to her lips and pulled the hood of her cloak closer to hide her bright hair. "Why can't we do it now instead of waiting?" he asked for the third time.

"I told you, I can't sustain it for very long," she said. "We're only going to get one shot at this. Besides, Baiyu hasn't even been brought out yet and we don't know where the Bag is."

Phoenix elbowed his way through the growing crowd, hunching his shoulders in a futile attempt to be less conspicuously tall. Everywhere, black-and-red clad soldiers eyed the milling peasants with suspicion. Tensions ran high. The crowd murmured and Phoenix overheard snatches of hushed, frightened conversations that told him the people of Xijing knew what was happening and didn't like it one bit.

"Y'know," he turned to mutter to Jade, close behind, "if I were the badguy, I'd be doing this little ceremony somewhere in private. Why the big song and dance? Why expose yourself to the chance of things going pear-shaped?"

She flashed him a tense grin. "I think it's written into his bad-guy subroutine to be showy. If it was all done and over behind closed doors, how would we be able to win?"

Phoenix paused, blinking in surprise. "I think you're

right, y'know. It's way too easy to believe in this 'reality' and forget that things here are, sort of, scripted."

Jade grimaced. "That might not be true in our case. I think we've established that none of the other gamers have been sucked into this." She gestured at the growing crowd. "There's always a chance that Zhudai won't stick to the script when the time comes."

"I'd say he's already deviated several times," he growled back.

She nodded.

Phoenix scanned the crowd again, wondering how many were spies and plants.

"Just a thought," he whispered into Jade's ear, "but won't Zhudai be expecting us to try and free Baiyu?"

"More than likely."

"Won't he be ready for us?"

"Probably," she agreed.

"So aren't we being just a *little* bit mad, walking into another trap?" he pointed out the obvious.

Xinyu, who was listening, leaned closer. "As Grandmother would say, *Those who hear not the music, think the dancers mad.*"

Phoenix looked sideways at her. "Thanks. That helped. Really."

She smiled in amusement. "Then how about: *Four things come not back: the spoken word, the sped arrow, the past life and the neglected opportunity.*"

He reached up to shove back his hair only to hesitate, remembering his Western looks. Instead, he tugged his hood closer about his face.

"OK, now *that* one I get: this is our only chance. Alright already."

"Enough philosophy." Jade shushed them. She looked up at the sun. "We all need to get into position now."

Phoenix gripped her arm. "You sure about this?"

She shook her head. "No, but we don't have a lot of

other options. Brynn and I'll be fine. Go." She made a shoo-ing gesture.

He looked at her for a long moment, wondering how much was truth and how much bravado, then shrugged, turned away. The whole plan hinged on Jade, so whichever it was; she'd better just make it work. He really hated having to rely on someone else at a time like this.

Jade and Brynn headed toward the dais.

With a sigh, Phoenix nodded to Xinyu and the two of them elbowed their way toward where Jade wanted them to wait. Somewhere, hidden in the nearby rooftops, Marcus watched over them all with his bow at the ready. They were not taking any risks this time. Well, Phoenix glanced around at the stiff-faced soldiers holding back the crowds, not *many* risks.

The palace gates opened. He groaned as more soldiers poured out. OK. It was all one big risk but they were out of choices. If only he had Blódbál.

"Is that Baiyu?" he whispered to Xinyu.

She stood on tiptoes to look over the crowd, nodding as a group of six soldiers emerged carrying a black-swathed box slung on bamboo poles.

"Yes. Zhudai will hide him from the sun until the *ri shi*. Only once the sun is fully obscured, will it be safe to free him long enough to kill him."

Phoenix followed her a few more steps as they gauged their distance from the dais and where the Life Daggers should appear. Their position had to be just right or they'd lose the daggers in the chaos their distraction would – hopefully – create.

Glancing up at the high palace walls, Phoenix's eye was caught by a flutter of golden cloth. A man, richly clad in yellow robes, stood on the defensive parapet, gazing impassively down at the gathering crowd. Several paces away, palace servants in red robes watched also, looking nervously back and forth between their master and the dais below.

Phoenix nudged Xinyu. "Who's that?"

Her eyes widened in surprise. "It is the Han Emperor himself. I heard he was in the city."

"So why doesn't *he* stop Zhudai? Surely he must know what's going on. Everyone in the crowd seems to. What's he waiting for? Why doesn't he just march on out and arrest him?"

Xinyu shushed him urgently, pulling on his shoulder to make him shorter again. Indignation made him stand too tall and he towered over the crowd.

"For one, the Emperor does *not* leave the Palace while he is in Xijing. It would be unthinkable for him to walk among the peasants." Her expression reflected genuine shock, so Phoenix didn't bother to argue. "And General Ban Chao, who leads the Han army, has been sent on a mission to the west. No one else is powerful enough to stand against Zhudai's personal forces."

Phoenix scowled. "How convenient."

"No," Xinyu shook her head seriously, misunderstanding his sarcasm, "I believe Zhudai fabricated the order to send the General away because he was gaining too much influence over the young Emperor."

Before he could reply, Xinyu stopped so fast that Phoenix bumped into her. She tipped her head to one side, narrowing her eyes.

"There," she pointed.

Phoenix twisted, trying to see around the milling masses. Sure enough, in the midst of this hot and very crowded courtyard, a small open space existed where one should not. It was as though people just didn't see the gap; or they walked through it but didn't stop. In spite of the pressure of thousands of bodies, this small space remained empty.

"How did you know?" He frowned at her. Then he recognised the signs. "You can see magical stuff, like Jade can?"

Xinyu nodded. "I have a very small gift. Enough to see the time pocket. I sense the time loop is almost closed." She and squinted up at the sun. "The *ri shi* is close. You must take your position and do your job. I will bring them to you." Standing tall, she kissed him on the cheek. "Good luck." She slipped through the crowd to stand beside the empty space, waiting for the Life Daggers to emerge.

*****

Beside Jade, Brynn craned his neck, trying to catch a glimpse of the palanquin holding Baiyu.

"Can you see a way to get close enough?"

Draped in black and carried by six burly soldiers whose muscles bulged with the effort, it was clearly no ordinary litter. The crowd parted slowly before it, opening a path to the dais with obvious reluctance. Jade discretely elbowed her way closer until they were in the front row. Baiyu's mobile prison would pass directly by.

She glanced up at the sun. "We've only got about ten minutes. It's going to be close. The cage is made of iron. I can feel it from here. Do you think you can do it?"

Brynn eyed the contraption. "I won't know if I can pick the lock until I see it. What if there's a magical part again? Will you be able to break it?"

Jade shook her head, biting her lip. "Zhudai can manipulate iron because he's not Elven. I can't."

"This whole plan will fall apart if we can't release Baiyu and give him sunshine time," Brynn warned.

"I know. I know." Jade frowned, thinking hard. The soldiers were only a few steps away. "We have to try anyway. Like Xinyu said: it's our only chance."

"Actually," Brynn corrected caustically, "Phoenix said that. Xinyu said something much more obscure."

Jade ignored him. She was busy muttering the spell she'd devised to get them into position. She yanked him closer just as the casting was complete. There was a barely-visible flash of purple-blue which quickly died to an almost-imperceptible shimmer in the air around them. The crowd surged forward. Jade and Brynn stepped out into the middle of the cleared path.

Nobody reacted. Not a head turned, not an eye twitched. Nobody saw them.

"Wow," Brynn breathed.

Jade made shushing motions. When they'd formulated this plan, she'd experimented with a new version of her shield spell. By altering the way it refracted visible light, she'd managed to make herself invisible. However sound was still an issue. If she made noise, it could be heard. She couldn't stop the flow of sound without stopping the flow of air molecules also. Since breathing was pretty important, she couldn't do that. So it was essential they remain silent until their task was complete.

This new invisibility shield also sapped her energy quickly. She could only maintain it for twenty minutes before utterly exhausting herself. In the presence of iron, it would be even less. They were working on a tight schedule and would be very vulnerable if anything went wrong.

Pushing the thought firmly aside, Jade dragged Brynn down to the ground. Together, they crouched, hidden in plain sight. The palanquin passed overhead and three pairs of legs marched steadily on either side, neither stopping nor hesitating. As the last one passed, Jade and Brynn stood up, moving to keep pace.

They clambered on board the litter, trying to make as little noise as possible. Jade smothered a gasp of pain as she grabbed an iron bar to haul herself up. Even through the black silk that covered the cage, the iron burnt her hand. Luckily, one of the soldiers grunted at the same time and shifted his grip on the bamboo pole. Their walking pace slowed as the soldiers strained to carry the extra weight.

Balancing on the slippery bamboo litter, Jade nodded

to Brynn. He quickly felt the bars beneath the cloth and shook his head. The lock was not on this side. It was frustrating but not unexpected. Jade signed that they should split up and go around the sides to the front. The lock was probably there anyway. It would be difficult to maintain two smaller shields with so much iron between them but the cage was narrow and this seemed the most efficient way to make sure they didn't miss the lock.

It was a harrowing walk. Twice Jade accidentally brushed the iron bars and flinched back, almost falling off. Her shields were stretched, twisted and put through a ringer by the presence of iron. It took all her concentration to maintain them. By the time she rejoined them and Brynn, at the front of the litter, she dripped with sweat and shook like a leaf in a winter gale.

Brynn gave her the thumbs-up when his fingers finally found the telltale lock. Jade concentrated fiercely. Every swaying motion of the soldiers provoked spikes of agony as metal sapped strength from her shield, burned and weakened her. Cautiously, she extended her senses, feeling the lock with tiny probes of magic - just enough to test it, hopefully not enough to alert Zhudai to their presence. She sagged and shook her head at Brynn. Zhudai had once again used magic. Even if Brynn picked the lock, there was no way she could break the magical component. It was firmly embedded in the iron of the mechanism. Zhudai had learned from his past mistake.

She glanced back over her shoulder. Even with the slower walk, they were only a few dozen metres from the dais. Zhudai had not yet appeared and the *ri shi* was still a good seven minutes away, if her Elven senses weren't misleading her. How were they going to get Baiyu free and into the light? Phoenix awaited her signal to start his distraction and for that, Baiyu had to be free.

Or did he?

She looked up at the sun, directly overhead now as

midday approached. Catching Brynn's eye, she pointed upward, at the top of the cage. He raised an eyebrow then, as she made scissor-like cutting motions with her fingers, he grinned in understanding. Slipping his dagger from its sheath, he stuck out a foot for a boost. She tossed him up onto the roof of the cage, dividing the invisibility shield at the same time. It was getting harder. She resisted the urge to grab the cage for support as her knees shook.

Seconds later, she heard a low laugh inside the cage. Baiyu's voice carried softly to her straining ears. "Well done, child. Leave the rest to me. Go."

Suddenly, the palanquin tilted, throwing Jade against the iron bars. She bit back a cry of agony, seeing the world through a red haze of pain. Oblivious, the soldiers mounted eight stairs to the dais before setting the cage down and stepping away with discrete relief.

Stuffing her fist into her mouth, Jade half-fell to the wooden floor, barely holding the magical shelter intact as the pain subsided. Brynn appeared at her side, helping her to stagger upright. Together, they headed for the stairs and escape. They had done all they could. Now it was up to Baiyu to absorb enough power to free himself and fight Zhudai when the time came.

Jade was so focussed on keeping their magical safeguard together that she almost tripped when Brynn tugged hard on her arm. Her foot hovered over the first stair but he pulled her backward. Dazed, she followed his pointing finger. Zhudai's foot was on the bottom riser.

Panicked, Jade backed away, looking for another way off the dais. There was none. The entire edge of the structure bristled with kneeling archers. They faced outward but there was not enough space between each one to squeeze a cat through, let alone two people. Even if they could get off the dais without knocking a soldier over, the space beyond was being kept clear by a solid double-row of more soldiers holding the crowd back.

They were trapped.

She bit her lip. Together, she and Brynn crouched in one corner of the wooden stage, still hidden but feeling totally exposed.

Zhudai mounted the stairs slowly, regally, as if he had all the time in the world. The *ri shi* was now only minutes away. Already a faint shadow began to darken one edge of the sun.

Fumbling in her belt-pouch, Jade drew out two needles of the Ephedra plant and a small portion of ginseng root. Brynn looked at her, frowning. He shook his head. Both he and Marcus believed she was strong enough without herbs. She knew she wasn't. She shrugged fatalistically and swallowed them with a grimace. This was looking like the final show-down and she'd already used a lot of magical energy on this shield. If they were going to survive at all, she'd need help. Now was not the time to be over-cautious.

The big question was: would Baiyu have the strength to free himself?

Zhudai stepped onto a small, raised platform at the northern edge of the dais – facing the palace. He raised his arms high, the long sleeves of his black and red robe fluttering like wings. All around, the crowd stilled, watching him with a kind of tense reverence; as if they were too afraid *not* to admire him.

Brynn yanked on her sleeve again and Jade looked askance at him. He scowled, pulling out his dagger and pretended to stab it fiercely into Zhudai's exposed back. Jade shook her head vehemently. She curved her left arm, miming a warrior's shield and pointed at Zhudai, shaking her head again. He got the message. The sorcerer took no chances: he had a personal shield up and Brynn's little knife would not penetrate it. The boy's shoulders sagged and he glanced dispiritedly at the black silk cage where nothing happened.

Overhead, the eclipse shadow was now clearly visible, like the first small bite nibbled from the edge of a large cake.

"Behold!" Zhudai pointed dramatically up. "It is the day of reckoning; the day when Dark obscures Light; when Death overcomes Life. It is the day of the *ri shi*."

There was a pause and the crowd held its collective breath, awaiting the punchline.

"And after the *ri shi*, is there not a rebirth? A time when life begins anew?" the sorcerer continued persuasively. "And should there not only be a rebirth of the sun but also a rebirth of this great Empire? Is it not a sign to us? A sign that it is time for a return to the days of glory and strength; the days when to be of the Qin people meant more than just paying taxes and farming the land for the ruling class; the days of *power* and riches for *all* the Qin? Is it not time for that?"

A swell of surprised, murmured agreement swept through the crowd. This was not the speech they had expected.

Zhudai clenched a fist and shook it at the palace. "It *is* that time and the *ri shi* is a sign of it. We can *take* that power back, my friends. Together, we can *rule* this great land – and many more besides. I have seen the vast wealth to be had beyond our mountains and I can make it *yours*."

The whispering increased as people caught the gist of what he was saying. Many cast uncertain looks over their shoulders at the Emperor, standing silent and unmoving on the parapet.

Zhudai spread his hands and the crowd quieted again, expectant now, rather than frightened. "What do you say my friends?" His voice was silk and gold. "Are you sick of working harder but having less?"

There were a few, half-hearted agreements shouted from the crowd.

The sorcerer raised his voice. "Are you tired of the

rich eating meat and dressing in silk while you eat broth and wear rough homespun?"

This time the swell of accord grew louder, more definite.

Now he shouted. "Are you tired of paying *taxes* so the Emperor and his cronies can live in luxury while you struggle?"

"Yes!" The throng united now.

"Are you!?" Zhudai waved his hands like the conductor of a mass choir. They responded in kind.

"YES!" A frenzied excitement grew. People began to shout and punch the air in anger, caught up in the mood Zhudai generated.

"Shall I fix it for you?" the sorcerer cried. "Shall I?! Say the word and I will *FREE YOU!*"

"YES!!" The crowd screamed, cheering madly, swept away by the excitement of the moment.

"Oh my god," Jade whispered. "He's not just going to make himself immortal, he's going to make himself Emperor of the world. Both worlds."

CHAPTER EIGHTEEN

Murmuring *heili-tala* beneath her breath, Jade sent a tight mind-communication to the others, hoping that Zhudai would be too distracted by his big show to notice.

Phoenix? Did you hear?

Yes.

Confirmations came in faintly from Xinyu and Marcus as well, overlain by horror from the Chinese girl.

Have you released my father?

I can't. The lock is magic as well. We've cut a hole in the top instead. He has light, it's just a matter of how long it takes him to recharge. The longer we can give him, the better, I guess.

Time for that distraction? That was Phoenix, doing his best to sound casual about what he had to do.

Jade chewed on her lower lip, watching Zhudai. The sorcerer glanced up at the sun but the eclipse was not yet complete. It would take awhile and he couldn't afford to expose Baiyu too soon. He turned back to the crowd, speaking again of freedom, equality and all the things he had no intention of giving them. They responded with frenzied support. He played them well but if he wasn't careful they'd try and storm the palace and he'd lose all his followers in one fell swoop.

We don't have the Bag yet. Hope surged as something caught her eye. Eagerly she recontacted Phoenix. *I can see it! It's on Zhudai's belt. It's outside his personal shield, too. By its nature, the Bag must repel magic that might disrupt its own field. My magic must be more similar to the Bag's than Zhudai's is or it would have done the same when I shielded and had it on me. Can you see it?*

Phoenix's affirmation came back to her, tinged with eagerness for action and impatience with her explanations.

Wait, she ordered. *Wait until the last possible moment. Wait until Zhudai is about to uncover the cage. Then do it. Give Baiyu as much extra time as you can. An eclipse doesn't last long. Maybe we can distract Zhudai long enough that he'll miss his chance.*

Got it, he confirmed. *Hey, where are you two?*

We're ok. You just worry about your job. Cutting off the connection before he could pester her with more questions, she looked at Brynn.

The boy nodded to show he'd heard everything. Looking again at the sun, Jade concentrated on holding her shield. Sitting crosslegged, she signed to Brynn to keep watch. Closing her eyes, she drew a deep breath, trying to relax and find reserves of energy deep within. Their lives depended on it and she was weakening.

*****

After Jade cut their mental connection, Phoenix watched Zhudai, the sun, Baiyu's cage and the crowd around in anxious turns. As an ever-increasing shadow slipped across the sun, Zhudai continued to exhort the crowd with promises of glory and riches. Baiyu's cage remained shrouded and the Chinese people grew restless. Up on the Palace wall, the Emperor stood, unmoving.

Damn. Baiyu was cutting it fine. Their whole plan hinged on his being free and strong enough to take on Zhudai in an equal match. It was very clear that Jade and Phoenix were not strong enough to overcome the sorcerer on their own. Without Baiyu this whole thing would become very, very messy.

The shadow of the moon inched further over the sun. It was very close to a full eclipse now and the crowd muttered, pointing. Bright daylight darkened to an uncanny, blood orange as the sun vanished. All that now remained was a very narrow, brilliant halo of red-gold around a perfect circle of darkness. It was both eerie and beautiful.

Phoenix dragged his eyes away from the sight and refocussed on his task. Slipping closer to the stage, he pulled out his last throwing knife from beneath his shirt and watched Zhudai move over to the cage. Hot anger surged as the sorcerer drew forth what looked suspiciously like Blódbál. Phoenix's own sword was destined to be the weapon that killed Baiyu? No *way*! Zhudai was *not* going to use Blódbál for something that evil. Not if he could help it.

Common sense reasserted itself. He had a job to do and now was the time to do it. Trying to get a grip, he took a deep breath to release the desire to run up and fight for his sword.

Zhudai's hand reached up to snatch away the black silk cloth.

Phoenix acted.

With more than a small twinge of regret, he hefted the knife, drew his arm back and threw it. Quickly, he ducked below the crowd, hoping desperately his throw was accurate enough. He had no more knives if he missed. No other options. Everything depended on this one throw.

A shocked gasp swept through the crowd nearest Zhudai as the knife sliced through the air – and through the bottom of the Hyllion Bagia dangling at Zhudai's waist. The dagger snagged in the silky cloth, cutting a gaping hole in the strange blackness of it, then fell to the wooden floor with a loud clatter.

Surprised, Zhudai glanced down and kicked the dagger away contemptuously. He peered into the crowd, obviously believing someone had tried to kill him. Phoenix ducked lower.

For a moment, nothing happened and Phoenix cast an anxious look up at the dais again. The black silk began to slither off the cage. If Baiyu wasn't ready yet…

Suddenly the thick silence was split by a scream of fear, mingled with excitement. The peasants around Phoenix began to yell, point and back away from the dais. He did the opposite, trying to edge closer while keeping an eye on Zhudai and the Bag. Crackles of purple-blue lightning flickered at the edges of the jagged cut in the bag. Hissing and snapping, they earthed themselves into the ground, struck a guard senseless, flung another off his feet. Something protruded from the Bag. Something large.

Realising a possible danger, Zhudai snatched the bag off his belt and flung it into the crowd. The peasants pushed back then stopped, staring in horrified amazement.

It was hard *not* to watch. Just as Brynn had once predicted, it seemed that everything anyone had ever put into the Hyllion Bagia came pouring, tumbling and crashing out of it at once. A near-hysterical cry of astonishment arose from the people nearest as trash and treasure in enormous amounts appeared in front of them.

Half a dozen or more bronze swords; a locked wooden chest and three bags of what might have been clothes appeared, clattering to the ground. They were swiftly followed by a confused jumble of weapons of all sorts from all ages: Roman, iron, bronze, swords, spears, even flint axes. The pile grew as what seemed to be an entire household of furniture appeared: two beds, a chair, a loom, any number of pots, pans and cooking utensils. A confused sheep bleated and staggered about, blinking in the light. Fleetingly, Phoenix wondered how long the poor thing had been in there.

The crowd overcame their initial fear and greed took over. Small squabbles broke out over items of value, rapidly escalating to all-in brawls as people fought over weapons and money.

Phoenix backed further away, watching in awe as his distraction took effect. His only regret was that he couldn't see the Horn of Aurfanon and there was little chance of finding it now. More and more people came crowding over to see what was happening. More and more fights broke out, spreading outward into the crowd in a wave of reaction. The bed rose up and wove its way through the crowd, carried on the heads of four determined people. He heard the distinctive tinkle of money hitting the ground and the crowd noise stopped for a second as the bag spewed forth thousands of coins of all denominations and countries.

That was the final trigger. Pandemonium erupted. People went berserk.

Up on the dais, Zhudai brandished Blódbál and shouted uselessly, his voice unheard in the melee. Even his guards wavered at the sight of golden treasures now tumbling down the growing stack of *stuff* that continued to emerge.

Phoenix looked up, the sun was still covered; Baiyu still hidden from sight.

Coming to a quick decision, Phoenix strode purposefully toward the dais. There was no chance of retrieving the Horn of Aurfanon from beneath the pile of treasure from the Bag. Blódbál was now their only hope. It called to him. He wanted his sword back. Now.

Phoenix, don't. It was Jade's voice in his head. *We're in a better position to get it for you. Just don't put yourself at risk for that damned sword. It's not worth your life. Go back and find Xinyu. We need those daggers and amulets if we want to get home.*

He paused in mid-step, wondering where the hell she was. Zhudai sheathed Blódbál and signalled to one of his guards, his face stiff with anger. The sword's call diminished, Phoenix considered Jade's words and saw their sense. After a brief, internal struggle, he gave in and spun around, hunting for Xinyu in the milling mass of dark-

haired people.
*****

Up on the dais, Jade watched Zhudai with such fierce concentration that it was a wonder he couldn't feel her gaze on his back. Her heart jumped to her throat when he grabbed the cloth over Baiyu's cage. It was too soon. Where was Phoenix? Then, when his throw was true and the distraction of the Bag's treasure finally took effect, she ignored it and kept watching the sorcerer. He was the key. She had to let the others do their jobs. Hers was to free Baiyu or prevent the ceremony, one way or another.

Brynn grabbed her arm and pointed urgently. Phoenix was elbowing his way through the crowd toward them, his eyes fixed angrily on Blódbál in Zhudai's hands. Frantically, Jade threw her thoughts at him, hoping he would be sensible – at least this once. Relief washed over her as he turned away.

"Do you think you can steal the sword?" she whispered to Brynn.

He sent her a doubtful look and shrugged.

"We need to try. Blódbál is probably one of the only weapons that actually *can* kill Baiyu – or Zhudai. Without the Horn it's our only chance." She looked quickly at the sun. It was still shadowed. How long did an eclipse last? "I've got enough strength to keep the shield going about another three or four minutes. We'll have to go now."

Brynn nodded, his young face turning hard as he sized Zhudai up. Together they crept forward, Brynn signalling to Jade which direction he wanted them to go. Jade's heart beat so hard she was certain it must be audible to the sorcerer as they came nearer. Zhudai conferred with the head of his guards, gesturing angrily toward the ever-growing, ever-spreading brawl that threatened to consume his audience.

Brynn stretched out his hand toward the sword hilt. They edged closer, stepping carefully, quietly, stealthily.

Two feet away, one, just a few centimetres more.

Brynn's hand was on the weapon. He nodded sharply and pulled. Blódbál slid easily free and into his hand, inside the invisibility shield.

The boy's face was a picture of surprised confusion as the sword tried its magical wiles on him. Fortunately, his was not a warrior's mind and the sword could not find a foothold in it. Brynn shook his head, blinked and grinned at Jade. She nodded approvingly and gestured. They needed to get away and quickly. The presence of such a large amount of iron *inside* her shield was draining the last of her power more quickly than she'd anticipated. They had to get off the dais.

They'd gone no more than a couple of steps when two things happened at once: Zhudai reached around to draw his sword – and found it missing; and Jade's shield collapsed.

She and Brynn stood, completely exposed, in the middle of the enemy, holding a stolen magical sword for all to see.

Before she could move, Jade found herself pinioned by two burly guards, her arms painfully twisted up behind her back; a knife at her throat. An arrow sang through the air toward her captors, only to bounce off a shield thrown up hastily by Zhudai.

Brynn, always quick on his feet, made a dash for the edge of the dais. At Zhudai's cry of outrage, the soldiers turned and spotted him. Hampered by the sword, the boy was easily caught – but only for a moment. The guard holding him gargled and fell sideways, an arrow protruding from his throat. Marcus had found a new target. Brynn sprang from the platform, casting a worried look back over his shoulder at Jade as he rolled to his feet. She tossed a thought at him.

Go. Go.

He nodded, sidestepping more guards and jumping

over several others who fell beneath more of Marcus' deadly arrows. Within seconds, the boy vanished into the chaotic crowd. Zhudai's guards were left peering vainly into it.

Jade fought to stay upright, her legs weak, the pain in her arms excruciating. Zhudai cast a swift look up at the sun. It was still obscured. Pulling out a dagger, he sent her a viciously triumphant glance as he whisked the black silk off Baiyu's prison.

Inside, Baiyu sat, perfectly motionless, his legs crossed, eyes closed, the backs of his hands resting on his knees, finger and thumb making a loose circle. His flowing, white silk shirt and pants were smoke and blood stained, his feet bare, his long hair tied back into a rough braid. Jade strained to see him. Was he well enough? Could he break free? Could he fight Zhudai?

Smiling with feral delight, Zhudai circled the cage, intent on his victim. His words reached Jade faintly over the angry mob noises around the dais.

"It is time, oh mighty white dragon."

Baiyu opened his eyes, looking on his childhood playmate with compassion and lingering sadness. "So it would seem, brother."

Zhudai spat. "I am no brother of yours. You betrayed our friendship. You betrayed me."

"No," Baiyu returned calmly. "You betrayed yourself. I did not accept the status of the White Dragon lightly, or happily. I never wanted power. The protection of these people is my responsibility, not my right. You never could understand that."

"You lie, Baiyu." Zhudai sneered. "You wanted the power, alright. You just felt guilty once you had it, but it didn't stop you from lording it over me every chance you got. You even used it to steal Hua Mei-Lien from me."

Baiyu shook his head pityingly. "She was never yours. We were married for over eighteen years, brother. I simply hid the fact from you for fear of what you would do."

Zhudai stilled as understanding and fury bloomed in his face. "No." He shook his head in denial. "It's not true."

"Pretty words are not always true; true words not always pretty; and yet," Baiyu sighed, "they are still true."

"No." Zhudai hit his dagger hilt against the iron bars, his anger ringing out across the courtyard like a bell. "You took my life, *my* path, the woman *I* loved. You took all of it. Now it is time for me to return the favour and watch you die. Your blood will give me immortality and the Empire. That is all the revenge I need."

"He who seeks revenge should dig two graves," Baiyu quoted, closing his eyes again.

"What are you going to do, meditate me to death?" Throwing back his head, Zhudai laughed. He pointed at Jade, struggling in the arms of his guards. "I have your would-be rescuers by the throat. No one can save you now." He opened the cage door. "Come, you fool, come and feel *my* power."

Baiyu's eyes flew open. For the briefest instant, he caught Jade's and she read some sort of message there. What was it? What did he want her to do? What *could* she do? There was iron at her neck and four strong hands holding her. How could she help? How could she get free when she was so weak?

Distracted, she almost missed Baiyu's move when it came. As soon as the prison door was fully open, Baiyu rose with fluid grace and strength. He seized Zhudai's knife hand in his own and wrapped long, strong fingers around the sorcerer's throat. Zhudai backpedalled, eyes wide, mouth gasping for air, muscles straining against Baiyu's unforeseen strength.

"No," Baiyu murmured. "I have held back too long out of pity and love, brother. Perhaps now it is time for *you* to feel the true extent of *my* power. Let us determine, here and now, who will have the balance of power in this world: Light or Dark."

CHAPTER NINETEEN

A strange, purple-blue haze shimmered around Baiyu. A matching one, tinged blood-red, enveloped Zhudai. The brother-enemies broke apart, glaring at each other. Zhudai flung his dagger aside. Baiyu nodded serenely. The magical distortion grew until Jade was forced to squint to see them.

There was a soundless implosion, followed by a mind-twisting warping of reality. She blinked. Where Baiyu and Zhudai had stood, were now two creatures of myth and magic: a white Chinese-style dragon and a huge, black-feathered bird.

Long and sinuous, the dragon raised his broad head and bared a mouthful of fangs at the bird. At a shouted order from Zhudai's guards, arrows rained down. They bounced harmlessly from his gleaming white hide. Defiantly, he reared back on two strong, hind legs, flexed the curved claws on his front feet and leapt into the air. Wingless, he flew entirely by enchantment, slipping through the sky like the fluttering white tail of a kite.

With a raucous cry of anger, the bird leapt aloft. The weird half-light of the eclipse reflected a dull orange off his jet feathers. A tongue of fire, aimed at Baiyu, gushed from his wicked beak. Powerful wings caused a downdraft that blew dust and pink flower petals into whorls and whipped Jade's hair into her face. Blinded, she turned her face away. When she recovered, the two supernatural beings soared high, engaged in a titanic battle far above the city.

In the courtyard, the crowd paused in their frenzy to watch in awe as their guardian and their Emperor's advisor battled for supremacy. A ripple of fear ran outward from the dais like a wave. As the Light and Dark war waged on high, people realised how exposed the courtyard was. At the edges, they slipped into nearby alleys, looking anxiously back and carrying pilfered treasures into the city and away from danger.

Still imprisoned by Zhudai's guards, Jade tore her gaze from the spectacle above. She had to escape if she could and this seemed like the best chance. Even as she searched the crowd for signs of Phoenix and Brynn, one of the guards holding her arm choked and grabbed at his shoulder. He collapsed to the wooden floor, another of Marcus' arrows vibrating in his back. Zhudai's shield was down. Time to act. The second man gripped her tighter but she saw a certain wildness about his eyes that spoke of conflicted desires.

"If you let me go," she whispered, "you might live."

He started, glanced hastily around at his fellow soldiers and swallowed hard. Then he stiffened. His fingers relaxed and he blinked at her before slumping to the ground with an arrow in his back. Jade snatched up his long sword-bladed staff and hurried toward the stairs.

The courtyard was almost empty of civilians now. Only Zhudai's soldiers remained, standing in clumps, staring up at the battle raging overhead. Jade passed unnoticed behind several as she made her escape and ran toward her friends. Phoenix, Xinyu and Brynn stood together, watching the sky.

"You ok?" Phoenix asked, sparing her a quick, searching look. He had Blódbál in one hand and held Xinyu's hand with the other.

"Yes," she nodded, joining them and turning to stare upward. "Our knives?"

"Not yet," Xinyu said shortly. "Not long, though."

"Where's Marcus?" Jade asked, still studying the heavens.

"Here." His voice sounded nearby.

She shot him a quick, welcoming look. "Nice shooting. Thanks."

His warm hand fell on her shoulder and stayed there. She entwined her fingers in his and squeezed gratefully, her eyes fixed on the conflict overhead that would determine the fate of this world and her own.

High above, the two tiny figurines came together and parted; attacked and split time after time. Had it not been so frightening, the spectacle would have been quite beautiful; an aerial ballet. Black feathers, white scales and drops of blood fell to earth like the first hints of spring rain. Xinyu bit back a sob and snatched up a scale, holding it in her fist like a talisman. Phoenix put his arm around her.

The adversaries dropped lower. Now their battle became clearly visible. Flame spouted from Zhudai's mouth, singeing the tip of Baiyu's tail as he twisted lithely through the air. Baiyu turned an impossible, inside-out loop and raked Zhudai's exposed belly with long claws. More blood spattered.

Zhudai soared high then folded his wings to dive from above and behind. The dragon rolled over, entangling his claws and tail in Zhudai's; his teeth closed around the feathery neck. They fell briefly, locked together, coming ever closer to the watchers below. Xinyu gasped as it appeared they would crash into the Palace that dominated the northern skyline. At the last second, the pair separated and soared into the air again.

Zhudai flapped away to the west before turning on a wingtip to arrow back toward the White Dragon. Baiyu coiled back on himself, looping around in dizzying circles. The great bird snapped his beak on empty air time and time again until he cried out in frustration and withdrew to regather himself. Hovering with rapid wingbeats, Zhudai waited for the right moment then spewed a narrow stream of flame directly across Baiyu's exposed flanks. The dragon roared in pain. Xinyu whimpered and hid her face in Phoenix's shoulder.

"Why is he a bird?" Brynn asked, shielding his eyes as the eclipse began, at last, to slip away from the sun. "I mean, I get it that Long Baiyu means White Jade Dragon but…"

Jade clutched at Marcus' hand. "He's right. We never translated Zhudai's name."

"So?" Phoenix wasn't so easily distracted. He jerked in sympathetic reaction as Zhudai's beak scored a painful strike to Baiyu's leg. The dragon twisted free, his tail slapping Zhudai in the eyes, blinding the great bird.

"Feng Zhudai translates to 'Phoenix Black Pearl'," Jade said, frowning. "'Black Pearl Phoenix.' But that means nothing, really. A phoenix is a bird in both our language and theirs but that's the only real similarity."

"The true Fenghuang bird," Xinyu said bitterly, "is meant to represent the Balance: both male and female. It is a bringer of peace. Zhudai is the 'Feng' half only. He brings only strength and power without the mitigating balance of love and compassion."

"It is strange, though, that the translations of both Baiyu and Zhudai contain your names," Marcus commented.

Jade focussed on him wonderingly. "I hadn't realised. You're right. White *Jade* Dragon. Black Pearl *Phoenix*." She looked back at the two enemies, puzzled. "But I still don't see the connection."

Phoenix waved a hand, cutting her off. He pointed. "I don't think you're going to have time to work it out now. Looks like things are ending. We need to move. They're coming down."

He was right. The battle sank closer and closer to

earth as the two well-matched opponents tired. The little group of friends headed for the dubious protection of the wooden dais. As Baiyu and Zhudai descended, it became clear that both were badly wounded. The White Dragon's left eye was gouged and bleeding profusely. Deep slashes were scored along the length of his body. Zhudai fared little better. Great clumps of feathers were missing, blood dripped freely from neck wounds and he favoured his right wing.

Suddenly, Zhudai lunged, latching on to the back of Baiyu's neck with his hooked beak, like a bird catching a snake. He dug strong, clawed feet into the dragon's supple spine and held on as Baiyu writhed and twisted in his grip. Locked together in mortal combat, the two spiralled ever closer to the ground. Baiyu turned, trying desperately to close his fearsome jaws onto Zhudai's legs. Too late, Zhudai released his grip. The earth shook and dust rose in a great cloud as Baiyu plunged to earth, almost exactly where his horrified young friends had stood moments before.

Jade gasped, rushing to Baiyu's aid, her Healer instincts fired. Xinyu beat her to it, running swiftly to her fathers' side. Light once more crept across the Palace grounds as the moon-shadow shifted and exposed a burning crescent of the sun. Slowly, dust and upswept pink petals, settled back to earth.

Above, Zhudai flapped his immense wings, circling once before soaring back into the sky. Banking, he swept low over the Palace walls, shrieking a harsh cry of triumph. Folding his wings, he dived sharply toward the parapet. The Emperor's servants realised his intention and ran to shield their master. They were too late.

Zhudai snatched up the gold-clad young man in his claws and struggled skyward again with his prize. He circled once more before swooping low over the courtyard and dropping the Emperor into the waiting arms of the red-

and-black clad guardsmen waiting there. Seconds later he returned, coming in to land awkwardly some distance away from where Baiyu lay. The air around him wavered as he morphed back into his human form.

Soldiers flocked to his side, kneeling before him in a show of abject devotion. In their midst was the young Han Emperor, glaring defiance at his treacherous advisor.

Oblivious to these events, Xinyu knelt, holding her fathers' hand as Jade and the others arrived. Tears poured down her dusty cheeks at the sight of his broken, bleeding body.

"Father, please," she begged. "Don't die. I can't fight him alone. Please. We need you."

Once more in human shape, Baiyu smiled painfully. "You are not alone. Look around."

Jade reached out her hand, intending to heal his many, ugly wounds but Baiyu pushed it gently aside. "Even death is not to be feared by one who has lived wisely, child. It is my time and I am ready." He grimaced, his one good eye closing.

"Father!" Xinyu stroked his forehead, weeping openly.

"There is not much time," Baiyu whispered, "and things still unsaid. Jade," he fixed her with a look of such compassionate understanding that she felt her heart stop for a second, "remember: it is not who you *are* that holds you back, but who you *think* you are *not*."

Blindly, Jade nodded, not really understanding.

"Phoenix," the wounded man gestured feebly for the warrior to lean closer, "if you are patient in a moment of anger, you will escape a hundred days of sorrow."

Phoenix frowned momentarily then his eyes widened and he nodded. His eyes flicked to Blódbál, held firmly in his hand, then to Marcus, who stared gravely back.

"Xinyu," Baiyu drew his daughter closer, "there is one more thing I must tell you."

She leaned in and he whispered in her ear. She pressed her lips together then nodded and closed her eyes as he touched her face, his scarred face gentled by love.

"Stand aside, fools." Zhudai's harsh voice interrupted.

Jade looked back over her shoulder, straight at the business end of a very long, very sharp spear. Phoenix lowered Blódbál and glanced back at Baiyu, who inclined his head wearily and released Xinyu. Slowly, the five friends stood upright, their hands raised in surrender. They were surrounded by dozens of armed guards and cocked weapons. There was no escape.

Jade caught Phoenix's inquiring look and shook her head. She didn't have enough magical strength to take on Zhudai and his men. He frowned, lips tightening.

"Stand aside and I may spare your lives," Zhudai commanded again.

Jade and the others edged back, followed closely by the tips of spears, swords and arrows.

Laughing, Zhudai limped forward to kneel beside his fallen foe. He looked up at the sun, still more than half-hidden in shadow.

"The Dark still overwhelms the Light. There is time." He paused, smiling coolly at his old playmate. "You fought well, old friend but not well enough. I have you. I have the Emperor. Nothing can stop me now. I will have it all."

Baiyu shook his head painfully, his expression peaceful even in the face of death and loss. "You will not have what you want most, brother. You will not have love."

Zhudai's face darkened. "I will have *everything*," he repeated forcefully.

Baiyu said nothing, merely smiling faintly, sadly. Zhudai made a small noise of frustration. Scowling he reached out and dipped a finger in the blood pooled at the base of Baiyu's throat. Examining the reddened digit curiously, he shook his head.

"Somehow I thought your blood would be…different." Shrugging, he muttered a short incantation. Red-purple magic arced from his fingertips to earth in Baiyu's battered body. Then, with an expression of deep satisfaction, Zhudai put his finger in his mouth and sucked it clean.

With a faint sigh, Baiyu's eye closed and his head lolled to one side. Zhudai looked down at him, his face revealing contempt mixed with a fleeting impression of sadness. His eyes narrowed and he surged to his feet. Sweeping the Emperor, captives and entourage with a look of triumphant arrogance, he threw his hands into the air and laughed aloud. A faint, red-purple shimmering enveloped him, brightening to a blinding, blood-red glow.

When it was gone, his robes and skin were clean, his wounds healed, his hair once more neatly bound. He was whole and undamaged. At his feet, his old friend lay lifeless; a broken, bloody husk.

Darkness had defeated the Light. Zhudai had triumphed. He was Immortal.

Jade looked down at the shell that had been Baiyu. Sickening realisation hit like a fist in the stomach. Baiyu *was* dead. She saw the same understanding turn Phoenix's expression into stony hatred. Without Baiyu they were, truly, trapped in this realm. His power had brought them here. His had to return them.

They had failed in their last Quest.

They could not get home.

Ever.

CHAPTER TWENTY

Hard on the realisation that their situation was now hopeless surged the familiar burn of anger and resentment. Heedless of the danger, Phoenix reached out and wrenched his sword from the guard who had taken it. The guard tried to reclaim it. Phoenix ran him through without hesitation or mercy. With Blódbál's insidious song of war back in his head, the strength of his anger mounted until he could barely think through the red rage. Baiyu was dead and Zhudai was responsible. That was all that mattered.

His action must have caught the sorcerer's eye, for Zhudai turned a contemptuous, sneering look on his captives. He considered Phoenix for a moment then gestured to his guards. Hesitantly, they backed away, leaving a clear space between Phoenix and Zhudai. Jade and the others were still securely held but Phoenix was now free to attack. Zhudai accepted a long, curved sword handed to him by his guard captain.

Phoenix hefted Blódbál and its song exploded with joyous disharmony in his mind, obliterating reason and clarity. After all, he thought dimly, there was nothing left to lose. There was no way to return home and Zhudai was going to kill them anyway. It was best to go down fighting.

Zhudai's heavy eyelids drooped as he considered the warrior before him. "So you think you have the skill to defeat me, boy?"

Phoenix didn't speak; couldn't speak through the veil

of hatred that clouded his mind. He was lost in anger: anger at Zhudai for taking away their last chance; and at Baiyu for dying and abandoning them; anger at everything and everyone in this unreal reality. It was time to fight; time to die. Nothing else was important.

He closed the gap between them with five swift steps, bringing Blódbál around in a vicious overhead strike. Zhudai blocked it, turning the blow aside with one hand and driving stiffened fingers into Phoenix's stomach with the other. Gasping for breath, Phoenix staggered back, clutching at frozen diaphragm muscles. Zhudai waited, sneering.

"You do not have what it takes to defeat me. You are lazy, just as your stepfather always said. Lazy and useless."

Anger flared higher. Phoenix struck again, more craftily this time. Faking another overhead blow, he changed direction at the last second, arcing the blade toward Zhudai's exposed neck. Once more the sorcerer blocked with ease. His elbow came up, connecting painfully with Phoenix's jaw.

Phoenix fell back again, shaking his head to clear the multicoloured lights of pain. Again he attacked; a flurry of blows that Zhudai deflected easily, each in turn. Nothing Phoenix did broke through his guard. Blow after blow was turned aside yet the sorcerer did not retaliate in kind. He played with Phoenix, drawing the fight out for his own amusement. That dim realisation heightened Phoenix's fury. He redoubled his efforts, striking faster and harder than he ever had before. No-one could withstand his frenzied attack, yet Zhudai did.

At last, Zhudai blocked and followed up with another elbow-strike to the exposed side of Phoenix's head. Phoenix stumbled back, half-stunned. He shook his head, trying to clear the ringing in his ears. It wouldn't subside. In fact, it grew louder but it now sounded more like someone calling his name from down a long tunnel.

Phoenix!

Phoenix. Listen to me!

Phoenix, please!

It was Jade's voice in his mind, not a delusion at all. Something of Phoenix himself surfaced briefly from beneath the sea of rage that swamped his mind.

What? Kinda busy here.

He didn't get to hear her reply. Zhudai chose that moment to launch an all-out assault. Phoenix could think of nothing except keeping his feet as Zhudai battered his defence with strike after strike, forcing him backward, step by step. His arm ached and lungs burned. His head rang with pain and the song of the sword. He couldn't keep this up much longer, even with the sword feeding him energy.

Phoenix brought Blódbál up in a desperate attempt to deflect a blow that seemed to come from nowhere. His heel caught on an uneven flagstone and he stumbled, falling to his knees. Blódbál was struck from his hand and flew free, skittering over the paving stones with the bell-like tone of a gong; a gong that rang a death knell. Panting, Phoenix knelt on the ground, the point of Zhudai's sword pricking the hollow of his throat. He looked up and saw finality in Zhudai's flat gaze.

Zhudai glanced at his audience and said something but Phoenix's mind was too clouded to hear it. The sorcerer seemed to be taunting someone but Phoenix didn't care. He wanted this to be over. Choking on hatred he gathered his remaining strength for one last attack. Even if he had to impale himself on the sword, he wanted, for just one moment, to get his hands around the throat of the man who had caused so much pain and humiliation. Just one moment.

Phoenix. It was Jade's voice again, faint but determined. *Remember what Baiyu told you. Patience in a moment of anger will save you a hundred days of sorrow.*

Be patient. Just for one moment.
*****

Jade watched in despair as Phoenix succumbed to Blódbál's berserker magic and attacked Zhudai. The flare of unreasoning anger in his face was impossible to miss. Even Zhudai saw and responded by toying with the young warrior as they fought. Time after time he did not take a killing opportunity when clearly he could have.

Desperately, she tried to reach Phoenix. She broke through, only to lose him as Zhudai renewed the attack and he surrendered to the sword's spell again. Laughing, the sorcerer forced Phoenix back until he tripped and fell only a few feet from where Jade and the others stood. Blódbál flew from his grasp, leaving the Phoenix kneeling before his enemy, death only inches from his throat.

Then Zhudai looked up and caught her eye. He smiled slowly.

"So you see, my dear. You could not defeat me with magic and this fool could not defeat me in the martial arts. I am unsurpassed. I am immortal. I deserve to be Emperor. *You* deserve *nothing,* for you *are* nothing."

Jade blinked, tears gathering as she finally faced the hopelessness of their position. He was right, she already knew she was not strong enough to beat him and if Phoenix could not either then what could they ever do? They were going to die here and she would never see her family again. She stopped struggling against her captors, her shoulders drooping in defeat. She had been stupid to think she could be good enough to succeed against a master sorcerer like him. She had failed…again. Now Phoenix would die.

Zhudai laughed softly. "Yes. You are a failure. You were never worthy and will never be worthy. Now you and your friends will die having failed completely and I *will* have my Empire."

Then, surprisingly, in the depths of the despair that gripped her, Jade heard a faint echo of Baiyu's last words:

it is not who you are *that holds you back; but who you* think *you are* not.

Blinding enlightenment flashed through her consciousness, clearing away the black heart of self-doubt. Belief. Self-belief. That was the key. Zhudai's and hers, both. Suddenly, like a door opening in her soul, pure joy flooded into her, filling her body with warmth and her mind with clarity.

It was so obvious. How had she missed it? It had been there all the time: Yin-yang. The symbol on their amulets; Balance and Harmony. It all made sense now. Light and Dark; Good and Evil; Dragon and Fenghuang bird. They were all two sides of the same coin. Together they were Balanced. Separately they skewed people and the world into wrongness and disharmony.

Renewed, Jade raised her head and smiled at Zhudai. The sorcerer frowned at her, glancing around, seeking the source of her sudden reversal. At his feet, Phoenix tensed and began to rise, his eyes fixed on Zhudai with singleminded intent. Jade flashed him a warning thought; a reminder. She saw the red rage drain from his face, replaced by reluctant comprehension.

She waited. There was a chance now. A faint one. She wasn't sure if what she wanted to do was possible but if it was, it would only be through teamwork. Now for her part.

Extending her senses, she sought the paths of energy that connected her to her captors, through their hands. It was the work of seconds to relax enough to 'feel' their life-force. In even less time, she had drawn enough of their brown-red energy to restore herself and weaken them without killing them. She shook their hands off, smiling a little as they stared at her in surprise before collapsing, unconscious, to the floor.

Zhudai's frown deepened. He jerked his head and four more guards laid hands on her. Jade's smile broadened.

Without hesitation, she drained their energy. They joined the others at her feet.

Zhudai flicked a peremptory hand at the men guarding her friends. The Emperor, Brynn, Marcus and Xinyu were held and knives put to their throats. Zhudai shortened his own arm, preparing to thrust his sword into Phoenix's body.

She hesitated. There were only two variables left. If her guess was right then it was really only one. She flicked a sidelong glance at Xinyu. The Chinese girl managed to smile, just a fraction; a knowing, wise smile. That was all the confirmation Jade needed. She stepped a little closer to Zhudai, distracting him. There was a shimmer of purple-blue near the ground beside Phoenix.

The final variable.

The time had come.

Perhaps sensing some disruption in his plans, Zhudai glanced back at the warrior. He caught the haze of magic near to Phoenix and saw the dim outline of two knives. With a faint, contemptuous smile, he lowered his sword and stepped back, arms outstretched.

Zhudai laughed. "Ahhh... You bring me the final pieces I need to conquer your world as well as my own. Thankyou." He sent Phoenix a mocking bow.

At Jade's unspoken instruction, Phoenix snatched the two Life daggers and the amulets as they appeared from Jade's time-pocket. He shoved the amulets into a pocket and knelt, waiting, a dagger now in each hand, watching for the right moment.

Zhudai raised his head, looking arrogantly down his nose at Phoenix.

"But do you really think you can kill me with those little things when the mighty Blódbál could not? Have you both forgotten what I am? I am Immortal! I cannot be killed."

Jade smiled again. "I think what you are, is a bit self-deluded but by all means, let's test that little theory."

She drew more energy from the guards around her friends. This close, she didn't even need to touch them, now she knew the trick of it. One by one they slumped to the ground, insensible. Her whole body thrummed with the power she now held.

"*Sky-hiti!*" Her spell drew an almighty lightning bolt from the clear sky. It exploded just an arms length from Zhudai, sending a shower of sharp stone fragments in all directions.

He remained unmoved, sneering at her. "Your aim has not improved, has it?"

"I wasn't trying to hit you," she returned calmly. "I was giving you a chance to end this peacefully. Look."

She pointed at his right arm; the arm closest to the shrapnel. Blood dribbled down the back of his hand. It dripped to the ground, staining the paving stones black.

Zhudai raised his hand and pushed his sleeve back, his expression shocked as he stared at the deep slice on his arm. Wildly, he looked around: at Jade, at Phoenix kneeling nearby and finally at Baiyu's still body.

"But... I...I spoke the Rite... I drank the blood of the White Dragon," he stuttered. "I am Immortal. I felt his strength flowing into me. I healed myself."

Jade shook her head, stepping closer. "You *believed* you'd inherited the strength of the White Dragon, so you *felt* more powerful. *You* have not changed. You're still as mortal as the rest of us. Belief was all you gained. Thanks to you, I then realised that belief is all you really need. I can beat you now."

"No!" Zhudai hissed, taking several steps back. "It's not true. I *am* immortal. I drank the blood of the White Dragon."

Xinyu tossed her head and moved to stand next to Jade. "No, you drank the blood of an ordinary man. My father passed on the inheritance of the White Dragon to me before you even touched him. *I* am the Dragon now." To prove it, she morphed into a lithe, smaller version of the Chinese Dragon they had seen before then back into her human form again.

Zhudai froze then his expression segued back into arrogance and he raised his chin defiantly. "It doesn't matter. I defeated your father; I can defeat you, girl."

He gestured to his remaining elite troops. They ranged themselves behind their master, weapons ready.

"It's true that you probably could beat Xinyu," Jade said softly, as Marcus and Brynn took up their positions on either side of the girls, "but can you overcome all of us, together?" She lifted her hands in preparation.

The sorcerer snarled, his black gaze sweeping the five companions. "I have more men. The odds are in my favour. I will *not* be overcome by low-life foreigners and children."

"Yes," Phoenix stepped up beside Marcus, his face calm once more, "I'm afraid you will, actually."

Zhudai growled his frustration, his hands crackling with power as he began another incantation. Grimly, Jade strengthened the shield around her friends. The spell Zhudai threw bounced off, earthing with explosive power into the stones at their feet. Pieces of rock flew into the air.

When the smoke and dust finally cleared, the first thing Jade saw was Zhudai's smiling face and his hand, outflung toward the wooden dais behind them. She glanced back quickly, her heart stuttering as she saw why he was so pleased. On the dais, composed and proud in the clutches of Zhudai's men, were the Han Emperor himself and Zhi Hui. Zhudai threw back his head with a laugh.

"I know you, you see. You are all weak and your weakness is that you care for others." He laughed again. "Now lay down your arms and surrender or they die."

CHAPTER TWENTY-ONE

Phoenix caught the swift look and even swifter thought Jade sent him. He nodded slightly in acknowledgement. It was a risk they had to take.   This had to end, and quickly. Jade's plan was the only option. He heard her mutter *kala* as she cast a spell on the guards holding Zhi Hui and the Emperor, time-freezing them so the soldiers couldn't physically harm their hostages but they still looked alert - enough to fool Zhudai for awhile, anyway. Now they just had to deal with the sorcerer once and for all.

"You're wrong, Zhudai," she said aloud. "Having people you care about is not a weakness. Being in a team makes you stronger. No-one succeeds on their own."

Phoenix stilled, feeling the power of her words, realising their truth at last. Slowly, he nodded his agreement. Marcus laid a hand on Jade's shoulder. Brynn twirled his sling.

"But," Jade sighed, "if that's the way you want it..."

Zhudai threw up a personal shield, its glimmer turning the air around him into a thick, purple-red haze. Jade tilted her head.

Now. Her thought came into Phoenix's mind.

All of them attacked at once. Brynn flung stone after stone at the remaining loyal guards to hold them off. Marcus shot his quiver empty then drew his sword and engaged any who came within range.   Xinyu morphed back into the White Dragon and dived from above, scattering the soldiers, sweeping them aside with great lashes of her tail.

That left Zhudai to Phoenix and Jade. Jade divided up her own shield into individual ones around each of the friends. Her expression showed pure triumph, as though she couldn't believe how simple it was, how much power she could now channel. Figuring he could rely on her to watch his back, Phoenix tucked the two life-daggers into his belt and made a dash for Blódbál, still lying on the ground near Zhudai. The sorcerer saw and threw a spell his direction. The force of it knocked Phoenix flying but Jade's shield meant he came through unscathed. He rolled to his feet, circling around to try and get at the sword from behind, dividing the sorcerer's attention.

Zhudai threw spell after spell. Jade countered each, casting her own with a wave of her hand, deflecting the magic back at his own men. The ground around them erupted as paving stones exploded into lethal debris. The soldiers withstood the onslaught for a few moments then wavered, broke and ran like frightened rabbits, abandoning their master. Left alone in the courtyard, Zhudai glanced around as though finally realising his vulnerability. His eyes narrowed in fury.

Everyone paused, watching the sorcerer cautiously. Phoenix crouched where he was, waiting with a patience he didn't know he possessed. His moment would come. A breathless, still silence fell on the courtyard, as if the whole world awaited Zhudai's next move. Warm spring sunshine poured down onto their heads in a benediction of life.

Zhudai gestured to the guards holding the Emperor. When they didn't respond, he made a noise of extreme frustration and threw everything he had at Jade instead. Flashes of red-purple energy rent the sky. The air tasted of electricity and blood. Her shields shuddered under the onslaught but held. Again and again Zhudai flung bolts of pure power at her; again and again she turned them back at him. He shifted his attention to the others, the Emperor and Zhi Hui. Jade must have strengthened the shields around all of them, for Phoenix now saw the world through a strange, purple-blue shimmer.

He looked over at her, seeing a hint of strain in her eyes. Even her newfound power must be stretched by the drain on her resources. Defending seven people had to be harder than attacking one. She still had limits. She probably couldn't take much more. Somehow, they had to break through and finish Zhudai off.

Catching her attention through the miasma of smoke and haze of magic, Phoenix drew his finger across his throat in the classic symbol to end it. She grimaced, looked down at her own hands then raised them. Her face revealed that, whatever she was going to do next, she did it with extreme reluctance. She closed her eyes, lips moving. Phoenix backed away. Even at this distance, even with the sound of Zhudai's magic crackling in his ears, Phoenix still heard her whisper.

"Hata."

A shaft of pure purple-white light shot from her palms, slicing through the air with a tearing sound that jarred Phoenix to the toes. He held his breath as it speared into Zhudai's shield. The 'destroy' spell smashed Zhudai's protective barrier into fragments and exposed him at last. Zhudai flung up a new one. Jade ripped that apart, too. Nothing protected him now.

Denied access to Blódbál by the raw power flying around the sorcerer, Phoenix decided he couldn't wait any longer. With or without the sword, he had to get to Zhudai and end it. Responding to Jade's thought-question with a terse command to drop the shield around him, Phoenix sprinted toward Zhudai, knowing Jade would not wish to kill if she could avoid it, knowing *his* time had come.

Are you sure? Her words in his head were distracting.

Phoenix growled in frustration. *I can't even touch him*

if I'm inside a shield and you know it. Drop the damned thing now!

Her purple warping of the world fizzed into nothingness just as Phoenix came within reach of Zhudai. The sorcerer turned on him with a snarl, drawing his sword and slashing in one smooth move. Phoenix ran on, spinning aside at the last second to avoid the slice at his stomach. He laid a hand over Zhudai's on the hilt, turned, twisted the wrist and shifted his weight. Zhudai flew through the air then, in an incredible display of athleticism, flipped and landed squarely on his feet, utterly unharmed.

Giving Phoenix no chance to recover from his shock at the manoeuvre, Zhudai launched himself, his sword a gleaming circle of death. Wary now that his personal shield was down, Phoenix leaped away, trying to get out from between Zhudai and Jade, hoping she could at least slow the man down. The sorcerer was cannier though, moving swiftly to keep Phoenix between himself and her magic.

Zhudai lunged again and again, almost like a fencer, careful not to over commit himself. Phoenix could do nothing but turn aside, barely avoiding the swordpoint time and time again. Underfoot, the ground treacherous with broken stone and holes. Watching the sorcerer closely, Phoenix backed three quick steps away. He reached down a hand and swept his fingers over the surface, feeling for what he wanted, rather than looking. His hand closed on a fist-sized chunk of rock. Zhudai saw and laughed, advancing to close the gap again.

Phoenix circled left. Zhudai followed, moving with the smooth, fluid grace of a trained killer. The sorcerer skipped forward, feinting with the sword then lashing out with a front-kick that almost took Phoenix by surprise. His reflexes saved him. He sidestepped, hooked his left arm under Zhudai's upraised foot and continued its upward momentum, hoping to drop the sorcerer on his head.

Zhudai pushed off the ground with his other foot and backflipped in mid-air, just missing the kick to Phoenix's chin before landing squarely on his feet again. Phoenix groaned. He'd only seen that done in movies. This guy was unbelievable.

The only chance he had was to close the distance and engage in close-combat, Phoenix watched for an opening. He threw the rock at Zhudai's head, hoping to distract him. The sorcerer simply flicked his fingers at it and it exploded into dust. That moment was all Phoenix needed. He hooked his foot under another stone and kicked it toward Zhudai along the ground.

There. Zhudai trod on the loose rock, lost his footing, glanced down and spread his arms to keep his balance. Phoenix rushed forward, closing the gap. Too late, Zhudai tried to swing his sword-arm in a strike at Phoenix's head. Phoenix caught the sorcerer's forearm on his own and levered it backward, pushing the sword away from his face and using his right hand to pull the elbow forward at the same time. Stretching out his right leg, he swept at Zhudai's foot and drove the sword-hand toward the ground with as much force as he could muster.

Again, Zhudai did the unexpected. In mid-fall, he somehow twisted out of the armlock. Turning, he hooked a leg around Phoenix's waist, and looped his free arm around Phoenix's neck from behind in a choke-hold. Phoenix felt the first stirrings of true panic. He had only seconds before sliding into unconsciousness. Seconds to break a hold that felt like an iron bar across his throat. Then his training kicked in. Still keeping Zhudai's sword-hand out of the way with his left, Phoenix reached up and back with his right hand. Stars sparkled behind his eyes as the blood-flow to his head slowed. Gasping, weakening, he scrabbled behind until his fingers latched onto the base of Zhudai's long black braid. As the day darkened, Phoenix dropped to his knees, pushed up with his left hip, bent as he fell and hauled on the braid as hard as he could. Zhudai sailed over his shoulder and landed hard on the broken stone a few feet away.

Gasping for breath, Phoenix staggered upright. Zhudai arose as well, his black eyes snapping with fury. The two circled warily again. Phoenix sucked great, heaving breaths into his starved lungs. Sweat ran into his eyes but he didn't dare wipe it away. His legs were jelly. This had to end soon.

With a sudden laugh, Zhudai looked down, hooked his toes under Blódbál's blade and flicked the sword up, into his waiting hand. A contemptuous flip of his wrist sent his own blade far away, out of Phoenix's reach. It skittered musically across the ground. Zhudai's smiled broadened then turned almost feral as the sword's song wove its dangerous message into his mind. With a sinking heart, Phoenix watched his mortal enemy lose himself in the berserk urgings of the Svear sword.

He pulled out the two Life daggers, the only weapons he had. Their small blades were all that stood between him and Blódbál's magic. Zhudai's swordsmanship was already incredible, even without the sword's encouragement. This was not going to be easy.

Phoenix drew a deep breath, relaxing his shoulders, extending himself, feeling the ground, tasting the air, staring through his opponent. His only advantage: Zhudai had no experience with how to control the sword. His only hope: that Zhudai would find it as difficult to manage as he had. It was a thin hope, as Zhudai clearly lacked the moral restraints of a normal person.

Even as Phoenix began to despair, he felt a half-familiar honey-warm strength seep into his limbs. Jade's voice percolated into his head with it.

Finish it, Phoenix. I have lent you strength but I can't do it for long. I'm running out of people to draw energy from. I've tried taking it from Zhudai but he stopped me somehow. It's up to you, now.

Phoenix nodded, grinning as the warmth of her spell spread into his whole body. The sorcerer moved with unbelievable speed, bringing Blódbál up in a lethal upward slice that would have disembowelled any ordinary man under normal circumstances. Phoenix danced out of reach, hoping for any opportunity to get to close quarters where the longer sword would be useless.

Quick as he was, Zhudai was faster, the sword descending from above almost before Phoenix realised it. It was only Jade's frightened warning in his head that gave him the chance to block. He raised both dagger blades, crossed, over his head and caught the full force of Blódbál's motion. The shock of it jarred through his hands, right down to his heels, almost collapsing his knees.

A wave of anger surged through him, so unexpected that it almost seemed to come from elsewhere. Phoenix shook his head, suddenly recognising Blódbál's song - only this time it came to him as the sword's victim heard it; full of helpless, hopeless anger at himself and his own inadequacy; a false anger to make him give up the fight.

More of Jade's honey-gold energy surged up through his belly to counter it. Phoenix growled. That damned sword was more trouble than it was worth. Straining against the sorcerer's strength, their gazes locked and Phoenix recognised the twisted, demonic expression in his enemy's eyes: it was rage; a fury so long-held, so deep-seated and so pervasive that it coloured everything; influenced every decision.

He was looking at a reflection of himself, when he had wielded the sword. It was a shocking image. This was who he had been; this was who he would have become if not for his friends. Cold sober, Phoenix knew he had to end it, and soon. Where he had had friends to bring him back to reality, out of the sword's grip, Zhudai did not. The sorcerer would never let go of the heady, berserker rage that filled him now; never stop pursuing them; never give up peacefully. This fight had to be to the death.

Sickened, Phoenix accepted what he had to do. He relaxed his arms a little. Zhudai's snarl became triumphant. The sword blade hovered just inch from Phoenix's nose. Phoenix twisted, shifting his weight, shoving away and, at the same time, snuck a foot out to hook Zhudai's in a leg-sweep. The sorcerer stumbled, managed a beautiful roll and sprang back to his feet, leaving Phoenix no advantage to follow up.

With a cry of rage, Zhudai hurled himself forward, Blódbál raised high above his head in a position no cool-headed swordsman would ever use. Phoenix saw the opportunity, risky though it was. As Zhudai began to cut, Phoenix ducked forward, into the attack, under the downward swing of the blade. His timing had to be absolutely perfect. He turned slightly, harmonising his movement with Zhudai's body. Then he drove his shoulder and both Life-daggers into Zhudai's exposed chest, using their combined momentum to fling the sorcerer over his hip. The daggers were torn from his grasp and something hot stung his arm as Zhudai rolled away.

Suddenly, it was over.

Zhudai climbed to his feet, Blódbál's tip dragging on the ground. He staggered toward Phoenix, a look of utter surprise on his face. He coughed, blood spraying from his lips. Then he fell to his knees, staring at the two, ruby-studded handles protruding from his body. There he sat for a moment, near the body of Baiyu, his childhood friend. Finally, life drained from his dark eyes and he toppled sideways to lie beside his blood-brother. Blódbál dropped from his lax hand, clattering discordantly against stone in the breathless silence. A gust of wind whipped a swirl of pink and white magnolia petals into the air. They settled softly on the bodies of Light and Dark, balanced, at last, in death.

CHAPTER TWENTY-TWO

It was not until much later that day that Jade and Phoenix finally had time to think about their own situation. The hour or so after Zhudai's death had been chaotic. Emperor Han Zhangdi thanked them sincerely but briefly, before being surrounded by a gaggle of anxious servants and returned to the Palace. Zhudai's personal guard were rounded up by the Emperor's men and placed under guard. Xinyu was whisked away to the Palace to confer with the Emperor about her new status.

Sidelined by the sheer efficiency of the Emperor's staff, Jade, Phoenix, Brynn and Marcus quickly realised they weren't needed and, for lack of anywhere else to go, wandered back to Zhi Hui's house.

The place had been trashed by Zhudai's guards but Zhi Hui and her servants were there, busily restoring it as best they could. She had philosophically accepted her son's death and was getting on with life. She waved them absently into the living area, where the four travellers sank onto cushions, weary and lost. Food and tea appeared. They consumed it in silence. Jade healed the deep slice in Phoenix's arm. Time passed. They barely noticed.

Finally, Jade raised her head and became aware of the gathering dusk outside. She looked at her friends. "So what do we do now?"

Phoenix shrugged. "Dunno. I guess, even though we stopped Zhudai, we didn't really complete the Quest. We didn't master the Yu Dragon. Anyway, with Baiyu gone, we are actually stuck here after all. I feel like we've come thousands of miles for nothing."

Zhi Hui, who had come in to light the lanterns and refresh their teapot, cackled. Shaking her grey head, she spoke to no-one in particular.

"One does not need to journey a thousand miles to find the truth within." The old woman shuffled out, leaving a confused silence behind her.

Marcus moved to sit next to Jade, sending her a warm, concerned look. "Things could be worse, couldn't they?" He put an arm around her shoulder.

She smiled at him and nodded wearily, leaning her head on his arm with a sigh. "I suppose so. It's just..."

"Just what?" he prompted.

"Just that I miss my family," she murmured, trying hard not to give in to worry again. She had learned so much today. It wouldn't do to let it slip away and fall back into old, bad habits. Self-belief. She had to remember that that was the key to success and happiness. True belief in herself and her own worth as a person – regardless of what others thought of her. If she believed in herself and always tried to do the right thing then she *was* worthy of happiness and love. If she believed in herself and worked hard enough, she could achieve anything.

"Oh!" She sat up straight as Zhi Hui's words sank in and the final piece of the puzzle clicked into place. "The Truth Within."

"What?" Phoenix asked yawning.

" We had to Master the Yu Dragon, you said."

"Yeah, so what?" He poked his finger into a dish of rice that remained on the table. "We never did work out how to do that, remember?"

Jade laughed, feeling tension ease in her chest. "But we did. First we had to consider the meaning of names, yes?"

The others nodded, clearly not following.

"Well," she continued, "the only names we forgot to think about were our own – yours and mine, Phoenix."

He frowned at her quizzically. "Ours don't exactly need translation: I'm Phoenix Carter, you're Jade Lockyer. They don't have other meanings."

"No," she agreed, "but remember how Marcus noticed our names appeared in the translation of Zhudai's and Baiyu's? Well, it's not just our *first* names." She pointed to herself. "Jade *Pearl* Lockyer. Feng Zhudai: Black *Pearl* Phoenix." She indicated Phoenix. "Phoenix *Drake* Carter – from the Latin "draco", meaning Dragon. Long Baiyu: White Jade *Dragon*. The answer was there all along and we were too slow to realise it."

"Huh?" Phoenix screwed up his face at her, evidently still not understanding.

"We never had to Master the 'Yu Dragon' and defeat 'Feng Zhudai'." Jade shook her head at her own blindness. "They were just a…a…metaphor. We had to Master and defeat 'Jade Pearl' and 'Phoenix Drake'. We had to master and defeat ourselves."

Now Phoenix sat up as well, catching on at last. "So today, when ...what…when I was 'patient in a moment of anger'; when I beat Zhudai even though he had Blodbal; I was really mastering myself? Is that what you mean?"

Jade nodded eagerly. "You mastered your own anger and did the right thing at the right time. You worked *with* us instead of on your own. You trusted us. And when I decided I *could* be strong enough do match Zhudai with magic, I defeated my own lack of self-belief. That was what has held me back this whole time. That's why I had to rely on herbs for strength. I've never *believed* I was good enough without them."

"And I was blinded by anger every time I thought people had left or betrayed me. Just like when my father died," Phoenix admitted softly. "When I let that go I could think clearly and see that I needed you; that we had to work together to beat Zhudai.”

There was a long silence as they contemplated his words and respected his pain.

Finally, Phoenix raised his head. “OK, so if that's true, maybe we did succeed in our Quest. So why are we still here and not back at home?”

Jade sighed heavily and sank back into Marcus' loose embrace. “I don't know. I thought maybe we'd vanish in a blinding flash of enlightenment when we finally understood, just then. Guess either I'm still missing something vital, or we are here for good.”

Phoenix leaned back also, intertwining his fingers behind his head and staring up at the ceiling. Brynn took out his little bronze whistle and piped a cheery little tune. Jade smiled. Marcus was right. Things could be worse. At least she still had all of her friends.

Marcus shifted position and frowned. He sat forward, reaching behind his back to pull something out from under the cushions - the Horn of Aurfanon. He turned it over in his hands then passed it to Phoenix.

“It was the only thing left of the pile that came out of the Bag. No one else seemed to be able to even see it. Part of the magic of it, I assume.” He smiled faintly.

“You never blew it,” Phoenix frowned at him.

“I didn't find it until everything was over,” Marcus said.

Brynn stopped tootling and looked at it curiously. “Maybe you should blow it now, just to use up the last time.”

Jade yawned. “We're not exactly in dire peril though, are we?”

“No,” the boy shrugged, “but you did say you wanted to go home. Maybe whoever shows up will be able to get you there.”

Phoenix punched the little thief on the arm, lightly.

"You trying to get rid of us after all?"

Brynn smiled wryly. "No, but I've finally realised that, as much as I'll miss you, you have homes and families to go back to. It'd be selfish of me to want to keep you here."

Jade reached over and hugged him. "Oh, Brynn. I'd miss you too but you and Marcus could look after each other. He'd be your family." Marcus nodded, leaning over to grip the boy's forearm in a gesture of equality and respect. Brynn quirked a small grin at him and nodded back.

"So should I blow it or not?" Phoenix asked, the Horn half-raised to his lips.

"May as well." Jade shrugged fatalistically. "Not much to lose, really."

So Phoenix blew and a pure, distant note rang softly through the house, raising the hairs on the backs of their necks with its eerie, otherworldly sound.

He stopped. The note continued for awhile before fading into the gathering gloom.

They all looked expectantly at the door.

Nothing happened.

They waited.

Some more nothing happened.

Phoenix sighed and gave the Horn to Brynn. "Oh well. You may as well keep it as part of your treasure, since you lost the rest of it when the Bag was destroyed."

A surreptitious, guilty look flitted across Brynn's mobile face. "Er... about that. I didn't exactly leave *all* the treasure in the Bag and the Bag isn't exactly destroyed, either." He pulled the Hyllion Bagia out of his shirt and held it up sheepishly for inspection. The bottom, where Phoenix had sliced it open, was once again whole; unmarked.

"How did you do that?" Jade asked in wonder, fingering the silky black material. There was no trace of the cut.

The boy shrugged. "Xinyu fixed it for me before she went to the Palace. I'd hidden most of my Egyptian stuff and our Roman and Indian coins before Zhudai took it off me, anyway. At least now I know exactly what's in it. Pity about all the stuff that came out, though. Such a waste of treasure."

"Hardly," Jade admonished. "The people here deserve it as much as you do. I had no idea Xinyu could do such powerful magic, though. I wonder if..."

The others didn't get to hear what she wondered. A new voice interrupted from the doorway.

"The answer is 'yes'," Xinyu said quietly, smiling at their surprised faces.

Phoenix leapt to his feet and strode forward, only to stop a few feet away, looking awkward. Xinyu wore beautifully embroidered, courtly robes of blue silk, a gold sash around her narrow waist. Her hair was done in an ornate style that glittered with gems and gold hairpins. She looked exquisite; untouchable. She smiled shyly at Phoenix and bowed her head a fraction.

"The Emperor has offered me the position of Grand Vizier," she said.

Phoenix shuffled his feet. "Er... congratulations?"

She shook her head. "I have refused, as my father did. Court life is too full of politics and machinations for the White Dragon to remain pure of heart. My place is amongst the people. I cannot protect them if I become the very Evil I am sworn to fight."

Jade got slowly to her feet. "I'm glad but what did you mean when you said 'the answer is 'yes'', before?"

Xinyu's sweet smile widened. "You were about to ask if I inherited enough of my fathers' magic to return you to your homeworld. Since you summoned me with the Horn's call, the answer is 'yes'."

Jade gasped, covering her mouth in shock. Marcus

stood abruptly and left the room without a word. She hesitated, wondering if she should go after him.

Xinyu laid a hand on her arm. "Do not worry. He will come back before you leave. Now, there are some friends waiting to see you off. The Horn called them as well. Outside. Come." She gestured for them to precede her out into Zhi Hui's small courtyard.

Now that she was listening, Jade heard a babble of voices, speaking in all different languages, rising as they tried to make themselves understood. A girlish giggle rang out. She exchanged astonished looks with Brynn as they emerged into the lamplit open space outside.

"Truda?" Jade gasped, catching sight of the young Norse goddess.

The redheaded girl tugged at the hand of her enormous father, who was deep in conversation with an attractive Egyptian woman. "Thor? Anuket?" Jade named them, astounded by their presence here, in China. "The Horn brought you, too?" They waved in greeting.

"Hey," Brynn pulled at her sleeve. "There's Asulfr, too, talking to Heron! And is that Vasi over there with …hang on, that's Cadoc! I thought he'd gone to Rome."

"And Aurfanon and Arawn, too," Phoenix added wryly. "Hey hey, the gang's all here."

Then they were in amongst friends, being hugged, thumped, hair-ruffled and kissed by one and all. Questions and answers flew in a confused jumble until Thor finally inserted two huge fingers into his mouth and blew an earsplitting whistle. Silence fell as even Arawn, mighty King of the Light Elves winced in pain and covered his sensitive ears.

"I think we all deserve to know exactly what has happened to you," the Thunder god said bluffly, "but perhaps it's best if just *one* of you tells the story. Brynn, I hear you're a fine sagatala. Will you do the honours? Someone get me some wine."

So, for the next hour, Brynn talked himself dry relating their adventures from start to finish. It was not without interruption as various audience members broke in to correct or draw attention to their own contributions, but at last the story was complete. Brynn sat down with a sigh of relief as the chatter began again.

Arawn approached Jade, his inhumanly beautiful features making her nervous all over again. He looked down at his daughter and smiled. "And so we meet again, as I foretold. You have done well, child. We are all proud of you."

Jade curtseyed deeply, blushing at his praise. "Thankyou but we couldn't have done it without help from all of you." He bowed in return, nodding at the others, hovering around, waiting to talk to her.

"Your time here is almost ended. A few moments more and you will have to leave. Say your goodbyes, child."

She nodded and reached out to hug him gingerly. The Elf-King seemed surprised then he returned her affection and smiled down at her, kissing her forehead lightly. "Your other-world father is a lucky man. You will be remembered, child."

One by one, the others came up to say their farewells.

Cadoc approached Jade and Phoenix and shook their hands, grinning. "Every blog and chat site out there is talking about you two. You're the only ones to make it all the way through, you know. This is now officially the toughest game ever written. I hacked back into the system and rewrote myself as a Non-Player Character after I got killed in Rome. Couldn't get you on any of the chatsites, so figured I'd come and congratulate you in person – kind of, anyway."

Vasi stepped in, holding Jade's hand and bringing it to his lips with courtly grace. "My lady, I had to beg Vishnu to send me here in his stead when I heard the call of the horn. I was too late to help you but if you should want to stay in this realm…" he let the sentence hang in the air between them.

Jade blushed and shook her head. "Thankyou, Vasi. You're kind but I-"

"But you're already taken." Cadoc stepped in and put an arm around her shoulders protectively.

Jade made a noise of protest. Vasi bowed and turned away, obviously disappointed. Cadoc dropped his arm, grinning at her discomfort. Jade punched him, hard. He winced.

"I didn't mean me, woman. I meant him." He jerked his head at Marcus, standing in the shadows behind her. "Although all bets are off when you finish and come back to the real world. I'll definitely look you up on the outside one of these days." He winked, saluted her jauntily and went to chat to Anuket, towing Phoenix with him.

Marcus approached and drew Jade aside. "Are you sure you have to go?"

She nodded, her eyes swimming in unshed tears. "I'll miss you so much, Marcus. I wish you could come with me."

He sighed. "And I. Could I not?"

She shook her head. "It wouldn't be fair to drag you into our world, even if it were possible - which I'm not sure of at all. It's more likely you'd just never make it through to my world at all and I'd be left wondering if you were alive or dead." She looked at him straitly. "I'd rather know you were alive somewhere and at least had a chance of happiness."

With a short nod, he held her face in his hands and looked into her eyes. "Then, good-bye, my Fair one. Be happy." Swiftly, he kissed her, his lips briefly warm against hers, his fingers holding her face gently. Then he was gone, vanishing into the darkness of the house without another word.

Turning away, she ran into a broad chest and sobbed into Phoenix's shoulder. He patted her back awkwardly until Brynn interrupted by tugging on her sleeve.

"I'd better go make sure he's ok," the boy said when she crouched and pulled him into a tight hug.

Jade dropped her arms and nodded, sniffing. "Look after each other." She wagged a finger at him. "And don't go stealing any more. I won't be around to rescue you."

Phoenix swatted him across the head. "She's right, kid. Be good."

Brynn ducked and grinned at them. "You know me. Always good. See ya." He kissed Jade shyly on the cheek, shook hands manfully with Phoenix and shoved his hands into his pockets. "By the way," he added, looking at Phoenix with his usual sparkle of mischief, "you beat me: eight to seven." Without a backward look, he disappeared into the house after Marcus.

Phoenix laughed.

Jade stood up, looking after them. "I guess that's that," she said, resignedly. "It's time to go."

"Yeah. Guess so," Phoenix agreed, still smiling. "'Sbeen fun, huh?"

She sent him a sour, resigned look. "You still have a strange sense of fun."

"Come this way." Xinyu appeared at his side and pointed toward the front entrance to Zhi Hui's house.

The old woman smiled and waved at them as they passed through, followed closely by the oddest entourage of gods and humans this part of the world had probably ever seen.

They made a merry enough group, traipsing through Xijing that spring evening. Thor, full of unfamiliar alcohol, led a round of singing. Thankfully, the rather rude lyrics were only understood by half the group. Everywhere they went, doors and windows slammed hastily shut as skittish citizens hid from the strange foreign devils that stalked their streets.

At last, they reached the palace and halted in front of the very servants' entrance through which Jade and Phoenix had escaped with Baiyu just the night before. Silently, Xinyu pointed at the distinctive, three-stone formation of the doorway.

"You *have* to be kidding," Phoenix complained. "How do we keep missing these things?"

Jade laughed. "We weren't exactly looking at the time." She turned to her friends, holding back more tears by dint of sheer willpower as she looked at them for the last time.

One by one, the gods, goddesses, mortals and Elves stepped forward and activated the Portal back to their own lands. In Cadoc's case, he just winked at them and vanished as he deleted himself from the game. That took even Thor by surprise but Jade decided it was too hard to explain.

Thor was about to step through the portal when Phoenix called out to him. With obvious reluctance, he drew Blódbál from its sheath.

"I guess I should give this back to you," he offered it once more to the Thunder god.

Thor took it between his great hands and turned it over. Finally, he grinned.

"This old thing? No, it's too small for me. Here," he handed it back to Phoenix. "I think there's someone else you know who can truly keep it under control, don't you? Someone who could use a good sword. Never thought it would end up in the hands of a Roman, though." He shrugged, waggled his great hairy eyebrows and stepped blithely through the portal without a backward look. Truda giggled, kissed Brynn on the cheek and waved as she dashed through after her father.

Jade caught Phoenix's look of surprised regret as he half-turned toward Marcus. "Marcus?" he asked, holding the sword out.

Hesitantly, the Roman boy took the handle, hefting it, testing the balance. He grimaced as the sword sang in his head. With a frown, he laid it back in Phoenix's hands and shook his head.

"Oh no, I saw what it did to you. Find another, more worthy."

Xinyu smiled. She stepped forward and laid a hand on the blade. There was a brief flash of brilliant white light, tinged faintly purple.

Dazzled, everyone blinked rapidly to dispel the glittering red afterimages. Phoenix swung the blade experimentally.

"What did you do? The song is gone! It feels...strange." The question sounded more sharp than he probably intended.

Xinyu bowed. "I merely took away its lust for blood. It is still unbreakable; still magic. It will simply no longer have power over its owner. They will control it, not the other way around. Now Marcus can use it with impunity, if he will."

"Well, if he won't then I will!" Brynn reached out to grab the handle, only to be forestalled as Marcus reached over his shoulder and wrapped his hand around the hilt first.

"I don't think so, little brother," Marcus grinned down at the boy. "You'd either chop your own leg off or mine. Come." He draped an arm around Brynn's skinny shoulders. "I believe we have some Romans to throw out of your country."

With a grave nod for Xinyu, a small salute for Phoenix and a long, slightly wistful look at Jade, Marcus ushered his young companion through the Portal, back to the tumultuous land of the Bretons. Maybe, Jade thought, in this world Marcus would even succeed and the Romans would never get their four hundred year dominion over

Britain. This world would certainly be a very different place in the future if that happened.

Finally they were all gone except Xinyu.

She bowed. "Now it is your turn."

Jade and Phoenix exchanged puzzled looks.

"But what do we do?" Jade asked, touching the stones lightly. She felt the magic pulsing through it.

"Give me your life-daggers. You don't need them any longer."

They handed them over reluctantly. Xinyu slid the blades into almost-invisible slots on each side of the doorway until only the hilts, decorated with now-dead rubies, protruded from the grey stone.

"Now, just hold your amulet in one hand and lay the other on the handle of your knife. Think of your home and say its name," Xinyu instructed. "The Gate will know where to send you. Goodbye and thankyou." She brushed Phoenix's cheek with a kiss and hugged Jade quickly.

Hesitantly, Jade and Phoenix both laid hands on their knives. Together they looked at each other, took a deep breath and said, "Cambridge."

The Portal flashed into life, its mysterious liquid-looking surface shining in the darkness.

"Wait!" Xinyu stopped them. "You do know you still have one task left to complete before you are truly home, don't you?"

"What?!" Jade and Phoenix exclaimed together.

"Nobody said anything about that. What is it?" Phoenix sounded outraged.

Xinyu blinked at his expression. "You must place the amulet where Jade will find it, of course. Otherwise none of this will happen. When you have done, the portal will open one last time to take you to your true home. After that, the portal will be gone and you will not be able to return here. Now go."

Confused, they stepped through the portal with no idea

of what would come next.

CHAPTER TWENTY-THREE

"Oh man, my head hurts," Phoenix groaned, sitting up.

He looked around, squinting against the too-bright sunlight. Where was he? It looked vaguely familiar. Slowly, sights and sounds that were, indeed, both familiar and strangely alien began to filter through the fog of disorientation. Recognition set in. He clambered unsteadily to his feet, staring about in disbelief. They were home.

He drew a deep breath of air, smelling rain and the acrid tang of smog. Nearby, a car engine revved followed by the strident beep of a horn. He jumped in surprise, turning circles in an effort to see everything. The skyline was jagged with houses and highrise officeblocks behind the trees that surrounded him. He was in some sort of public park.

He rubbed his eyes, finding it hard to believe he was back in the real world. The colours seemed too bright; edges too sharp; sounds too loud. It made his eyes and ears hurt as well as his head. Wonderingly, he knelt down and picked up a discarded drink can. It felt real. Too real, almost, as though his senses weren't used to this much input and were having trouble coping.

Someone coughed and moaned behind him. Jade probably. Yes, there she was, pushing long, pale hair aside so she could rub her forehead. She leaned up against a three-stone portal – a park decoration that looked eerily out of place in this modern world. Almost as out of place as she looked, herself.

Phoenix replayed what he had just thought, trying to work out what was wrong – for something was very wrong. Jade glanced up at that instant. Her eyes widened. She looked at him first then at the buildings then back at him.

"B..but…" she stammered, pointing at him before catching sight of her own hands. "But…I'm not *me* and you're not the real you, are you?"

Then it hit. Phoenix reached up and touched his own face, feeling the long hair, the scar on his cheek, the leather and rough linen of his clothing. They were still in their avatar bodies. He was still a warrior and she a Half-Elven Spellweaver from another realm entirely. But how?

Jade sank to the ground as though her knees had suddenly given way – which they probably had. Phoenix joined her gratefully.

"I don't understand," she said. "How are we home but in the wrong bodies? And *why?*"

"Xinyu did say we still had to put your amulet where you would find it," he reminded her.

"But I could have done that when I got back any…oh." She sat up, staring around. "No, I couldn't, not unless we're back in our own world but not in our own *time*. She said the portals would take us to our *true* home after we'd completed the task."

"Huh?" he said intelligently. His head throbbed.

"When I found my amulet," she explained, standing up and hauling him to his feet, "it had to have been put there *before* my family moved into the house. So this has to be at least a year or two *before* the time we were playing the game. Do you get it?" She glanced around, trying to get her bearings. "We have to find my house and put my amulet in the cupboard so I can find it in two years. That's the only way to complete the loop. Come on. I'm pretty sure it's just a block or so this way." She tugged on his arm.

Phoenix stayed where he was, gazing at his own toes as an awful thought froze him in place. He raised his eyes to Jade's.

"No, I don't think you've got it quite right."

"What do you mean? It must be right. We put my amulet in place and it's over." She stood before him, hands on hips.

"No," he repeated bleakly. "Didn't you say you'd found the amulet on a broken chain?"

"Yes but..."

"It wasn't *your* chain, was it?"

She shook her head, so he continued, wishing with all his heart that he was wrong but knowing he wasn't.

"It's my fathers'. We have to put *my father's* amulet in place for you to find."

"But-"

He cut her off short. "It must be. It explains why his amulet disappeared the day he died. It explains why this park looks so familiar. My mother brought me here after the accident. We planted a tree over there in his honour." He pointed at an open patch of ground near the swingset. "Most of all, it explains why the police reported two strangely dressed people with him at the car accident site as they arrived. *We* must be those two people with him. *We* have to go and take the amulet from my dad. Today must be the day he dies; almost three years before we ended up in the Game."

Jade covered her mouth with her hand in distress. "Oh, Phoenix, I'm sorry. Oh no. What do we do?"

He shrugged bitterly. "We do what we have to."

She nodded, her green eyes clouded with worry for him.

"This way." He began to walk quickly in toward the city, setting his face against the tumult of emotion in his chest. Jade hurried to keep up.

They were silent awhile then Phoenix glanced up at the sun. "It's almost noon and that's about when the accident happened. We'll have to run."

Together, they began to lope in the same ground-eating jog they had used when they first travelled in 80AD England. This time it was to a far grimmer, more certain destination. Finding a pathway, they dodged pedestrians, joggers and cyclists with single-minded intent, ignoring curious stares at their outlandish costumes. Someone even called out a laughing compliment on their cosplay. It seemed surreal. Their own world felt as foreign now as 80AD had almost four weeks before.

Finally, they reached a set of traffic lights and Phoenix skidded to a halt, looking around. He nodded.

"This is it. In a few moments, a guy will go through a red light and run straight into dad's car coming this way." He pointed. Closing his eyes, he scrubbed a hand through his hair and turned to Jade in anguish. "He'll die of internal injuries and bloodloss from a severed artery in his leg, before the paramedics can even get him out of the car. They get here too late because another accident on the freeway causes a traffic jam and because the car is so damaged they can't get him out fast enough."

He looked out at the flowing traffic for a moment then shook his head. "It's not right. It's not fair, Jade. I have to stop this from happening. I have to save him if I can."

She grabbed his arm. "You can't, Phoenix, don't you see? There's no way of knowing what causes the accident. If you try and stop the driver, you may end up actually *being* the thing that makes him run the light. You can't interfere. No matter what you do, the accident will still happen. It has to, because it *has*. But if you end up *making* it happen, you'll never forgive yourself."

Phoenix hesitated, trying, through the turmoil in his heart, to understand what she was saying. It had a kind of twisted, paradoxical logic but a huge part of him still wanted to *do* something; anything to save his father.

It was too late, he realised, hearing a gasp of shock from Jade as she looked over his shoulder at the intersection behind him. A squeal of tyres and the godawful rending crash of metal and glass shattered the peaceful morning. Someone nearby screamed. There was a brief silence, followed by the sound of metal twisting and breaking as Alex Carter's car spun out of control and slammed into a light pole.

"Oh god," Phoenix murmured, turning to see the devastation for himself.

His knees weakened at the sight of the so-familiar white sedan, bent around the pole. He couldn't move.

Jade pulled on his arm. "Come on, Phoenix. We have to go. Oh shut up, woman!"

Startled out of his shock, Phoenix looked at her. Jade had snatched a cell phone out of a hysterical bystander's hands and was dialling the emergency number even as she raced toward the wrecked vehicle. Speaking rapidly, she gave clear, concise instructions to the emergency response team.

Next, as Phoenix stood frozen, afraid to look inside, she stood beside the car and peered in. The window had shattered but the door wouldn't open, crumpled as it was. She tore a wide strip off the bottom of her long silk shirt, knocked out the rest of the little squares of window glass with her elbow and leaned inside for a few moments.

"Help me with the door, Phoenix," she ordered.   "I can't quite reach the necklace."

Numbly, Phoenix added his massive strength to her Elven one and, together, they wrenched the door from its hinges.

She leaned into the car for a minute. Then she stood up and gestured for him to replace her. She was pale, her hands spattered with blood. As he passed her, she opened one hand. There, glittering in the palm, was his father's amulet; twin of the one she wore around her neck.

Shaking, Phoenix managed a nod and bent down. He had to see his father alive, just one last time. At least he could say goodbye, even if Alex Carter didn't know who was saying it.

"Da...Alex?" He looked down at his father's bruised, bloodied face and almost broke. It was all so much more horrifyingly real than in the digital world. More so because it was someone he loved so much; missed so much.

"Help..me." Alex Carter's head lolled to one side.

Phoenix reached in and supported it. "I'm here," was all he could think of to say. "I'm here. It'll be ok."

A blood-streaked hand grabbed weakly at his wrist. Alex's blue eyes opened for a moment and stared intently at his son without recognition. Phoenix swallowed hard against the lump of pain and tears in his throat.

"Tell my wife..." his father said faintly. "Tell her I love her...and my son, Phoenix. Tell him, too. I'm so proud of him...so proud..." his words trailed off, his eyes rolling back in his head. His mouth fell open, the hand clutching at his son's wrist dropped limply to his lap.

"No!" Phoenix yelled. "Don't you dare die on me. Not again." He leaned in, trying to unclip the damaged seatbelt; to lift the mangled steering column pressing onto his father's legs; trying to haul his father out - without success. There was just no way to get him out of the wrecked car without help. Help that would come too late.

Finally, defeated, Phoenix dropped his head onto his arm and cried the tears he had never let himself cry in three long years. Eventually, the pain in his chest eased and he looked up again. There was only silence from inside the car.

A siren wailed in the distance, coming closer. Slowly, Phoenix eased his father's head back onto the headrest and stroked his dark hair once.

"Goodbye, Dad. I love you too."

Finally, with love and regret, he let his father go. The anger was gone now, too; at last he could accept what had happened.

Jade reappeared at his side, the phone now back in the hands of the hysterical woman, who gaped at her in bewildered anger.

"We have to go, Phoenix. The police are coming." Gently, she towed him away.

Again in silence, they jogged down the street toward her house. Phoenix couldn't yet think beyond what had just happened.

They reached her soon-to-be house and knocked. No one answered. With a swift look around, Jade ran to the back and jemmied open a small window to the master bedroom ensuite.

"Mum and Dad never got this fixed," she explained as they slipped inside.

Phoenix just followed along, numbly observing as she riffled through a pink-flowered jewelry box on the dressing table. With a small cry of triumph, she produced a green velvet jewelry bag and emptied its contents back into the box. Dropping his father's amulet into it, she pulled the ties shut and hurried toward the front of the house. Phoenix trailed behind.

By the time he reached her, she had already opened the hidden cupboard and was carefully stuffing the bag into its hiding place. That done, she cocked her head as though listening.

"I hear a car. Let's go."

Seconds later they were back outside, strolling along the sidewalk as though they hadn't just committed a break and entry offence. Jade swiped futilely at the bloodstains on her shirt. Phoenix looked blankly at his hands, still covered with his fathers' blood. Jade took one of them in her own. He stared at her.

"I'm sorry, Phoenix," she said, her green eyes worried

for him. "I tried to Heal him but," she spread her hands, "I don't have any magic here. I'm sorry."

He shook his head, a strange calm washing through him. "It's ok. Really." He smiled wearily. "Let's get back to the Portal and go home."

EPILOGUE

Phoenix opened his eyes and stared blankly at a white ceiling. He drew a slow breath, tasting the chemical tang to the air; hearing the soft beeps of machines close by. His body felt strangely limp. Experimentally, he lifted a hand. Long-unused muscles protested. Gazing in wonder at his own strangely unfamiliar fingers, Phoenix took in the IV drip attached to his hand and finally understood.

He was back in his own body; in a hospital. That explained the noises and smells and the weird feeling that his body was, somehow, too small and too weak. It didn't explain, however, what had happened. Had the whole trip back to 80AD just been some vivid dream? Had he just been feverish? Had he imagined the entire thing? It must have been some sort of hallucination. He must have been in a coma or something. It was the only logical explanation. How else could he have stepped through the portal in the park and ended up back in his own body?

"Phoenix, honey?" His mothers' voice drew his attention. Gwen Carter's beloved face, careworn by worry, hovered over him.

"Hi Mum." His voice came out rusty with disuse but she understood and burst into tears.

Gathering him gently into her arms, she rocked him as she had when he was small and hurt. He let his head rest on her shoulder, breathing in the familiar, secure smell of her skin.

Eventually, she let him go but kept hold of his hand. Nurses and doctors came and fussed over him for awhile. Finally they left the pair alone and Phoenix was deeply grateful. Their forced joviality got on his nerves.

"What happened?" he managed to ask, annoyed that he felt so weak.

Gwen dried her eyes and sniffed. "Nobody really knows. You were playing that computer game I bought for you. When you didn't come down after dinner, I came up to find out how you were. I found you... unconscious... on the floor." She wiped away more tears and cleared her throat. "You've been in some sort of coma for days. The doctors couldn't find out why. We had no idea if you would ever wake up!"

"Sorry mum." Phoenix found himself apologising.

She laughed tearfully. "It's hardly your fault. Just don't do it again! You frightened the life out of me. Oh!" She jumped from her chair. "I must go and tell Allison you're awake. It will give her hope. Will you be alright for a little while?"

"Sure. But who's Allison?" Phoenix struggled upright. "Why would me waking up give anyone hope?"

"Oh." Gwen appeared surprised that he didn't know. "Another girl was brought in the same day as you, with exactly the same symptoms. I've become quite close to her mother. She's been such a wonderful support. She's hardly left Jade's bedside, even with six other daughters to look after. She's just in the room next door. I'll only be a moment."

With that breezy comment, Gwen flitted from the room, leaving Phoenix bereft of speech and stunned. He flopped back onto the bed, shaking.

Had it all been a dream or not? He had to find out.

Determinedly, he slid out of bed, leaning heavily on his drip stand for support. Step by shaky step, he made his way out of the room, trying to ignore the breeze that crept in through the back of his hospital gown.

Pausing outside his room, he listened for his mothers' voice. There it was. Slowly, he inched his way down the corridor, using the wall to hold himself up. It took awhile but his muscles slowly got used to being worked again. He just felt like they were the wrong muscles – so pathetic compared to his avatar's body.

At last, he made it to the next room and turned the corner. A moment of amazed silence fell as everyone stared at him. Phoenix was acutely conscious that at least four beautiful blonde girls looked at him curiously, along with an older woman he took to be their mother. Gwen, who stood next to a curtained off bed, rushed over.

"What are you doing Phoenix? Let me get a nurse. You need to get back into bed. You're not strong enough yet." She scolded lovingly.

The curtain around the bed twitched back. "Phoenix?" An unfamiliar voice called his name with familiar inflexions.

There, sitting up in the starched white surroundings, was a girl about his own age. Small boned and dark haired, the only recognizable thing about her was her green eyes.

"Jade?" he whispered, incredulous. "Is that you?"

Her thin face split into a huge grin. She nodded, her short wavy hair bouncing.

Their mothers exchanged bemused looks over their heads.

Phoenix turned to his. "Mum, I know this will sound odd but can you guys give us a moment?"

Gwen looked back and forth between her son and Jade and shrugged. "I guess so. Come on Allison. Let's go find Hector and get some coffee. Come on girls. Tell me how your school dance went."

Jade's mother kissed her daughter on the forehead, brushed back her hair and nodded reluctantly. With inquisitive looks, the gaggle of girls and women traipsed out.

Phoenix sat on the edge of Jade's bed, sighing in relief. He peered closely at her.

"Is it really you? Did it really happen?"

She nodded again, drawing a thin silver chain out from under her hospital gown. Dangling at the end of it was her half of the yin-yang amulet.

"Mum said every time the nurses took off our necklaces, we went into cardiac arrest. We died, Phoenix. Several times each. They had to keep putting them back on to bring us back."

"So it was real then?" He couldn't get his head around it.

She shrugged. "What's reality? I know I felt it, tasted it and remember it as clearly as I do this life. That makes it real to me. Marcus once laughed at the idea that his world could be make-believe and I realised then that there was no way I could prove his wasn't real."

"But all the things we did; all the stuff we destroyed – Stonehenge, the temple in Egypt," Phoenix protested. "We can't have made it happen in *this* world, too."

"Why not?" Jade said intently. "Who's to say how it happened? Remember that we came back to this world in our avatar bodies, somehow. Maybe what we did in the other world *did* affect ours. Who knows?"

Phoenix suddenly laughed. She raised an eyebrow.

He grinned. "I'm just wondering if, one day, when they dig up Emperor Qinshihuan's tomb, they'll find Brynn's name where he scratched it into the wall when he was bored."

Her eyes crinkled in amusement. "Or maybe they'll find the rest of that treasure under the step-pyramid in Egypt."

Phoenix's head hurt. He scrubbed a hand through his greasy hair and sighed. Jade's eyes lit up.

She laughed. "Now I'm certain it's you. You do that

all the time, you know."

He grinned weakly. "Yeah, well you have some notable habits, too."

"Ha!" She folded her arms, pretending annoyance. Then, with a shy grin, she touched his fingers. "We four made a pretty good team, didn't we?"

"Yeah," he replied. The sadness of losing Brynn, Marcus and his father had not yet eased. He saw it reflected in her eyes and forced a smile. "Don't think I'll be playing any computer games for awhile, though."

Jade shook her head vigorously in agreement. There was a noise in the doorway. She looked up, her face lighting up with recognition.

"Dad! Come and meet my friend, Phoenix. You know his mother already - Mrs Carter."

A cultured voice sounded behind him and a tall, thin, dark-haired man appeared at the bedside, smiling indulgently down at his daughter.

"Of course I do. Phoenix." He stuck out his hand and Phoenix shook it. "Nice to finally meet you awake. Ah, here's someone else who's glad to see you again."

A gentle hand fell on Phoenix's shoulder. Twisting his head, he turned…and looked into the haunted, grateful blue eyes of Alex Carter.

"D..Dad?" Phoenix managed to stutter the word, "but..but..how? I don't...?" He turned back to gape at Jade.

She grabbed his gown and pulled his face close to her mouth, her soft words meant for his ears only. "Evidently someone told the paramedics about that accident on the freeway and put a tourniquet on his leg to stop the bleeding. So the ambulance got there in time, this time. And you ripped the door off so they could treat him fast."

Phoenix looked at her, then back at his father, still unable to believe it. His heart pounded so hard he could barely breathe. Tentatively, he put out a hand and laid it on his father's broad chest, feeling a matching heartbeat there. Alex smiled and wrapped strong arms around his son, holding him tightly. Hesitantly, Phoenix did the same, wondering if this were just still a dream and he would vanish. How was it possible? How could his real father be here? Where was Jacob in this world? Had the last three years just never happened or would he wake again and find *this* wasn't real, either? Leaning back, he stared up at his father's beloved face in disbelief.

Alex smiled down at his son and smoothed his unruly hair back. "I'm glad you're awake at last. You had us worried." He cleared his throat and looked around, a sheen of tears in his eyes.

Jade's father stood next to her, his arm protectively around her shoulders. She smiled up at the Carters, one hand still fiddling with the yin-yang amulet around her neck.

Alex Carter spotted it and nodded. "Oh yes, Hector has just been telling me that you said you found my necklace in an old cupboard where you hide from your sisters."

She hesitated then reached up to unclasp the hook. She slipped it off the chain and dropped it into his palm. "Sorry. I should have given it to my parents straight away."

He fingered it and smiled a little. "From what I understand, you were home alone, so you couldn't have – and I believe it has saved your life several times in the last few days – although the doctors still scratching their heads over exactly *how.*"

He glanced at Phoenix then at Jade. With a decisive nod, he handed the little charm back to her. "Keep it. I'm just glad you're both back, safe and sound. I have a feeling its time with me was over and it was meant for you next, anyway."

Jade stammered a thankyou and slid it back onto the

chain with a faint sigh of relief.

Alex smiled down at his son and squeezed his shoulder. "I understand the doctors also have no idea why playing the same computer game should have caused you both to fall into a coma, either. Any ideas?"

Phoenix could only shake his head, still speechless at the sight of his father, alive and well.

Alex Carter looked swiftly at Jade then met Phoenix's disbelieving gaze with one of unexpected depth and understanding.

"As an old buddhist monk once said to me: isn't it funny, how often we meet our destiny in the very place we try to hide from it?"

THE END

Hope you enjoyed Book Five. That's the end of the series.

APPENDIX

The **Karla Caves** in India were begun approximately 200BC by Buddhist monks. They are a spectacular set of hand-carved temples, dug into the volcanic rock of the Western Ghats mountains. The most impressive is the principal cave in which is the largest **Chaitya** among Buddhist cave in the country, being 15meters wide and 16 meters high. The most remarkable feature of the cave is its arched roof supported by wooden beams which have astonishingly survived the onslaught of elements for more than 2,000 years. The Wooden Umbrella above the Chaitya is unique in the Buddhist caves around the world. There is absolutely no sign of any corrosion.

The **Emperor Qin shi huan (or Qin shi huang)** lived from 259BC to 210BC. He was king of the state of Qin ("Chin") from 246BC to 221BC, when, after many years of bloody conquest, he became the first to unite the country under one Empire. He established standards of government, money, taxation, laws and administrative systems. He built the first version of the Great Wall. For his tomb, he had thousands of life-sized warriors, horses, chariots and entertainers made from terracotta. They were buried around his tomb near Xi'an.

Forgotten for thousands of years, the terracotta armies were re-discovered in 1974 and are still being excavated and restored today. The Chinese have not yet excavated Qinshihuan's tomb, which stands as a hill about 1 kilometre away from the buried warriors. Writings from not long after Qinshihuan's death describe the interior of the tomb as having a miniature map of his empire laid out on the floor, with rivers of mercury and star patterns embedded in the roof with diamonds and pearls. Studies have shown elevated levels of mercury in the soil around the tomb, so this may be true.

The **Qing Ming Festival** is a Spring festival for the celebration of the renewal of life after winter and lasts for several days. It's official beginnings date from several centuries after 80AD, but it undoubtedly replaced an earlier festival of similar nature.

The **Han family** took over China as the ruling clan in 206BC and ruled until 220AD. It is commonly considered to be one of the greatest periods in the history of China. Even today, a large majority of the people refer to themselves as the 'Han people'.

During the **Han Dynasty**, China officially became a Confucian state (following the philosophy and teachings of Confucius) and prospered domestically: agriculture, handicrafts and commerce flourished, and the population reached over 56 million people. Meanwhile, the empire extended its political, cultural influence, and territory over much of Korea, Mongolia, Vietnam, and Central Asia before it finally collapsed under a combination of domestic and external pressures.

The original site of the Han capital of **Chang'an** was first located 3 km northwest of modern Xi'an. As the capital of the Western Han Dynasty (206BC- 9AD), it was the political, economic and cultural centre of China. It was also the eastern end of the newly established Silk Road, and a cosmopolitan city comparable with the greatest cities of their contemporaries in the Roman Empire.

After the Western Han period, the Eastern Han government

(25AD-220AD) used Luoyang, three hundred kilometres to the east, as the new capital and renamed Chang'an to Xijing (Western Capital).

Emperor Zhang of Han (hàn zhāng dì), (57-88) was an emperor of the Chinese Han Dynasty from 75 to 88. He was the third emperor of the Chinese Eastern Han Dynasty. Emperor Zhang was a hardworking and diligent ruler. He reduced taxes and paid close attention to all affairs of state. As a result, Han society prospered and its culture flourished during this period.
During his reign, Chinese troops, under the leadership of General Ban Chao, progressed far west beyond the Caspian Sea. These military expeditions into the far west established direct contact with the Parthian Empire and sent an official embassy to Rome.

One of the great **Chinese inventions, paper**, dates from the Han Dynasty, and is largely attributed to the courteunuch Cai Lun (50 - 121 AD). By the first (1st) century BC, the Chinese had discovered how to forge the highly durable metal of steel, by melting together wrought iron with cast iron. There were great mathematicians, astronomers, statesmen, and technological inventors such as Zhang Heng (78 - 139 AD), who invented the world's first hydraulic-powered armillary sphere. Zhang Heng's most famous invention was a seismometer with a swinging pendulum that signified the direction of earthquakes that struck locations hundreds of kilometres away from the position device. Zhang Heng also argued that light emanating from the moon was merely the reflected light that came originally from the sun, and accurately described the reasons for solar eclipse and lunar eclipse as path obstructions of light by the celestial bodies of the earth, sun, and moon.

A **Solar eclipse** can only occur during a New moon, when the moon's orbit brings it into a position to pass between the Sun and the Earth. A total eclipse of the sun can only last a maximum of about 7 minutes.

Grief. Throughout the books, Phoenix has to deal with grief over the loss of his father and various friends. Grief is real and can be broken down into five basic stages. Everyone goes through them, although perhaps not all of them. The feelings also come back over and over, gradually getting less intense as time passes.
Stages include:
* Denial - eg "This can't be happening"
* Anger - eg:"Why him? It's not fair!"
* Bargaining - eg: "I'll do anything to have him back; take me instead!"
* Depression - eg: "I'm so sad, why bother with anything."
* Acceptance - eg: "It'll be ok. I can't change it, so I'll have to live with it."

Eastern Philosophy. Various Eastern/Asian philosophies throughout the ages have produced a number of wise sayings. Buddhism, Zen Buddhism and Taoism are just a few of the fascinating Eastern philosophies that influence the world today.
Some of their more famous sayings include:
Count not what is lost but what is left
Pure gold does not fear the smelter
The diamond cannot be polished without friction, nor the man perfected without trials
The man who strikes first admits that his ideas have given out
When the mantis hunts the locust, he forgets the shrike that is hunting him
Only when all contribute their firewood can they build up a strong fire

Only he that has travelled the road knows where the holes are deep
When your horse in on the brink of a precipice, it is too late to pull the reins
It is the beautiful bird which gets caged
Four things come not back: the spoken word, the sped arrow, the past life and the neglected opportunity.
A wise man makes his own decisions, an ignorant man follows public opinion
There are many paths to the top of the mountain, but the view is always the same
Those who hear not the music think the dancers mad
He who seeks revenge should remember to dig two graves
The great question is not whether you have failed, but whether you are content with failure
A man must despise himself before others will
Some roads aren't meant to be travelled alone
If you are patient in a moment of anger, you will escape a hundred days of sorrow
If there is beauty in character, there will be harmony in the home, If there is harmony in the home, there will be order in the nation, if there is order in the nation, there will be peace in the world
Often one finds one's destiny just where one hides to avoid it
Holding on to anger is like grasping a hot coal with the intent of throwing it at someone else; you are the one who gets burned.
Great anger is more destructive than the sword
It's not who you are that holds you back, it's who you think you're not.
Even death is not to be feared by one who has lived wisely.
Happiness is a journey not a destination
In the practice of tolerance, one's enemy is the best teacher
True words are not always pretty; pretty words are not always true

Do not stand in a place of danger trusting in miracles
The beginning of wisdom is calling things by their right names
A journey of a thousand miles begins with a single step
Fall seven times, stand up eight.
One does not have to journey a thousand miles to find the truth within

Discover other titles by Aiki Flinthart at:
http://aikiflinthart.weebly.com/

Connect with Aiki on Facebook

The 80AD series
(YA Adventure/Fantasy)

80AD Book 1: *The Jewel of Asgard*
80AD Book 2: *The Hammer of Thor*
80AD Book 3: *The Tekhen of Anuket*
80AD Book 4: *The Sudarshana*
80AD Book 5: *The Yu Dragon*

The Kalima Chronicles
(YA Adventure/Fantasy)

IRON (Book 1)

ABOUT THE AUTHOR

Aiki Flinthart lives in Australia. In between running a business and being with her husband of many years, she pursues writing, archery, knife-throwing, martial arts, art, music, bellydancing and watches too much television. After many years of writing for her own amusement, she finally decided to write for others' – and discovered it was even more fun.